THE MAN
IN A HURRY

PAUL MORAND

THE MAN
IN A HURRY

Translated from the French
by Euan Cameron

PUSHKIN PRESS

LONDON

Pushkin Press
71–75 Shelton Street, London WC2H 9JQ

Original text © Editions Gallimard, Paris, 1941
Afterword © Michel Déon, 2009
English translation © Euan Cameron, 2015

The Man in a Hurry was originally published
as *L'homme pressé* in France in 1941

Afterword by Michel Déon was first published in
Lettres de château by Michel Déon, Gallimard, Paris, in 2009

This translation first published by Pushkin Press in 2015

This book is supported by the Institut français
(Royaume-Uni) as part of the Burgess programme

INSTITUT
FRANÇAIS
ROYAUME-UNI

0 0 1

ISBN 978 1 782270 97 3

Frontispiece: Paul Morand © Harlingue Viollet

Set in Monotype Baskerville by Tetragon, London

Proudly printed and bound in Great Britain by TJ International,
Padstow, Cornwall on Munken Premium White 80gsm

www.pushkinpress.com

CONTENTS

THE MAN
IN A HURRY

To Hélène Morand
... but does one dedicate a book
to the person to whom one dedicated one's life?

P.M.

PART ONE

A Cracking Pace

CHAPTER I

A T THE POINT at which the road reached the top of the slope and was about to dip down on the other side again, the man jumped out of the taxi without waiting for the driver to brake. He went into one of those suburban taverns where in the summer you can have lunch with a view and where you can dine in the cool of the evening. With an anxious step, he charged down the path lined with box hedges and rushed over to the terrace. There was such a contrast between the sweltering, glare-filled outskirts of the city and the still, stony silence of this panorama that he stopped in his tracks. Paris fanned out beneath him; an incline plunged towards the Seine, hemmed in by the hills of Clamart and the heights of the Sénart forest. The eye could look down from Villeneuve-Saint-Georges as far as Kremlin-Bicêtre. He took a seat at a metal table and clapped his hands. Twice, he glanced at his watch, as if it were a friend. Nobody chose to bring him a drink. Finally, a waiter in his seventies whose rheumatism was aggravated by working at night came to wipe the table with a duster.

Why, since he had achieved his aim, did the visitor appear disconcerted?

The sun was still lighting up the sky, while below, darkness had already fallen; driven from the heavens by sudden flurries of light, rather like an actor unable to make up his mind whether to leave the stage, at nine o'clock the sun was lingering in the summer dusk, drowned in a rosy mist.

The customer without a drink cast his eye over the surrounding tables; all around him people were dining; at that time of the year refugees (everyone was exclaiming rapturously in Central European languages) had come to graft themselves onto the old Parisian clientele of lovers, boozy wedding parties and entertainers for whom Sceaux and Robinson were a rustic extension of Montparnasse.

The man kept turning around, as though he were being followed; twice he looked to see whether his watch had anything new to tell him. He had scarcely been sitting down for more than a minute or two than he clapped his hands again, prodded the hobbling, elderly waiter, and insisted on having something to drink.

Behind the lady at the bar, who was totting up numbers, a whole array of aperitifs was displayed. The visitor gazed at the cordials and coloured alcoholic drinks with melancholy, with longing, with love. His legs began to quiver; his knees knocked together; he clenched his fists, did his best to resist, sighed, and all of a sudden yielded to his desire, abruptly giving way to his impulse, and dashed over to the shelf; his arm brushed against the tiered cake that was the barmaid's hairdo, he snatched a bottle of quinquina at random, slipped a finger into the handle of a beer mug as he passed the trolley, having also grabbed a soda siphon with the other hand, hopped down the two steps and collapsed into his chair. After having poured the soda water and the Dubonnet into his beer mug—simultaneously, to save time—he gulped it all down.

Only then did he realize that he had never been thirsty.

"May I, monsieur, at your table be seated?"

The customer looked the newcomer up and down.

"Is it to sketch a portrait of me? No one has ever been able to draw me, I warn you; I don't keep still."

"Allow me to introduce myself: Doctor Zachary Regencrantz, from Jena. Here is my card. Yours, please? Your behaviour has greatly interested me, Monsieur… Monsieur Pierre Niox. I have been observing you ever since you entered the restaurant. Fascinating! My attention was drawn by your extremely sudden appearance on the terrace. I saw the way you bounded in! Your impetuous movements struck me, a specialist in the study of impulsive movement and the anatomy of reflexes, as most unusual and not at all in keeping with their aim. They had originality and even beauty. Rather like a panther leaping on a mosquito. Ha! Ha! Ha!"

The doctor held forth in measured tones, without beating about the bush, proceeding as though on tiptoes in a language which he was clearly more accustomed to reading than speaking; he lost his balance over the slippery syntax and recovered as best he could.

"So far nothing abnormal, my dear monsieur. I classified you straight away among the paroxysmal-needing-to-satisfy-himself-quickly-subjects, having initially imagined that you dashed in so that you could shorten the distance that separated you from the moment at which you could drink, since thirst seemed to be the *Mittelpunkt*, the core of your activity. But this new incident—one that would readily require clinical observation and even perhaps a substantial monograph—is that having satisfied an apparently burning desire, but which in reality was not burning, you have not so much as touched your glass, as it were."

Pierre scrutinized this Regencrantz with the friendliness one feels for someone who talks to you about yourself, even though in theory he did not care for people touching him or murmuring in his ear, but he was used to Jews who, when they speak to you, always look as though they are buying something or telling you a secret. Pierre felt himself being stared at intently by a pair of blue eyes rimmed with gold; the eyes of a 100-year-old man in the sallow face of a skier. Very white teeth shone from skin bronzed by altitude; the doctor's tan was not as well preserved as it had been and was starting to turn green in patches. A nose like a bishop's crosier protruded between two cheeks that at the most serious moments always looked as though they were about to burst out laughing. Regencrantz scratched his skull, which was covered with a pale moss that was all the more unusual because the hair on his head had taken refuge in his ears and his nostrils.

"Sit yourself down, doctor. I'm going to give *you* a consultation. I am neither worried, nor paroxysmal, nor impulsive, nor overwrought. I am perfectly healthy."

"We shall see."

"Were I on my own, I would feel marvellous; but there are other people."

"*Halt!* All my patients say the same thing: 'Doctor, I'm a victim…'"

"I'm not a victim, I'm a martyr."

"Ah, there we are. You can tell me what it is that is bothering you."

"My misfortune is to be precise. My life is spent waiting. You see, this evening I was meant to meet a friend here. Where is he? He is where everyone is: elsewhere."

"One question I shall ask you: are you enthusiastic?"

"No. Normally quite indifferent, and even apathetic."

"Do you believe in the afterlife? Do you talk with God?"

"I reckon that, having tricked me by bringing me into the world, it's for Him to get in touch first."

"And do you believe in progress?"

"What do you take me for?"

"Is your restless activity of the metaphysical kind? I mean: polypragmosyne?"

"Don't look for a moral cause, most honourable doctor, you won't find anything. It is not because of any acquired wisdom that I move quickly, I do so instinctively. The only explanation is that I possess a fatal gift, as the romantics used to say: that of mobility. I am cursed with moving at a galloping pace in a universe that moves at a trot."

"You are like the alchemists who used to see all the principles of the properties of the body in quicksilver. Have you always been so… impatient?"

"Me, impatient? But I'm so patient that I sometimes have convulsions as a result."

"The expression gave me away. Can you say in French: 'How long have people appeared slow to you?'"

"Always have done. Well, actually, no. I'm not really sure."

"You imply that your subconscious"—the doctor laid stress on the word with a very Germanic relish for terminology—"prefers not to remember. You don't know, but it knows and it has to speak out. If you would care to see me again, we shall collaborate on a methodical observation of your good self, which will lead us to throw some light on your nature."

"But I'm not ill!"

"Who mentioned illness? I certainly don't want to treat you. If you want to charge around like that, you're perfectly entitled to." (And with his hand the doctor imitated the throw of the javelin.) "I am simply trying to find out for myself, and I say once more that your case is interesting, that there is an original personality within you. The way you took flight, a moment ago, was admirable, and your agility and your lightness were exemplary. This is not a fatal gift in the least, I can assure you, it is a gift pure and simple."

"You make me very happy, doctor."

"My first diagnosis is that you are not living under a curse, as you say you are. No more than other men. You are actually rather better built, more athletic, and your reflexes, which are made of saltpetre, deserve my careful study. Call me from time to time, especially at moments of over-excitement, and we shall chat. Here is my address."

"Wait, doctor, don't go. This time you're the one who's in a hurry."

"Very well. I'll stay and listen to you. For myself, I have my entire life, when I am able, for organized leisure time."

"Very well, then listen: my profession is that of an antique dealer; except on rare occasions, I never buy later than AD 1000. I am known for the Carolingian period. I have never sold anything later than thirteenth-century, unless it was a fake, and in that case one returns the money."

"All that is a long time ago when people did not run as fast as you!"

"Yes. I said the same thing to myself last week, at Mount Athos, while inspecting a Byzantine ivory piece smoothed over by the centuries. All the same, one has to move quickly, with bric-a-brac as with everything else, and particularly in my area. Why? Because there's a regular demand and a steady market for eighteenth-century objects, whereas with the Middle Ages it's less reliable than the most active gold mine: I watch my customers rushing from Scythian art to Gandharan; six months later it's Pre-Columbian that's in vogue and Mycenaean that's out of favour."

"Might that not be the fault of young hotheads like you, Monsieur Dynamite?"

"No, it's my customers' fault. My clientele are as scarce as they are select. They're difficult and anxious. They are made up of those spurious sages, those devotees who run museums, and the demanding newly rich. Who is more excitable than a collector of objects from the Middle Ages? He strides across the centuries as he would streams. Could anyone be more volatile in his moods? I've been dealing with that sort for fifteen years now…"

"Without adopting the required philosophy?"

"Philosophy has no more to do with resignation, doctor, than eloquence has with the art of saying nothing. On the contrary, it's in so far as I'm a philosopher that I feel revolutionary."

"You told me that you are fit and well?"

"What I told you was that I was strong and from good stock. We are all made up of the same atoms that move around at the same speed and yet no one manages to keep up with me. Some mistaken adjustment must have been made at my birth. Explain it if you can. I'm aware of a discrepancy between my own rhythm and that of my environment. One of the two has to give way, either I succumb or else I teach my contemporaries, who really do mope about like snails, to follow my pace. Ah! The slowcoaches!"

"A good thing you're not a dictator. You'd be conducting a *Blitzkrieg* every day!"

"What can I do?"

"Improve yourself."

"Why *me*? I have to put up with people, because my fellow citizens have retained, in this tormented century, the pace of a former age. I admire people: they seem to have time for everything, they move forward on a horizontal plane; as for me, I have the feeling I'm constantly falling, as in dreams; when I was born, I fell from a roof and I could see all the floors going by and the ground getting dreadfully closer. I reckon speed is the modern form of sluggishness and I know that I'm obeying the true momentum of the universe and that I'm the only person who can feel that I'm obeying it. Why change? Why would I change, since it's not my mistake?"

"With mental dramas there are never any exterior causes."

"Tell me straight away that I'm mad. You've already treated me as if I were a case of paroxysm, doctor! I'm very upset."

"Please don't paint such a bleak picture, dear Monsieur Niox. I spoke not of tragedy, but drama, for drama has its comical side."

"So I'm a clown?"

"Our initial relationship this evening stems from a scene that can be characterized as basically comical. Your taking flight, so out of proportion to your supposed thirst, would have made anyone laugh. (You yourself were compelled to laugh.) But nevertheless, I think I may be permitted to look beyond this superficial comedy."

"The martyr?"

"No. But a personality who has been affected as far as sexual attraction is concerned, who has been badly bruised, who is probably courageous and quite capable of playing the hero in some modern adventure or other. Along with the word 'drama', I used the adjective 'mental'. I would have done better to use the word 'spiritual', yes, spiritual drama, *ein seelisches Drama*. You are entitled to believe that, had you simply gulped down your aperitif like a raw egg, I would not have spoken to you. Gluttony can be of no interest to me, it should be classified under hysteria; thirst, a primitive impulse, would have justified your haste and would thus have removed its grandeur and its importance. I would have expelled you from the pathology amid general indifference. It is only in proportion to the pointlessness of your actions and insofar as the spirit within you will do its best to shake up matter, that you deserve to be considered as a work of art or feature in the clinician's notebook, which often amounts to the same thing when it is a question of achieving the truth. But whatever the motivation of your behaviour, you are a truly veritable sphinx as far as I am concerned. You state that there is a conflict between you and the others? Very well. Who is right? Whom should I blame and whom should I absolve? In this debate I wish to make a judgement. Paris, an *ancien régime* city, is an excellent climacteric resort for the observation of human beings, for, like all the old capitals, it is the refuge of oppressed sensibilities, of those who ignore rules and of the cripples of the present age. Why does Paris have such a great reputation among us? Because it is a city of nervous upheaval and moral tumult. Here, monsieur, we must assert the profundity of this city that is supposed to be superficial and that has invented so many vices and so many styles. I wish to take advantage of my stay in Paris, while awaiting my transit visa for New York. I am noting things down. Later, I transfer them to index cards. Who knows whether I am not already able to recognize the symptoms of a new and, to us Germans, undiscovered passion?"

"Are you still talking about me?"

"Possibly."

"Then you will be disappointed, doctor. Just content yourself with this evening's episode."

"I want to do better."

"My autopsy?" asked Pierre with a laugh.

"Ha! Ha! Ha! Your autopsy! Ha! Ha! You are laughing, Monsieur Niox. *Sie gehen zu schnell!* You are going too fast!"

Regencrantz got to his feet.

"Man is a magnetic needle that is never still," said Pierre.

"Except at the pole…"

"Yes, indeed! Amid the polar ice, in death… Death which is nothing but a word! I drink to our life, doctor!"

"*Prosit!*"

CHAPTER II

CONFINED TO PARIS all afternoon, Pierre had been longing for fresh air, and being eager to sample the cool of the evening, he was consumed with the desire to go up to the woods at Robinson. But now that Regencrantz had left him, all he could think of was sliding downhill again towards his bed, like a river; he tumbled down the slope at full speed so that he could sleep.

The concierge just has time to catch him as he speeds by and to hand him a message from Placide.

"Monsieur Niox, from your colleague. It's urgent."

Pierre tears open the letter in the lift and reads it between floors: *"Latest development,"* writes Placide, *"the house that was not for sale is for sale; but there's not a moment to lose. Phone me this evening when you get home."*

"Not a moment to lose!" Pierre exclaims. "Marvellous! When do we leave?"

He rings Placide, who agrees to come along with him. Tomorrow morning at six o'clock, it's settled, they will both be on the road.

In bed, Pierre manages to fold himself in three in such a way that even when he is lying still he seems to be making a perilous plunge. He concentrates, then relaxes into a soliloquy: "Pierre, think hard before you fall asleep and before waking up and finding out you're a landlord. Pierre, you're going to tie yourself down! You're taking root. You're settling down. You're becoming stable! Your agile legs are going to bind together like those of a stone god! Your rushing stream will end up in a lake, in a bog. Is it possible? You, owning a house! You should know that there are snails that die crushed by their own shells! Are you going to swap the turmoil of a free man for the turmoil of a home owner? Think carefully while it's still dark before collapsing into a deep sleep. Up till now, what do you own? Treasures that are in any case not yours and which would fit into a single suitcase. You are one of those men who don't have any excess baggage.

"Here, in three lines, is the inventory of your belongings:

"A game of chess made of rock crystal, said to be from the time of Charlemagne (ninth-century), deposited in a bank in Buenos Aires. That's the large piece.

"A Byzantine vase (sixth-century) with a winged sparrow hawk mounting, in bond in New York.

"An illustrated manuscript known as the Ratisbon Gospel (1025), on gold and violet parchment, on loan to the Bodleian exhibition.

"A Greek paten (Mount Athos, sixth-century) in safe custody at Spink's of London.

"Six gold Théodebert sols, Merovingian coins (sixth-century).

"A Carolingian comb in the shape of two confronting birds of prey, bought in Brussels three days ago.

"A small golden bull on a pearl necklace, excavations from the valley of the Indus (fifth-century BC).

"These latter two pieces are in Paris, on your bed, the bed on which you will fall asleep if this continues because inventories are the best soporifics. When one possesses such compact wealth in such a minimal amount, it's pointless to encumber yourself with a house."

"Excuse me," Pierre says to himself, "I also have four Frankish sarcophagi, three Syrian twisting capitals, a porphyry Lombard armchair. (*A snore.*) And a black-and-white mosaic waiting for me in a garage in Antioch. These scattered pieces that risk being lost justify the purchase of a house. (*Another snore.*) Furthermore, a Roman cloister is not a house, it's more a work of art than a house. No, it's not a basilica, I'm exaggerating because I'm beginning to feel sleepy… It's a cloister. Let's think more slowly. But when you think slowly, you fall asleep. How boring it is to sleep!"

Pierre switches on the light again.

"I like counting the hours of the night: if I sleep I'm robbed of these precious hours. Sleep is unjustifiable."

Pierre falls asleep; not for long: the thought of his future acquisition wakes him up after ten minutes.

"This cloister really does exist and I'm soon going to take possession of it, unless the owner asks me to pay too much. All I have are the banknotes I earned yesterday; I'll take the whole wad just in case; perhaps it will be enough."

Pierre pictures himself three weeks ago on a flight from Marseille to Salonica, about to embark for Mount Athos and go to the cloister of Xeropotamos where the priests offered him the paten that is now part of his inventory. He had left Marignane at dawn and was flying over the Var. For a moment, the plane was hedge-hopping over the Maures hills. To his right, the Îles d'Hyères stretched out, to his left, the Alps. Beneath Pierre's feet, less than fifty metres beneath him, amid the tangled mass of trees, far from any roads and surrounded by scrub, he remembered perfectly having spotted a clearing; in the middle of this clearing, like a reliquary lying on green velvet, he had noticed, buried amid the rosemary bushes, a most exquisite Romanesque chapel, every detail of which his hawk's eyes immediately registered. "I have an excellent visual memory," Pierre often used to say; "It's the memory idiots have, *but* I have it; or rather: *and* I have it."

Primitive art is rarely exquisite; that is precisely what made him fall in love with his cloister. In the rising sunlight, this miniature chapel appeared brand new and as though it had barely left the donor's pocket. A thousand years had passed over it without it getting at all grubby; on the contrary, the stone looked as though it had been washed by the dawn. Between the blades of the propeller that drew him onwards, Pierre could make out every detail of the small stone steeple; beneath the undercarriage, the bell-tower and its lantern, like a cow with its calf, the thick walls and the apse that was rounder than a crinoline, passed by. "A manure cart was coming out of the porch, from which I concluded, even before the wheels of the monoplane had robbed me of my discovery, that the chapel was deconsecrated, that farmers used it, and that they might possibly relinquish it were I to offer to buy it. At that decisive moment, the last object to register on my retina was an ancient basin, in the middle of the courtyard, which I thought might serve as a drinking trough.

"Very well, I did what Lindbergh did when prospecting the Mayan temples that overlook the Guatemalan rainforest: I jotted down a rough sketch on my knees, with reference points and information provided by the pilot. The trees beneath us were the Dom forest; the beach to our right was Le Lavandou; the Provençal villas on the hillside,

Bormes." On arriving at Brindisi two hours later, during a miserable wait (journeys by plane are spent waiting!) Pierre had dispatched a telegram to Placide. The reply reached him in Athens:

"*Chartreuse du Mas Vieux, eleventh-century. Stop. Not for sale. Sorry.*" And now, here was the Mas Vieux for sale!

Pierre goes to sleep so as to prepare himself the better for his next raid. It's not so much a rest as a gathering of momentum. This man who is unable to keep still is not even grateful to the little cloister lost in the depths of the Var for having waited 1,000 years for him.

Placide has one cardinal virtue: punctuality. Here he is now with Pierre on the RN6, at six o'clock in the morning, sitting in a convertible which Pierre is driving at breakneck speed. Orly airport tilts back, Ris-Orangis rears up, Melun subsides, Fontainebleau throws open its forest to allow them to pass through; the mileposts flash past them, the advertising hoardings make them offers, the bends hug them, the downhill slopes prepare an easy incline for them, the uphill ones flatten out gently beneath their wheels, Sens cathedral proffers its two towers to them, Joigny calls to them on their way: "Lots to see in Auxerre!" and Auxerre, which they stride through like Gargantuas, sends them off to Saulieu; they swallow up Dijon and they bolt through Lyon on their flying jaunt.

Placide chats away like a cantankerous magpie. Whereas Pierre has spent his thirty-five years getting steamed up, his colleague, rival and friend has spent twenty-eight doing very little. Pierre's dark hair blows in the wind, whereas Placide is bald. Pierre thinks straight, sees straight, walks straight; Placide, who has become short-sighted and stooped through reading, moves in zigzags: he has small, shaky feet, puzzled hands and a mischievous face. Pierre has an instinct for things and Placide is highly erudite. Pierre became involved in Roman art at the age that Placide was leaving the École des Chartes.[1] Pierre drives and Placide is driven.

"I'm looking forward with much impatience to our meeting this evening," says Placide. "The owner of the chapel, Monsieur de Boisrosé (armorial bearing of Santo Domingo), is an elderly Creole preoccupied with his health and self-preservation; he's so slow he's unable to complete his sentences; neither are you, you're so quick. It will be a treat for me to see you together."

"So convey to me still further what you know of this matter, my dear."

Placide speaks as Madame de Sévigné writes, and Pierre, who is a tease, replies in the same vein, when he is in a good mood.

"We were disinclined to sell, but the local maidservant appears to have had her say."

"I should be extremely happy to cast my eyes over her, this girl, however fearful she may be."

Placide shrugs his shoulders:

"She is. It will teach you to make fun of me."

With his little finger in the air, Pierre, out of pique, pretends to take a pinch from an imaginary snuffbox.

"Well, no actually. The maidservant is extremely pretty and you will be delighted to make her acquaintance," Placide retorts. "But I am fearfully anxious that M. de Boisrosé may change his mind," he adds treacherously, thinking solely of spoiling his friend's pleasure.

"The main basis upon which I build my hopes is the care they have taken to call us by telegram, even though the word telegram sounds offensive here!"

And Pierre laughs, pressing his foot flat on the accelerator.

"Can we not stop soon? I'm so hungry," Placide sighs.

"It's impossible if we want to be in the Var by this evening. I fully intend to become the owner before dinner! When I do something foolish, I like to plunge in head first."

Placide sighs in desperation:

"You think of yourself as punctual," he says, "but you're missing what's important, which is the punctuality of the stomach."

"It's because I need you to be light, so that we can refuel en route."

Placide adopts a tight-lipped expression:

"I had thought, dear friend, that you were taking me along as an expert in Roman art and not as the speedster's mechanic. What a mad obsession not to stop at a petrol station!"

"Ah no! That's not all. The woman in a nurse's blouse, with her big red stick, irritates me; she's a chatterbox and never has any change. The petrol pipe she brandishes is always too long or too short; it's also ridiculously narrow; the air goes into the tank while the petrol spills on the ground. It's stupid! The pipes are always too narrow, whether it's a pipe that drains out, a pipe that pumps in water or the neck of a bottle, a human larynx, or an oesophagus tube. Come on, get a move on, there's not a drop left in the tank."

"You're going to make me reach out over the hood at a hundred kilometres an hour and risk breaking my neck… It's cruel and dangerous. Slow down, for goodness' sake, slow down!" yells Placide.

"Me! Slow down!"

"My cap!"

"So, are you sitting in the dickey-seat? Fine. Now, listen to what you have to do: the fifty-litre can is under the back seat. Found it? Fine. I'm watching you in the rear-view mirror: take the funnel. Have you got it? That's perfect! So, third step: lean out over the right-hand side of the car. You're right's not on your left! Don't fall out! Unscrew the cap. No, of course there's no danger! Just hold on with your foot and cling on with your left hand while you're in space… Well done! You see, Placide, saving ten minutes is child's play!"

Placide crawled back to his seat with some difficulty and sat down again beside Pierre, his face white from fear and the wind, his ears as red as a clown's.

CHAPTER III

"From here on, the road is no longer suitable for cars," said Placide. "The gravel crumbles beneath the wheels and if we go any further we'll risk thousands of punctures."

They step down and stride over the roots of a carob tree laid bare by the rain. The pitted track has become a stream. Pierre runs, followed by Placide who, in the woods, with his large head framed by a blond beard, looks like one of Snow White's dwarfs, though without their lightness of foot.

"I feel as though I'm in a Turkish bath. I'm sweating like an alcarraza."

"Onwards!" yells Pierre.

"Let me stop for a second."

"Must one stop over so minor a matter, Marquise? Onwards!"

The cork oaks, stripped to a man's height of their outer layers, display the red innards of their robust bark. Their cracked crusts, with their spongy slabs rounded like tiles, are piled up at crossroads.

"A forest that's ripe for a fire. All you need is a match," hints Placide, annoyed at having to do up his buttons again as he runs.

"If my house burns down, so much the better! It's unusual for a landlord to have a Wagnerian death."

The harbour at Hyères rises up to meet them through the pine grove. Lizards rush out, stopping right in front of them, on slabs of pink sandstone. A flock of red partridges, the same colour as the sandstone and the cork, cross over the stream and retreat into the oleander bushes that have reverted to the wild. Lizards and partridges are the only recognizable creatures encountered during the first thirty minutes of their climb, spent stepping over heather, laburnum and clumps of rosemary.

"Let's keep Gratteloup hill to our right. We're on the right track, assuming there is a track," said Placide. "I remember noticing those veins of white marble in the sandstone."

Small clouds scurry above them, floating over the lighthouse and dissolving far away in the sea mist. The woods scramble across the hilltops, those fiery, twisted, miserable woods of the Midi, those small forests that never grow to their full height, but repay their sparse nourishment with balsam and perfume. Far below, between the trunks of the trees, the golden curve of a beach can be seen: it is Le

Lavandou, and behind it lies Cap Bénat with its scrubland; in the background are the Îles d'Hyères, which the setting sun is lulling to sleep in a crimson light fringed with violet.

"Oh! How beautiful it is!" Pierre cries out. "My God, it's beautiful. Here's my hermitage, I recognize it. Here are the two cypress trees marking the entrance, on either side of the cart track. My plane flew over this precise point!" he exclaims in his enthusiasm.

Apart from a ring of agaves and prickly pears, the building, constructed of such a brightly coloured stone that it looks as though it were new, stops beside a drop. It clings to the slope; it cleaves to some splendid thick rows of Aleppo pines in one of those luminous landscapes that rarely experience the splatter of rainfall. The olive trees have taken it upon themselves to settle around the oil mill; they display their greying leaves crowned with tender green shoots at a time of the year when the young, bitter olive has not yet turned a shade of violet. The cicadas can be heard… A Galilean peace.

Pierre and Placide enter a courtyard that has the stench of that quiet, silent existence of those farms where the labour takes place in the fields. An alcove bereaved of its saint. A black and white cat, paws folded, sleeps on the sill of one of the small columned arches that pierce the walls of the ancient chapel. For the old *mas* has its own very primitive Romanesque chapel, and also its leper house, which has been turned into a stable. Farmers have clumsily hacked out doors and windows from these thick eleventh-century walls that are so sparing of light and access. The mistral has torn off the shutters that have fallen onto the dry grass and which nobody has picked up. Nothing that the later centuries have added to the original building, which was designed to be low, compact and smooth as a pebble, has withstood the elements. On the contrary, everything that is ten centuries old appears new, not least the layout of the stones that are greenish-grey and flecked with silvery mica like those *piedras de plata* in the Andes that the conquistadors mention. The drinking trough is a sarcophagus in which the profile of the abbot can still be seen, an African abbot perhaps, thick-lipped, with negroid features. The bell-tower has lost its bell; it stands above a roof bereft of all its colour due to the sun, with the ribs of the tiles eaten away by yellow lichen: tiles that have been fired and refired and which sound hollow when pecked at by the beaks of the white doves, turned pink in the setting sun.

"It's the lair of the owl and the nanny goat's palace!"

They mop their brows with their ties and rest on a bench which gets so hot at midday that no one can sit on it, a bench that retains its heat all night long.

In the darkness, through the open door of the former leper house, the stable can be seen, and in the shade, a cow swinging her tail as though it were a fly-swatter. At their feet lie a demijohn corseted in rust and an old saucepan full of holes, once used for the chickens. Along the wall, close to the door of the chapel, beneath a thick-shaped, squat arcature with a full tympanum, stands one of those carts that are used in poor countries. It is tiny, like all those ploughing tools in the South of France which, compared to the equipment used in the North, would look like toys were it not for the fact that, worn, scratched and chipped by flint stones as they are, they reveal how much hardship and effort was involved.

"I'm madly happy!"

Pierre is already laying an owner's hand over the sandstone that copper sulphate has turned green in places. There's a surprising silence in this courtyard, where the only sound comes from the water of the fountain.

"And what a fountain! Porphyry from Egypt. Look at the Greek Cross."

Their voices echo. An invisible dog barks. From a low door a woman comes out to meet them. She's a stocky peasant with hair made frizzy in places by a perm several months old, accentuating her Phoenician features. Joints made of steel, bare legs, a working woman's hips, a powerful

neck leading down to firm, gypsy breasts. No thighs, but-
tocks that begin at the back of her knees, and feet that are
planted firmly on the ground and attached to her legs by
large, rustic limbs, in pure Mediterranean style.

She had been expecting them, for she had dressed up:
a very clean yellow shawl and some lipstick.

They shake hands.

"Did you receive my reply to your telegram?" asked
Placide.

"Yes, yes indeed."

"Is Monsieur de Boisrosé in?"

"He's in, of course, but… he's tired."

"Well, he must rest, good God," said Placide in placatory manner; "we shall see him later."

"I repeat, he's very tired. Don't you follow me?"

"Not very well. Is he asleep?"

"He's doing more than sleeping, the poor fellow, he's
fainted."

It's not easy to extract much from this Provençal woman
who is on her guard. She sizes Pierre up, she sits in judgement. She has been waiting for these visitors too intently
to divulge matters all at once.

"A fainting fit?" says Pierre anxiously.

"He's been coughing now for some days, and he has a
stitch in his side that makes him double up."

"Pleurisy, his heart must have given out on him," says Pierre.

"His heart was thumping away last night! It sounded like the old motor in the well. Monsieur was having too much fun working!"

Pierre and Placide glance at one another: "Have we arrived too late?" Cow-like, the woman reads their minds easily. Naively, she forgets herself and replies aloud:

"He's already lost his mind four times in two days, the poor fellow. But he won't pass away without having chatted with you."

"Is he on his own?"

"Do you think I'd leave him! The lawyer, Maître Caressa, is keeping him company. Come in. I'll go and warn him."

She is no longer speaking like a maid, but as the mistress of the Mas Vieux, with the authority of a proprietor. One can sense that for years this scrupulous spider has spun her web here. She loses no time, certain that death will promptly reward her patience. Her future as a careful, prudent girl is at stake at this moment. She has worked long and hard preparing for this and the machine is set and running.

The two Parisians walk into the main room while she rushes to the bedroom. They look down and smell the tiled floor, brightly polished with linseed oil, and they look up at the old rafters of the house laid bare by the plasterwork;

the rotten beams and planks of wood, the corner posts, as well as the crossbars and struts, the whole framework of the room consists of ancient joists riddled with woodworm in which cheese-mites dwell, those grubs that inhabit olive trees and that cause sawdust to fall on you when you step too heavily. The room has two shades: milky, whitewashed walls and tables blackened by smoke and the stain of oil used at meals. The soberness of an orthodox cloister; and the railway timetable for Sud-Provence for an icon.

Pierre nudges Placide's elbow and points to a fireplace with a rounded hood and small columns supported by cushions filled with leaves.

"To think that I'll be able to make a fire in a real Roman fireplace! A Roman fire!"

And, indicating a heap of heather roots, pine needles and cones:

"Here, you won't be able to criticize me any more for pouring petrol on the wood to make it burn quicker! The fire will catch alight all on its own with these olive twigs. Have you ever seen olive wood burn, Placide? It's full of blue and green glimmers, like rum punch."

The beaded bamboo curtain quivered: a man appeared.

"Gentlemen, I have the great honour. I am the lawyer, Maître Caressa," he said solemnly. "My client has come to his senses."

"Ah, is he better?" said Pierre.

"No. He won't see the sunrise, unfortunately." The doctor was quite clear. "Monsieur de Boisrosé", he affirmed, "will pass away during the night."

The lawyer made as though he were tapping his heart, indicating how difficult his client's breathing was, then, squeezing his throat, he pretended he was suffocating.

"Yet Monsieur de Boisrosé seemed to be in very good health?" Placide interrupted, very politely. "Might we know what it is that is sending him to the grave?"

"Chronic pleurisy that has become acute; he has had four attacks in a few days. And to think that this fine man of ancient lineage, gentlemen, and courtesy itself, wanted— and it was his own expression—'to die without causing any fuss'!"

"May we still take our leave of him?" asked Placide as a matter of form. He was beginning to amuse himself at the sight of Pierre in convulsions.

The maid heard them as she came back into the room:

"Ah, monsieur, it's as if he were losing his wits. Come and see him as quickly as possible."

"Right away," said Pierre, "let's not waste any time."

Maître Caius Caressa cast a lengthy glance at the maid and said nothing. He bore the ugliness of several generations with assurance. His height, his heavy black shoes, unique in a region that wore espadrilles, his black suit, his civil service hat that lay on the table, his sclerotic mulatto's eyes that were a brighter amber than the glue of the fly-paper that hung from the ceiling—everything about him revealed a man who was wily and powerful. He looked like one of those effigies of princes dubbed "the Bad" by their subjects that can be seen on the back of disused coins.

Pierre and Placide, who were only familiar with a few roguish crooks from business consultancies on the Côte d'Azur who tossed words around, remained silent in the presence of this witness to a secret deed that smelt of conspiracy.

"Mademoiselle Hortense informed me. She told me that you would like to buy the Mas Vieux."

"The sooner the better," said Pierre.

"When your colleague came to see Monsieur de Boisrosé a month ago, the farm was not for sale. But as soon as my client became aware of the warnings from heaven, he wished to put his affairs in order. The Mas Vieux is a lovely piece of countryside."

"The price?"

"A very reasonable and moderate price. It's not on the road, of course, and there's no pergola, but you will produce ten tons of cork oak a year, enough to supply the whole coastline as far as Bormes with corks, floats and soles. And two earthenware jars of oil a year."

"And there's water," added the maid. "All the frogs throughout the summer are proof of that."

"The price?" Pierre repeated.

The lawyer was not accustomed to these sudden stops and starts. His eyes flashed and then dimmed.

"You must understand the situation. Monsieur de Boisrosé is sixty-five years old. A former judge in Martinique, for twenty years he has been separated from his wife who lives in Saint-Germain with their three daughters. On the death of their father, they will inherit. However, Monsieur de Boisrosé would like to recognize the loyal service given to him over several years by Mademoiselle Hortense Pastorino. Not being able to bequeath the Mas Vieux to her, he wishes to sell it during his lifetime; as long as he goes on living. He is an indecisive man and it took the arrival of the priest for him to make up his mind."

"I will pay in cash."

"The woods are full of amanita, bolete, parasols. Do you eat mushrooms?"

"I only like ceps."

"There are some here that are as fine as those at Sospel. But they need rain…"

"When are we going to sign?" said Pierre impatiently.

"… can you tell the difference between the poisonous and the edible amanita?"

"And you, Maître Caressa, can you tell the difference between a man who is in a hurry and a local village buyer?"

Pierre turned towards the maid, took her by the arm and led her over to the window.

Maître Caressa smiled at Placide and shrugged his shoulder.

"He's a lively fellow, your friend."

If the lawyer, who normally watched his words as carefully as one would watch over someone who was dying, had struck up a new conversation, it was because he wished to do so. He, too, was in a hurry to sign, but for selfish reasons he bided his time, exerting his renowned patience upon others. Out of the corner of his eyes he watched Pierre peering intently at the maid, while she was frowning and looked as though she were about to burst into tears from irritation and emotion. Her gaze was lowered and she was wringing her wrists like a bookbinder shuffling pages. She was actually crying. Then her face lit up.

"Do you like hunting?" the lawyer asked Placide. "There are hares here as big as mastiffs. And foxes. And squirrels. Squirrel is good to eat."

"I only shoot with a bow," Placide replied modestly.

Pierre and the maid rejoined them.

"It's done. We're in agreement."

And in the way one says: "Sit down, the soufflé is ready now!" the lawyer added:

"Pleurisy doesn't wait."

Here they are now in Monsieur de Boisrosé's bedroom. He had regained consciousness. His bony face, with its lined features, was sunk into the pillow. Spluttering, the sick man raised himself up as they entered and his head did its best to lift itself above the eiderdown, rather like the head of a Chinese torture victim trying to free himself from the cangue. Short of breath, his nose pinched, his hands wringing the sheet—everything pointed to a human being on his last legs. He recognized Placide, greeted him with old-world courtesy, said hello to Pierre and bid them sit down.

"Monsieur, all that remains is to sign," said the lawyer.

"I am happy to sell the Mas Vieux while I live to whomsoever would like it," the sick man, short of breath, whispered with difficulty. "I should nonetheless like to be sure…"

The lawyer, dry as a for sale notice, cut him short.

"To wit," he began: "a personal property, seven rooms over a cellar, fifteen hectares planted with one hundred and twenty olive trees, one hundred and fifty almond trees and vines, two water tanks…"

"… sure that the money will be immediately…" continued M. de Boisrosé in a feeble voice.

"… sheepfold, chicken run…"

"… It's very important…"

"… pine grove…"

"… paid to…"

"Don't interrupt me, Monsieur de Boisrosé… Workshop, wash-house…"

"My only demand, payment in cash…"

"Agreed," replied Pierre.

"It's because I want to recognize above all…"

"You're talking too much, you're exhausting yourself, and you're preventing us from completing."

"One more wish," the dying man went on in a suddenly steady voice: "I put in the electricity myself; I need to explain to you, monsieur, how it works."

"Ah, this electricity! He wore himself out installing it," the maid groaned.

"We shall never get through everything. It's getting dark. You oblige me to request that you keep silent, Monsieur de Boisrosé."

"It's horrible," Pierre muttered to Placide.

Then the thought occurred to him that the lawyer must

know what he was doing and that this brutality towards the dying was necessary. As the end approaches, one's thinking must grow confused; instead of becoming simpler, everything probably becomes complicated, and there must be doubts, qualms and alterations that affect everything. Lawyers are used to dramatic situations. This old grafter knows his job, but it's appalling nonetheless.

"Come on now, sign."

And Maître Caressa took out his pen.

Pierre admired the waxen hands of the dying man with their slender fingers that seemed to be busy undoing life's last threaded knot. A gold signet ring bearing a coat of arms slipped down his bony finger and stopped at the last phalanx. Monsieur de Boisrosé traced his name without raising his pen, allowing it to drop on the line three times, not having the strength to lift it up.

"It's as though there were a fog over my eyes…"

"Do you see the cross… *Read and approved*. Sign over the cross."

"What a word to end on!" sighed Pierre, who felt nauseated.

"Wait. I have to leave the room before it is signed," said Maître Caressa, wearing a grim expression. "I am here as a friend, for you are conducting a private agreement and not a notarized deed."

"What should I do with the money?" asked Pierre.

"Give it to me," said Monsieur de Boisrosé hastily. "You can ask Maître Caressa for the receipt and the title deeds."

The lawyer left the room.

"Love the Mas Vieux as I have loved it," said Monsieur de Boisrosé as though he were showing someone round his den. "Monsieur, nothing could give me greater pleasure than to see you there. I have, however, one favour to ask you…"

He was breathing with difficulty. His death rattle could be heard rising and falling, like a pea in a pea-shooter.

"I shall not be long in taking my leave of you. Therefore, do me the kindness of allowing me to die here in peace. Don't worry. I can see you are speedy, but I shall be no less so. It is just that it would make me unhappy, feeble though I am, to have to leave this bed and this house now."

Monsieur de Boisrosé's chest made a sound like a reed-pipe; he gazed at the pearly landscape that was rapidly fading, the tall pine trees, the moist eyes of his maid. In thanking Pierre, who had agreed to this final wish, he added:

"You see, monsieur, she and I, we have spent our best days here."

CHAPTER IV

T HE FOREST WAS DARK, but the road plotted a clear-cut course through it like chalk upon a slate. A silky moon, forecasting the mistral for the following day, appeared over the vines and lit up the path. Pierre and Placide found their way to the car in the darkness. When the headlights were switched on, the nocturnal crypt was suddenly transformed into a marvellous white palace.

"And now," Placide said, "we shall have a good dinner, take a filtered coffee beneath the plane trees of Aix with its beautiful fountains, and sleep at last for as long as we wish."

"We'll be in Paris—Porte d'Italie—by dawn," Pierre replied laconically.

Placide felt crushed and did not utter a word; his mouth open, revealing a spaniel's pink tongue, he was dreaming of revenge that deep down he knew to be impossible: at La Londe, he would call for help and Pierre would be forced to stop; at Grimaud, he would find the means of puncturing a tyre; at Ollioules, he would stun him with a punch; at Orange, he would murder him. Finally, he said:

"Allow me to light a pipe, at least!"

"A cigar," said Pierre. "That will make you feel as though you had had dinner. No? Do you really want your pipe? Then squat down beneath the dashboard to shield it from the wind."

"Slow down, for heaven's sake, slow down," Pierre yelled despairingly. "I've bumped my forehead!"

"Get yourself a tinder lighter that won't go out, you idiot; whoever heard of carrying a petrol lighter in a car."

"Not everyone has time to waste like you, inventing things that save seconds," said Placide sourly.

The green dials on the dashboard lit up the lower parts of their faces: Placide's bearded chin, looking like that of a Swiss mercenary grown plump from licking Charles V's saucepans, and the neat, chiselled chin of Pierre Niox.

"My curiosity never stops being aroused," said Placide, now back in the Grand Siècle. "What do you do with the seconds that you save?"

"I create minutes from them," moaned Pierre.

He was beginning to have had enough of Placide, who was continuing with his critical reflections:

"How on earth is it possible to buy a property in less than two hours!"

"A great deal of time lost, actually," muttered Pierre.

"Poseur!" said Placide, furious at having to shout, which rather cramped his style.

His own particular talent was for conversation, with its innuendos, allusions, insinuations and subtle, treacherous remarks. A master at fencing and needling, and dropping stink bombs, he was prevented by the car from hitting the mark, but he was too irritated to remain silent.

"No sooner have you bought the Mas Vieux than you're running away from it," said Placide, going on the attack straight away. "You're tying a weight around your neck, my friend! To say nothing of what it's going to cost you. It's money thrown away."

"That's why I'm going back to Paris," said Pierre. "I'm going back to get some funding…"

"… as well as a trustworthy gamekeeper, to keep away poachers; and a supposedly honest tenant farmer; and a household of caretakers with fewer than eight children. I envy you, dear Pierre. You'll enjoy your property in a comfortable, respectable way; you'll sip your Chartreuse like a good Carthusian monk; you'll draw up your specification, cultivate your memory and reap the benefits."

"Bloody hell!" cried Pierre, stubbing out his cigar, which would not draw, on the windscreen and putting it back, unlit, between his quivering lips.

"You don't know, you'll never know, how to smoke," said Placide disdainfully. "A cigar burns through its ash; at a hundred kilometres an hour, it's a heresy. A Havana comes from the land of indolence and nonchalance; yours is horrible to behold, full of little red holes, and it's making your lips black. Ugh! In circumstances like these you'd do better to take up the pipe."

"I inhale too much; I'd char the wood in one day."

Placide let out a long, affected sigh:

"My friendship for you, which no one can doubt, permits me to ask you an indiscreet question. May I? I should like to get to the heart of the Pierre Niox problem."

"There is no Pierre Niox problem," Pierre said tartly.

"But there is, there is! There is the unknown x that drives you. It can't be feelings, you don't love anyone; nor self-interest, no sooner have you earned money than you throw it away; nor sensual pleasure, you take no notice of anyone; nor vanity, you only have to look at yourself. Could it be Certainty, one of those abstract principles upon which people base their lives when they are young and foolish? No, you spent your philosophy classes playing football. Could it be *carpe diem*?"

"Your Horace drives me mad at least as much as you yourself drive me mad," Pierre interrupted. "He is the father of every Latin aphorism quoted by those who don't know Latin. No, I'm not a pleasure-seeker, still less one who experiments."

"Would you be bothered by the notion that our days are numbered? For it's true: they are, from our birth. Come now, respond!"

"Respond to what? I've never asked myself all these absurd questions."

"Tell me why nothing ever connects or holds together when you're around? It's constant confusion, with every minute sweeping the previous one away with an enormous broom; with you, dear fellow," Placide went on, intoxicated by his florid style, "moments overlap one another like waves, each forcing its crest into the other's foam; the present tumbles instantly into the future; I even doubt whether the present exists for you. A fearsome demon is pursuing you. And the name of this demon?"

"The wind."

"Pierre, I'm talking to you seriously."

"Very seriously: the wind, or, if you prefer, my creative energy. As a child, I was taught to jump. 'Use your creative energy!' my father would cry. 'Where is my creative energy?' That produced laughter and I felt ashamed; ever since, I've known that my creative energy was within me, in me alone, and that it was a marvellous potential source of power, always available to me, which grown-ups had probably forgotten how to use since they never seemed to run or jump. As I grew older, I could feel this expendable force beneath my feet; other people expend it in goodness, in the will-to-power, in concentration, in spiteful behaviour or in foul language. I expend it in speed. I am a man of prompt expedition, as your Madame de Sévigné would say. In a word, a precursor: 'I run ahead', it's etymology."

"Would you be really annoyed if the world went at your speed and caught up with you?"

"No danger of that. Whenever that happens, I'll have been long dead."

"And have returned to nothingness?"

"Who knows? There may be a reward up there for those who have spent long enough in Gehenna waiting for others, a paradise where buses and women arrive on time, and speeches take up ten words, where causes and effects go hand in hand, where the alpha collides with the omega and where God—"

"God is above Time," said Placide, out of his depth.

"Not at all! God is Time. If he's invisible to us, it's because he moves too quickly. To be able to see him, one would have to move as quickly as he does: that's what Eternity is. The other day, a train was pulling out; 'Ah,' cried the child sitting nearby, 'look, the trees are walking!'

So with the other life: it will be the turn of stationary things to start walking."

"Watch the bend!" yelled Placide. "Your door's about to open, for heaven's sake! Your speedometer's marking one hundred and sixty! And you don't drive as well as you think you do."

"*Quickly and badly*, that's my motto!"

"An epitaph more likely."

"Epitaphs are the mottos of the dead."

At that moment, after a surge of speed, Pierre was negotiating a bend. The beam of the car's headlights lit up a square shape that was not moving and badly parked. It was a large truck without rear lights that had pulled up on the road. Pierre slammed on his brakes from a distance of thirty metres.

Suddenly they had all the time in the world, more than a fifth of a second, to contemplate the twin tyres that loomed up, to take a careful look at the jack perched under the axle of the broken-down truck and the thick plank beneath it, as well as the faulty tail light and the number of the police car covered in dust that they were about to crash into, all presided over by a tarpaulin the colour of a bat. They took the time to read each letter of the name of the transport company, to consider almost nonchalantly each blade of grass and the enormous spare wheel by the side of the road, and the merest insect on this warm night made Amazonian by the proximity of the Rhône; they saw their lives flash by, were able to think about their future, about the gendarmes who would soon arrive with a box of bandages that lacked the required medicaments, about the curious bystanders, about the very haughty neighbours.

With a bold swing of the steering wheel, however, Pierre managed to avoid the worst, the local ambulance, the hospital bed and the temporary burial chamber at Saint-Vallier cemetery. Due to his quick reflexes, they were let off with a brand-new wing that still smelt of the workshop and cellulose paint. But, this battered wing being one of those improvements of current automobile construction that wrapped itself round the headlight, the light immediately went out, followed by the other one.

The night was resplendent, very dark and close-textured; the stars shone, you could hear the wide Rhône flowing over its cool bed and you could sense it between the tall poplars and the mooring stakes.

"And here we are," muttered Placide, quivering and trying to be composed.

"What a fine river!" said Pierre. "At last some water that moves quickly!"

"We had a lucky escape. The scoundrel who was driving that large truck must have been off drinking or asleep!"

said Placide indignantly. "That's a bad deed that deserves a proper whipping."

"Come now, control yourself, Monsieur de Grignan!"[2]

"And where is there a garage open at this time?"

"You're sure to find one tomorrow morning."

"But until then?"

"Settle yourself into what's left of the car. Take my overcoat."

"And you? Where are you going?"

"To Paris," Pierre said simply. "You wouldn't want me to wait, would you?"

And he set off into the night, walking in the middle of the road, at a rapid pace, dragging deeply on his chewed-up cigar.

CHAPTER V

I T IS MIDDAY. Madame de Boisrosé, naturally, is in bed, for she scarcely ever rises from this bed; she is unable to sleep in it and even though she is drowsy and constantly tired, she spends night and day trying to sleep. Nothing is more exhausting than being unable to sleep; there is a horizontal weariness that active people will never experience.

The sun skims the imitation Louis XVI bedroom furniture and flows into the tepid atmosphere; the damp logs sparkle in the stove, mingling humidity with the heat, causing a season of Caribbean rain to pervade this Saint-Germain apartment.

The Boisrosé family, who have lived there since the separation decree that had caused Monsieur de Boisrosé to retreat to his refuge at the Mas Vieux, leaving the three daughters to their mother, are holding a daylight wake in honour of the deceased. On hearing of his death, the four women, who had not set eyes on the old hermit for nine years, discovered an immense love for him. Separation, jealousy, quarrels and resentment do not preclude love, a reptilian fondness that bites its own tail and feeds happily from its opposite end. What the Boisrosé ladies enjoyed most about this bereavement was the nervous shock and the tearful stimulation aroused by the unexpected event, the notion of sorrow fomenting grief itself, or rather a magical elation similar to the outbursts at Negro funerals, all culminating in a French apotheosis of family-mindedness. During his bitch of a life, Monsieur de Boisrosé had let out numerous sighs; only the last of these was heard.

"Poor Papa died all on his own," sobbed Fromentine.

"Without having seen the old colony again, or the Trou Dauphin," said Hedwige.

"Without a bit of warm earth for his final resting place."

"He would have preferred the sailors' cemetery or even the Negro one to a grave in France!"

"He died of grief; I, too, will die of grief; one never dies of anything else," said Madame de Boisrosé.

Lying across her mother's bed, Fromentine was allowing her mascara to run like watery pitch down her lacklustre cheeks. Her red hair blazed. Sitting on the floor, dark-haired Hedwige, her back to the base of the bed, looked like a funerary allegory, while Angélique, her blonde head buried against Madame de Boisrosé's cheek, made up the final panel of this three-coloured, domestic carrying of the

Cross. Nothing could stem the tears of these four women, who rake up old memories and end up crying over themselves—that bottomless urn—nothing, that is, unless it be the smooth expanse of their Creole nonchalance in which everything they feel or undertake gets buried in the sand.

Once they had all wept and sobbed a great deal, once the emotion of the morning had subsided—something that was regularly provoked by the arrival of Angélique, who lived in Paris, who had not been able to cry at home during the night, and who rushed off to her own family as soon as her husband had left for the office—once this daily memorial service had lasted long enough—and it had been going on for three weeks—they realized that midday had struck and that it was high time to prepare lunch, which today happened to be peppers with sweetcorn.

While Angélique was laying the table and Fromentine was greasing the frying pan, Madame de Boisrosé whetted her appetite by polishing off a box of chocolates. She was a woman of forty-eight who, on days when she washed and daubed herself with white, managed to look only sixty, for among Creoles nature works twice as hard. Madame de Boisrosé ruled over her three daughters in the manner of the Sun King. The three Boisrosé girls would be famous for their beauty had they ever encountered other people, but they knew no one. They lived in Saint-Germain, a town that is nonetheless connected to Paris by ninety trains each day, as though they were living in a field of sugar cane. No news penetrated there, they received no communications from either the outside world or the present day; they bloomed amid an inaccessible and inflated collective happiness. The eldest daughter (twenty-four years old), the only married one, is called Angélique; the middle one (twenty), Hedwige; the youngest (eighteen), Fromentine.

Not daring to call their mother Mummy, they have given her the nickname of Mamicha. Just as primitive religions avoid giving their god a name out of extreme respect. Bonne de Boisrosé is certainly the object of such basic idolatry. For her daughters she is the water goddess, the cow goddess, the tree goddess. And just as a tree in autumn towers over ground that is strewn with its fruits, Bonne, sitting on a pile of cushions, watches her daughters daily as they sprawl at her feet, on her bed, adoring her; and serving her according to a certain number of rituals applied regularly and at random in life which they sometimes refer to with an anxious smile as the Rule.

The Rule assigns all household duties to Angélique. To her belongs the household washing, the ironing, the sewing machine, the kitchen; no one sautées or braises except under her direction; it is she who deals with the daily woman; from her generous hands flows the bleach; the food and the drink are her responsibility; she alone has the keys of the cupboards, the recipes for gherkins and the authority to decide whether a sauce shall be spicy or vinaigrette. But, like a chatelaine who permits servitude, she relinquishes the desserts to Fromentine. Her authority ceases with rum babas, madeleines, brioches and macaroons. Angélique looks after the tinned food. Angélique sometimes looks after her husband too, but having exhausted her domestic energy at Saint-Germain, she is so indolent and lethargic with him that he knows her only as an odalisque.

Hedwige, for her part, tries her hand at household accounting from the moment she jumps out of bed. She has scissors for the rent coupons and also for cutting out patterns for the family's dresses. She occasionally settles one out of every ten bills. The gas and electricity meters impart their secret tariffs to her. She sorts out the Boisrosé library, which even contains some books; she changes the needles on the gramophone. She also answers letters because hers is the most legible handwriting. Hedwige buys the lottery tickets. From her height of five foot seven, she discusses tax affairs with the inspector, who is only five foot tall.

The Rule requires that Fromentine, on behalf of the Boisrosés, should maintain contact with nature, sporting activities, flowers, fruits, bouquets and secateurs. No doubt because she is the least natural of all of them. She is the one who puts seeds in the pipit's cage, the little warbler from the tropics that chirps at the tiniest ray of sunshine. Every Thursday morning, she sets off for Paris and alights at that exotic aviary that is Hédiard's and, like the conquistadors in Seville, she brings back palm oil, potatoes and groceries. As soon as she is informed about a delivery of mangoes (mangoes from Guinea in summer and mangoes from Venezuela in winter), she buys bags of them. In this way, she serves the community while simultaneously gratifying the never-satisfied family appetite for expenditure (an appetite that is assuaged equally well with centimes as it is with banknotes) for a couple of days.

Young and beautiful, these three girls worked hard and never stopped blessing their mother for having brought them up without cares, without religion and with barely a thought of a dowry. But if one of them had a problem or felt upset, it was enough for her to set foot in Mamicha's bedroom to find peace and feel well again. Like a miraculous idol, Mamicha accepted everything and gave nothing away, but she was able to cure. She took upon herself the responsibility for anything to do with medicaments; and also with justice; she dismissed all appeals as squabbles, for the sake of general well-being.

Cleopatra dropped a pearl into vinegar, poured the vinegar into a vessel, and drank from it. The Boisrosés fit into this brief legend: Fromentine, the youngest and most beautiful, is Cleopatra; Hedwige, the most brilliant and sensitive, is the pearl; Angélique, the most caustic, the most fermentative, the vinegar. And what part does Bonne de Boisrosé play if not the vessel?

Bonne de Boisrosé was neither good, nor loving, nor intelligent; she was neither kind nor energetic, quite the contrary, and yet her three daughters, so different from one another, would have willingly agreed never to marry, or to die in torment, if it brought their poor mother comfort and happiness. Beneath the convenient label of filial love, she had inculcated in them a whole host of taboos and impulses that were as irresistible as the laws of gravity. No one had ever observed in Bonne that joyful self-effacement that most mothers display as their children grow in strength and beauty. The more her daughters progressed, the more assured the Mamicha-like demands and her domineering, radiant and foolish personality became. For there is a fragile power to old age, a stubbornly brilliant ineffectiveness, a frail domestic blackmail that novelists and historians, those Siamese twins of our age, must take into account.

This plump, bedridden dwarf had given birth to these three girls, the shortest of whom was five foot seven tall. When they were all together, one was reminded of the Sibyls

in the Sistine Chapel: everything was there, the proportions, the bones, the way they carried their heads. They
could not handle a broom or a saucepan without looking
as though they were holding cornucopias or sceptres. It
wasn't a hat that they should have worn on their heads,
but a circus tent. Fashion did not trouble them for they
were in vogue at every level. For such women, no men exist
these days, and particularly not in France. The Boisrosé
girls had no success because in our country popularity
wears size thirty-six clothes and size six gloves, because
success, like harnessed lightning, is a very delicate thing.
Failure awaited them; they were unfortunate in their size,
because what is very large either gets damaged or lost, be
it the Nile among the desert sands or Jean Mermoz[3] in
the ocean. The Boisrosés were like those vast Aubusson
tapestries, those gigantic seventeenth-century chests that
used to be sold at auction extremely cheaply because no
one had a lorry driver to transport them nor an apartment
in which to keep them. Comparable to allegories, these
human creatures were simple and indecisive, very different
from those allegories that possess neither simplicity nor
mystery and have their names inscribed at the bottom of
their dresses. From the Sibyls, they borrowed a vague and
sombre aspect; they were the gaudy ornaments of a temple
invisible to the non-initiated, the temple of the Mother.

They were female Knights Templar, the Porte-Glaive sisters of the uterine order.

"Hurry up, children," called Bonne; "Madame de La Chaufournerie is due at two o'clock to pay her respects to me on the death of your father and we still have to have lunch and tidy up. Hedwige, my pink dressing gown."

"You're not going to get up, Mamicha?"

"What, with my hacking cough and my wretched mortgage, debilitated and thrown into confusion by this news! It's catastrophic! It's crucifying! One of these days, I'm going to pass away!"

"Mamicha," wept Fromentine, "how can you frighten us like this? You, die! But then we'd all die."

"I'm in a bad way; I've got such a raging temperature you'd have thought a spider crab had bitten me! And I have to think of everything, get everything ready, take stock of our situation; do the balance sheet!" (Bonne loved words that she did not understand). "The Anse sugar refinery in Mustique is in a mess and the indigo factory has collapsed. Where are we going to get any money? My brain goes to pieces as far as figures are concerned. And to cap it all, here's your father selling the Mas Vieux and dying immediately afterwards."

"Very well," exclaimed Fromentine, her eyes gleaming, "that's where there's some money!"

"What a scatterbrain you are, girl! You never listen to serious conversations, your head's upside down. Haven't we said over and over again that this money was never discovered? Hedwige, get the cards quickly! A pack of fifty-two; I'm going to see what they have to tell me… and also an aspirin, no, some paraffin in a little *verveine* instead. You'll find some in the small medicine cupboard. Fromentine, get a move on!"

A spluttering sound could be heard coming closer and the platter of peppers with corn made its entrance. Angélique, sweating from the kitchen fumes, a cotton scarf around her head, a magnificent enchantress, was holding the pan, the handle of which she had wrapped in a lace handkerchief so as not to burn her fingers; Fromentine, like a choirboy, was carrying the can of oil, the palm oil that was an essential ingredient of the Boisrosés' diet.

Once lunch was over, Madame de Boisrosé, her pack of cards in her hand, started weeping again while playing "Napoleon's Tomb" at the same time.

"My adorable little Mamicha," said Hedwige, cosseting her, "don't cry any more, we'll take care of all your worries."

"I'm mourning your poor Papa who loved us so; his

last thought was for us, you can be sure of that. Ah, what a great heart and what a mind!"

"So where could Papa have hidden those millions of francs?" Angélique asked dreamily. "In a hole in the wall, or in a hollow olive tree?"

"He gave them to his mistress, of course," Madame de Boisrosé wailed tartly. "To that whore who hoodwinked him. His last thought was for her, no doubt about it, and his last will too."

"Things like that shouldn't be allowed. What Papa did was disgraceful."

"Don't say that, Angélique, don't show disrespect to your father. Hilarion was not a wicked man, but he was weak with women; they took advantage of him! One after another, the whole gang of them were there... and he didn't even get a good meal!"

"I've got an idea," Hedwige announced. "I'm going to go and find the purchaser, this Monsieur Pierre Niox. I shall explain to him that this business is illegal and since he must be an honest man—"

"Honest? An antique dealer? Look at your uncle!" cried Bonne. "That's a ridiculous plan."

"Are you going to forbid me?"

"No, I don't forbid you. Look under the bed, Fromentine, the jack of clubs is missing."

CHAPTER VI

FOR YEARS Pierre's household duties have been performed, and performed badly, by Chantepie. Lame from having fallen off a ladder, dressed in clothes that are too long for him, his tie askew, slow and undignified, squalid and penniless, an eavesdropper and someone who is insistent without being over-zealous, Chantepie is the link that connects the domesticated chimpanzee to the domesticated man. A committed capitalist, Chantepie goes out every afternoon to check the Stock Exchange prices; and also, since his food is paid for at a fixed rate, to squabble with the animals over the scraps from the horse butcher on which he survives. Pierre kicks him out of the house at least once a month, but Chantepie refuses to leave, offering to stay without any wages, which disarms his master. Furthermore, Chantepie lends him money and their accounts are so muddled that Pierre doesn't have time to examine them and so he settles them all in a single payment. The patient man always wears down the impatient one.

"Chantepie, my slippers!"

His slippers have not been polished, any more than his clothes have been brushed, his breakfast prepared, the logs sawn or the wine put into bottles. Rather than see him dawdling over these duties, Pierre attends to them himself; Chantepie follows behind listlessly, makes comments from a distance and watches as the lightning storm passes by. Pierre thunders and roars, but Chantepie doesn't hear him because he is deaf. He lives locked into his own deafness just as Pierre is locked into his own frantic pace: all disabilities are prisons. It is due to his imperturbable lethargy that Chantepie has been able to remain with Pierre, who would have driven any other servant mad.

Chantepie was nothing more than the ghost of a former hotel manager; his instincts were wholly antiquated. He neither stole nor pilfered; he would even have preferred to die of hunger when confronted with delicacies, like an elderly dog that is used to retrieving without biting. He never made use of his master's cellar to get drunk, but drank a foul pear cider sent to him from the depths of his native Brittany. A few drops would be enough to make him fall over; once on the ground, his rheumatism prevented him from standing up and he would remain there, like a tortoise on its back, until Pierre came to pick him up. Moaning like a child, he allowed himself to be moved as he whined, "Monsieur is so kind!"

For all these reasons, Pierre kept Chantepie, or more precisely, Chantepie kept Pierre.

The impatient man washing himself is a sight to behold.

"What delays us so much," Pierre says to himself in a loud voice, "is that we only do one thing at a time. And that we hesitate between various actions. It has taken me twenty years to devise a system for myself and to improve my speeds, but how many gaffes I still make: I remove my pyjamas to get into the bath; I then realize that I have left the soap on the washstand… Chantepie, my soap!"

And Chantepie brings some logs.

"I put my pyjamas back on because I am cold; I trip over myself because my shoes get caught in my trouser leg."

"Monsieur should always wear slippers," observes Chantepie, who indulges his master's quirks, "much time would be saved; monsieur would be able to get his foot in and out more quickly."

"We shall have to do away with these pointless vestiges," Pierre goes on. "Let's start by numbering each movement: *one*, remove the razor blade and take advantage of the fact that my legs are of no use to me at that moment to flex my instep, which will lessen the time spent on my physical exercises; *two*, screw the razor with my right hand between my thumb and index finger, while the left hand squeezes the sponge in the hot water; *three*, shave in the bath and thus avoid the time wasted with the water."

Pierre is famous among his friends for the speed at which he shaves himself, two minutes twenty-eight seconds, a record that has never been beaten.

"*Four*, comb your hair while drying yourself at the same time... No, let's pause a moment, because putting a shirt over your head means having to comb your hair twice. Chantepie, put on a record, and quickly!"

Pierre always has music playing, having read in books by Bedeau that it speeds up human efficiency.

"Having shirts that button up from top to bottom? Madness! Eight buttons means eighteen seconds lost each day. I've already got rid of sleeve buttons and those dickey shirt-fronts that waste your time, and there's no point in replacing them with other buttons. Putting your shoes on while doing your tie up at the same time, that's child's play. And now for trousers. All my trousers are fitted with zip fasteners."

"The days that the zips get stuck, monsieur loses an hour," Chantepie remarks, "and I get the blame."

"Buy me some mechanic's overalls!"

"That's not what monsieur should be wearing! A man like monsieur..." Chantepie sighs as he pretends to sweep with a broom that hasn't a single bristle.

Ever since he was at the *lycée*, Pierre used to dazzle his friends not so much on account of his high marks but because he already had as many braces as he did pairs of trousers, ready to be put on simultaneously. The others, with their single pairs, were well behind their impetuous classmate. Pierre had learnt at an early age the lesson of Fregoli's dazzling displays on the stage of the Olympia, and he remembered his childish admiration when the brilliant performer would suddenly loom up stage right dressed as a conductor, vanish again while still continuing to talk to himself, only to reappear stage left thirty seconds later wearing a low-cut dress; at the end of the show, the backdrop curtain would be raised revealing, hanging from strings, 101 amazing costumes surrounded by an array of accessories: the conductor's tailcoat along with the white gloves and the baton, and the ball gown together with the fan and the reticule. At military school, the squad of trainee officers traditionally remained in bed when the morning drum sounded and did not get up until the order came: "Everyone downstairs!" In Polytechnique jargon, that was called dressing in "quick-time". Pierre owed his popularity to the fact that, although he was last out of bed, he was the first one downstairs. It was the absolute tops, "super quick-time"; he had achieved this pre-eminence through a whole series of inventions: collar attached to the tunic, boots full of talcum powder worn without socks; he also went to bed half dressed. Later on, he resorted to lighting a cigarette while unfolding his newspaper, to opening his post while making a phone call, with the receiver held to his ear by a raised shoulder beneath his chin.

"There we are. I'm ready. A quarter of an hour would have been enough; it's not bad, but it means an hour gets lost every four days, which amounts to about ninety-six hours a year devoted to cleanliness. What a waste of valuable time! One trembles to think of it. How wise I was to give up massage and manicure! The toothbrush still plays tricks on me and so does the toothpaste tube, which always bursts at the bottom. These small luxuries must be sacrificed to the greater luxury that is time. It's the incidental things that mainly get me down: the brilliantine, the tweezers, etc. There would be good reason to see all this in a sordid spirit of economy of movement: doing away with gargling, for example; not sniffing water through the nasal fossae any longer; putting the *métro* tickets in my wallet beforehand."

Here is Pierre Niox standing between two mirrors, the one above the mantelpiece and the one on the wall. Not that he has stopped to look at himself, but while he is in this locality, let us try to grasp this elusive man from both angles. Pierre has washed his hands, but naturally he has not had time to dry them and he is doing so by waving them around like puppets. It is a good moment to examine this example of "instantaneous man" and we shall not have a similar opportunity later in the day because Pierre is catching the eleven o'clock train to Brussels. The slanting light reveals him to be slender, with smoothly rounded skin, a decently shaped face, a prominent nose and surprisingly fine light-blue eyes beneath some swarthy black hair.

The bullet that is fired from the gun does not ask itself whether it is going to make a hole in a cardboard box or shatter a skull; neither does Pierre. Reading this, you might think of him as daring. "There goes a confident man," people will say, "who is not going to make a mess of things." Quite the contrary, Pierre is timid because his haste has caused him many a failure alternating with huge successes. And the moral of this story shall be to show that the impatient man is punished more frequently than he is rewarded.

Let us return to the pose: Pierre has the figure of a fencer painted for the Salon des Artistes Français in about 1895, with his locks and moustache newly waxed. With his restless hands, his tremulous lips, his very dark skin beneath which many very dark feelings stir, he could only be French. His clothes are moulded to his body and it would be impossible for a dog to bite him by seizing the seat of his trousers or his sleeve, so neat and precise is the cut.

He walks with his hands plunged into the back pockets of his trousers, which accentuates the hollow of his abdomen. His stomach is concave and below it a watch chain glitters, casting a cold gleam over his Spanish Christ-like body.

Pierre is now reading the newspaper. Or one could say it is reading him. It has thrown itself upon him and is devouring him. He starts at the back page, just as he begins his letters with his signature and the address on his envelopes with the name of the town or the postcode. He can't help it. He can never help it. Continuing his perusal of the daily newspaper, he finally reaches the bold headlines on the front page and the editorial, makes a ball out of such fine prose and rolls it across the room. This habit dates from the time that Pierre owned a cat and would try to amuse it. But the cat was not amused; the cat remained forlorn, being of a contemplative breed that loathes impulsive people. The cat puts up with noise as long as it is a sound that is repeated. Being nervous, noise upsets it. The cat is purring at the moment. The cat always lives in the here and now whereas Pierre always lives in the following day. The cat thinks and doesn't move except to defend itself. The cat simmers and never boils over. The cat is a compact creature, a slow-cooking stove. Pierre's cat would look at its master (though is one ever the master of a cat?) with regret. He had an accommodating nature, but, having put his tail over his eyes to keep out the daylight and settled himself comfortably for the morning, he disliked Pierre's sudden disorderly entrances and exits. If he were drinking his milk and Pierre suddenly leapt up, he would flatten his ears, lower his tail and stand sideways to drink while keeping watch with an anxious eye; then, his appetite diminished by this galloping, which caused the floorboards to quake, he would set off sadly, with a drip on his chin, to shelter beneath the chest of drawers. One day the cat had had enough. He left via the balcony and vanished.

Having thrown away his newspaper, Pierre checked his watch: "Losing five minutes reading the paper is insane!" He thought that the best way, in accordance with the principle of *two things at once if possible*, would have been to read it while on the lavatory. A brilliant idea: print the dailies on toilet paper. Furthermore, Pierre never took long over these tasks; among his friends it was a classic joke:

"He does his main business faster than others do their lesser one!"

Pierre looked at his watch again. He lived with his eye on his wrist. Impossible to give a picture of him without this familiar gesture: his arm thrown forward to reveal his wristwatch, then folded and quickly raised towards his face so that he can read the dial. This ever so emancipated man was crucified upon the two hands of a watch; he felt ashamed of this, but has shame ever cured a vice? These tiny scissors carved his day into seconds, each of which, by dint of being too precious, comprised a total which, along with the others, was completely intolerable. On rare occasions, he became aware of his haste and was astonished by it: "Why is it that my heart is beating as though I were running to a romantic assignation whereas I'm simply going to call on my shoemaker? There must be things to slow up the systole: a false clock? Or false time? After all, we artificially create an hour in summer." At moments like these he considered himself ridiculous and promised to live a calmer life; but he only succeeded in filling his day by wandering around pointlessly in order that he could savour its actual duration, its duration pure and simple. (In such a manner did all Henry Ford's activity, the working hours he saved, lead to the distractions of a man of straw, to lessons in the minuet.) Placide, who was consulted one day, had suggested some remedies: a sea voyage, during which everything is adjourned (Ah! lower the anchor, otherwise I'll leap over the guard rail!); shows with long intervals (Oh! better to kill the usherette!); angling (until the sight of the float bobbing about on its own reflection makes you feel ill); shooting (hours spent swivelling on your shooting stick while the gamekeeper grumbles: "It's due to the wind that's changed direction, nothing else is going to come over today"). Why not have one's hair cut? laughed Pierre (No friction, no singeing, no drying, no this…, no that…, and especially no conversation!); wait at the counter of a bank (a French one); immerse yourself in reading *L'Illustration* at the dentist's ("Sorry, I had a lady from the country with a large boil"); regattas (All right, let's be off! The breeze is dropping now!)

"No, we'd have to find something far more ridiculous to block out the passage of time completely: total abstention from all activity. For what consumes us is not so much forced or prolonged waiting as those imperceptible pauses and automatic gestures that make holes like a sieve in one's day: chewing food, sharpening a pencil, sticking stamps, groping about for the button in a lift, signing a registered letter, filling the radiator with water, waiting for a dog to have done its business, comforting a woman…"

Pierre looked at his watch for the tenth time.

"I don't believe it! It's stopped. Chantepie, what time is it? What, you haven't wound up the drawing room clock! Chantepie, you must mend your ways! As soon as I have some money I'm going to buy myself an automatic clock."

"As they say where I come from, monsieur, men are not made for time, but time is made for men…"

A ring at the doorbell interrupted the manservant; he disappeared, but came back bringing a scrap of paper with a name written in pencil.

"It saves having to have visiting cards," he said disdainfully.

Pierre read:

MADEMOISELLE HEDWIGE DE BOISROSÉ

Pierre immediately took the usual precautions. He had a whole arsenal of defensive procedures with which to protect himself from bores: he hid the chairs in a way that would deter the visitor from settling down permanently, he opened the windows to let in a chilly breeze; the lady would not stay for long. In order to be safer still, Pierre donned a fedora (it was simply a sign that he was about to go out, for he put nothing on his head outside and generally he wore no over-coat because of the time it took getting into the sleeves). He grabbed his gloves in one hand and his umbrella in the other.

He glanced again at the piece of paper, his eyes fixed on the name.

"This visit may produce cheap cards, but a wealth of tedium," he thought to himself.

He almost said "I've gone out", but he could sense the presence on the other side of the wall of a solitary woman who would be determined and would return.

"I will see this lady," he said, dismissing Chantepie, who was standing to attention.

Hedwige entered. Hedwige in mourning in the totally white room; merely the simple, slow movement of her feet, with just enough delicacy to make her gait seem beautiful. Unaware of what he was doing, Pierre laid his hat on the table; this woman had something about her, but what was it? Hedwige removed her veil. The crêpe material, emblem of that which no longer exists, had the ability to move Pierre deeply. This cinder-like substance, worn in mid-morning over this youthfulness and beauty as though to cushion the shock, attired Hedwige with a Spanish modesty, and endowed her with the melancholy of a grave that is never visited. This tall young woman, an exquisite image of misfortune tinged with the leaden effect of crêpe, resembled a pole flying the flag at half-mast.

"It is you, monsieur, is it not, who bought the Mas Vieux from my father, Monsieur de Boisrosé?"

Pierre admired the pearl-like complexion, not yet ravaged by the sun like the skins of fashionable girls, but so opaque with light and freshness; the slight quivering of the crêpe, its waviness and the rustle of its black material, screening the light, succeeded in enchanting him.

"It is you?" Hedwige asked again.

"Yes, mademoiselle," said Pierre automatically.

A curious feeling came over him; he felt disengaged, freewheeling, and was descending effortlessly, as though in a dream, into a sense of unfamiliar well-being. This blindingly white room, which he had just emptied and allowed his ally the cold to come into, was turning into a warm Oceanic night. Pierre was discovering a part of himself that he was unfamiliar with and in which he moved with surprising ease. He happened to notice himself in the mirror and he thought he had changed, become more attractive in appearance, more imposing. His eyes met Hedwige's.

"Why are you laughing?" he enquired.

"Because you had forgotten I was there; I saw you in the mirror: when one looks at people face to face one can see them, but when one looks at them in the mirror one understands them."

"What you say is not at all foolish," said Pierre. "Do you read much?"

"Never; I don't like cutting the pages."

"I cut them with my finger."

They burst out laughing, both of them delighted to be laughing simultaneously over something so deeply ridiculous. A picnic-like gaiety spread through this room in which the onlooker would have seen only a tall girl dressed in black and a tall young man in grey, four walls that were so white that they gave you a pain in the optic nerve and the sinus, a steel desk, two telephones, some electrical wires, an electric heater and some wax-cloth curtains.

Hedwige slipped her finger under the white crêpe band beneath her chin, which was strangling her laughter. This reminded her that she had come dressed for serious matters.

"Monsieur, I hope that you won't be offended if I take the liberty of asking you a few questions."

Pierre made a polite gesture.

"To whom, please, did you pay the money for the Mas Vieux?"

"To your father, naturally."

"And do you know what he has done with it? Whether he has paid it to the lawyer or to someone else?"

Pierre was evasive:

"Goodness me, how should I know?"

She pursued the matter:

"You were probably in my father's bedroom, since he was very ill. Did you not notice anything?"

"Is this a cross-examination?" said Pierre.

These questions were becoming annoying.

"This money…"

Pierre could feel the pressure almost physically, as though he were being woken up; his nerves strained to resist; he remained motionless for a brief moment, then suddenly something clicked inside him and the whole machinery started up: time, which for an instant was suspended in mid-flight like a bird gliding, was set in motion; once again, Pierre had re-engaged the clutch. In a trice he glanced at his watch, tossed his cigarette away, rang the bell and without waiting opened the other window and both doors, shouting:

"Chantepie! Chantepie, my watch has stopped yet again." (He shook his arm as though he were drowning.) "What time is it on the kitchen clock?"

"It says almost midday," Chantepie replied.

"A taxi, right away!"

"Are you in a hurry?" asked Hedwige in astonishment.

"I've only got time to dash… Don't worry, I'll be back… tomorrow or the day after… I'll call you on the telephone… we'll sort it all out," yelled Pierre, who was already descending the stairs, one sentence on each landing. (Ever since he was at the *lycée*, he had held the record for descending the staircase.)

Once he was downstairs, Pierre stamped around in the porter's lodge, fulminated on the pavement, stood in the very middle of the road, complained about the concierge's husband who didn't know how to run, dispatched Chantepie to search for a second taxi, then eventually jumped into a cruising cab without waiting any longer. He set off just at the moment when both taxis arrived outside his door one after the other, one with the concierge on the back seat, the other with Chantepie perched on the running board, both of them waving madly, but ineffectively.

"He's a lunatic," said the taxi driver.

"He's a butterfly," said Chantepie poetically.

"He's a nincompoop," said the concierge.

CHAPTER VII

THE EARLY AFTERNOON SUN beamed down on the snow with which a gust of slanting east wind had prematurely whitewashed Paris; the snow kept nothing to itself, it reflected the warm light, now grown cold, in every direction, emphasizing aspects of the houses, darkening the bare trees, transforming pigeons into crows, tinting blonde girls into Negresses and brushing the whitest dogs with a coat of saffron yellow. The cars were causing the ice to crackle and were tracing flourishes in the streets. Concierges were scraping the doorways with coal shovels while melting stalactites dropped on their heads from the tops of cornices.

Meanwhile, at Saint-Germain, the minutes ticked by sluggishly. (The Boisrosé ladies, a curiously lethargic crew, pay no heed to passing time, nor to celestial trajectories; they could not care less whether it is the sun or moon that is reaching its zenith and, according to their whims, they can transform the brightest day into dusk by drawing the curtains, or the darkest night into a blaze of electric light.)

Although the afternoon had scarcely begun, the only light in Madame de Boisrosé's bedroom, where all the shutters were closed, came from the tiny flame of a silver night light; in this half-light, Angélique, seated on her mother's bed, her huge dark eyes ringed like Saturn (and, anyway, she always looked as though she had just come back from some unheard of, if not undreamt of, saturnalian gathering), was gazing at herself in a looking-glass.

"Be careful, Angélique, you're going to drop it; a broken mirror brings seven years' bad luck," said Bonne.

Angélique nodded vaguely. Nothing can be more misleading than a woman's looks: Angélique, the reasonable one, the good housekeeper, always seemed to look distraught, dishevelled and absent-minded, more like a character in a play than a woman. Yet she led the most ordinary of lives and there was nothing unusual about her apart from this amalgam of mother and husband, of free love and conjugal duty. For the Boisrosés, marriage was a necessary but transitional rite and procreation was a sort of impregnation, however contrived, prior to which the male was unnecessary, and after which he was abandoned. Scarcely had the wedding photographer snapped for all eternity Angélique's white satin dress alongside the morning coat and gaiters of the Polytechnique graduate who had thought naively that he was entering the Boisrosé family (one doesn't enter this family, one is born into it), than Angélique had returned to the roost and gone back to her mother's house, a step that so many women threaten and so few carry out. Angélique spent the required regulatory time lying alongside her husband, a period that was further reduced by the telephone which, though it has no power over the body, liberates the soul, allowing the married daughter to maintain nightly contact with her family through the intermediary of obliging neighbours (the Boisrosés had no phone) who didn't even mind being woken up occasionally, such was the Boisrosés' gift for having things done for them by everyone. In the morning, barely had the husband selected as the lesser evil had his breakfast, than Angélique went back to her old pattern of life until it was time to go to bed again. This brief nightly absence, a sort of gaseous migration of a body, which did not undermine the family's integrity or the abiding maternal authority, had no effect on conjugal relations. Angélique had no children.

According to the Boisrosé doctrine, as received from heaven by Bonne and revealed on some unknown mountain in Sinaï, love was the sole betrayal. Angélique had never been guilty of it. Neither would Hedwige ever sink into this quagmire. Never would she, like an unhooded falcon, set off for the open sea with some young male creature without coming back at the set time to sit at her mother's knee. But they were less sure of Fromentine. The fact that she was eighteen, had a prying and inquisitive temperament, a certain exploratory boldness, and a pride that prompted her to advertise her dangerous beauty to other people, suggested tendencies to cut herself off from her roots and to be drawn to the outside world. She was crazy about dresses, and wealth would have pierced her with its arrows had she ever experienced it; but she knew of it only through a sort of unconscious nostalgia and through that natural inclination that impels beautiful girls in the direction of rue de la Paix and avenue Matignon. The Boisrosé family, it goes without saying, watched over her, each of them taking turns to supervise Fromentine; and it was the suitors who were the losers, as were the matchmaking ladies, to their brief shame, and the jewellers who lost income. Just in case, in the unlikely event that the danger should become real, Bonne de Boisrosé kept a secret and dependable weapon in reserve: fainting and death which, if resorted to, immediately brought about remorse from the sinner, and resurrection. She was unparalleled in her ability to use her weakness in an intimidating manner. Pupils at the Conservatoire working on excerpts from *La Dame aux camélias* for their exams would have benefited from taking lessons in dying from her. Let us add that she rarely needed to pull out all the stops; the threatening remark, the last paragraph of the Rule, always sufficed: "I shall die". This graveyard blackmail, with its indulgent description of funerals to come, deciding upon the ceremony, the announcement of the death, the burial, the Mass and the liturgical hymns, not forgetting the invitation cards, the shroud, the procession… had the lugubrious ability to upset the three daughters. Far from familiarizing them with an eventuality that, when all is said and done, is completely natural and even inevitable, this far too frequently evoked prospect had transformed what for normal people is a sad and quickly repressed thought into anguished neurosis.

A ring at the doorbell, hurried footsteps, a cheerful passing remark aimed at the cleaning lady—it's Hedwige; she enters the room, her body radiating the pure, icy air she has absorbed.

"There you are!" said Angélique lazily. "What time is it? Oh, you've brought the cold weather with you; have you had lunch?"

"Yes, I've eaten some pistachio nuts. There are a few left over, here, take them," she says as she empties her bag on the bed. "Quick, Fromentine, relight the stove, I'm frozen. I've been dashing around all morning."

"Tell us, tell us!" Fromentine (on her knees) cried. She is blowing on the embers to revive them. "Have you seen the new perfumes? Where are the samples?"

"Just a moment," said Hedwige, who was fumbling in her pockets, in her handbag, in her blouse and finally in her brassiere, from which she extracted them. "They're marvellous, smell how sweet they are. I've also brought white nail varnish. You have to put it on first before the red, it stays on better. It's American."

A huge sigh from Bonne interrupted this information.

"Mamicha, at least you're not feeling ill, are you?" Hedwige called out anxiously. "I'm going to make you feel better straight away, my darling. I've got some good news for you. Monsieur Pierre Niox is going to sort everything out."

"Is he going to get us the money?"

"I don't know, but as he was leaving he said: 'We'll sort that out.'"

"He'll pay for the Mas Vieux twice to please Hedwige," said Fromentine straight away.

"I hope, my child, that you didn't give this stranger the impression that we are arguing over your father's legacy with a servant. We do not come from such a grand background that we can do such things without any shame."

"But, Mamicha, I had to talk to him about the sale. We're not interested in it ourselves, but we need money. He certainly understood…"

"What makes you think that he understood? What did he say to you? Tell us everything."

Hedwige opened her mouth, searched for the words and realized she had nothing to say. Fortunately for her, Fromentine cut in:

"First, tell us what he looks like. Describe him. Is he handsome?"

"He's ugly," Hedwige said slowly. "He's ugly and he makes one feel dizzy."

"Dizziness, that's light-headedness. Did you find him attractive, Hedwige?"

"Be quiet, child," said Bonne, immediately concerned. "Come now, Hedwige, let's start again. Repeat to me word for word your conversation with this gentleman, Monsieur Niox."

"He's not exactly a gentleman," said Hedwige (she was groping around trying to find the right description). "He's a young man. He dresses oddly. His windows were wide open and it was very cold."

"So he offered you a chair and you said…"

"He didn't offer me anything; there were no chairs in the room."

"I don't understand," said Madame de Boisrosé, genuinely amazed. "How can a room not have any chairs?"

"It was his office. I didn't like it," said Hedwige in the same slow, reticent tone of voice. "A totally bare room in which there was nothing to hold on to: neither furniture, nor mouldings, nor cornice, nor door handles. Everything was white, too, as if it was made up of six ceilings."

"You must have felt like a fly in there," Fromentine burst out laughing, "and wondered whether you were upside down. I can see why it must have made you feel dizzy!"

Hedwige glared at her in annoyance and turned to her mother, who asked her to begin at the beginning, from the moment he greeted her.

"He didn't greet me," said Hedwige, "at least not that I remember. For a long time he didn't say a word to me, then we spoke about various things… things of no interest…"

"What, you didn't explain the situation to him?"

"Yes, of course. I told him everything. There's no point in my repeating this story, which you know by heart," said Hedwige, who was feeling unusually irritated.

"There is a point in our knowing what he replied to you," said Angélique ironically.

She fixed her gaze on her sister. It had not escaped her that something was missing here.

"You shall know very shortly, my dear," said Hedwige, "because he intends to ask us to meet him. For the time being, I'm tired and I don't feel like talking. I'm going to have a rest."

And she slipped into the maternal bed, fully dressed, having kicked off her shoes with the heel of her foot and sent them to join her sisters' shoes in the middle of the room. (The Boisrosés were constantly removing their shoes everywhere, in the car, under the tables, in church and, rather more reasonably, at home; this dissoluteness was part of the Rule. What with these pairs of shoes scattered over the carpet, the place looked more like a Christmas hearth, a flea market or the entrance to a mosque; and there was no more characteristic sound made by this colonial family than the noise of large bodies causing the floorboards to bend beneath their bare heels.)

At about six o'clock in the evening, Fromentine was the first to wake up and she went to light the fire. She threw balls of paper which she moistened and put out to dry in the sun before stuffing them into her oven. The stove was an ugly little barrack-room model in which all the Boisrosé family's refuse was burnt. For, to the great astonishment of the dustbin collectors and the rag-and-bone men, this family never put their rubbish out on the street, not even the bones of a leg of lamb. In this slow combustion oven they burned the remains of what they consumed, which is to say almost nothing. Coffee was their principal gastronomic treat and even then it was Uncle Rocheflamme who almost always brought it, obtaining it from the Trou Dauphin by way of a former slave of the Boisrosé family who had become First Secretary at a Caribbean legation in Paris. Bills, which were anyway quite rare, made no impression on these single women, and the taxman himself, a person of devilish ingenuity, had a hard time making sense of their cloistered existence, which displayed no outward signs of wealth and was far more deprived than that of the Carmelites from the nearby convent whose chanting they could hear.

"Fromentine, the *Figaro*," Bonne commanded.

Fromentine read page two of the *Figaro* aloud. They loved the lists of wedding presents. Her sisters listened, seated on the floor, polishing their nails; this ceremony, which began at the four corners of the room, ended with a gathering of the Boisrosé girls on the maternal throne, and towards evening, since they were cold, with them all lying in a row beneath the old, moth-eaten squirrel-skin blanket that served as a bedcover. For, incapable of standing up to their mother's "What, you're going to leave me here!", they had one by one given up whatever they were doing. One hour later, there could still be heard:

"Marquis and Marquise de Z… a fan, Baronne W… a gilt dressing case, Vicomte B… a hunting print."

Since this breed of tendrils cling to one another, and these magnets magnetize themselves and magnetize each other, they had reverted to their blissful easygoing Creole life, which they had scarcely abandoned for a moment on their arrival in Paris. Four heads on the pillow: one grey, one brown, one blonde, one red, lying beneath a box-wood Christ, who looked astonished at the sight of these human beings who had reverted to nature. Next to the crucifix was an almanac from which not a single page had been torn out for eight months, which indicated the total contempt of the Boisrosés for the divisions of the calendar. Reconstituted as it was in this way, the mother cell borne on this motionless palanquin was now shut off from the world; it was a return to the embryo, to silence and the solitude of foetal life, to love in its most elementary form.

Shortly before dinner, Uncle Rocheflamme came in dragging his feet, like someone whose life was at an end, but no one paid much attention. With his pumice-stone complexion, his Gallic moustache, his blue Viking eyes and his inside-out clothes, Monsieur de Rocheflamme had only had to cross the road to be with his family: he lived opposite in a flat from which he carried on, without a licence, the occupation of man of the world, earning outrageous commissions for small pieces of marquetry furniture which colleagues left with him "as a minder", to use the jargon of the Salle Drouot.[4] His name, which brought to mind the Palaeozoic age and fermenting flint stones, scarcely accorded with his chilly, Swiss Guard-without-the-feathers personality. Nothing else was colourful about him apart from his knowledge of eighteenth-century furniture. Having no one with whom to converse about the engraving of Gouthière's bronzes, Monsieur de Rocheflamme allowed his sister to make decisions on every subject except on the roasting of coffee beans, about which he had ideas that, for once, were not fully formed. Apart from this, he was one of that vast herd of idiots who, in a coagulated voice, hand back their newspaper once they have read it. Nobody asked him anything. His presence was an absence. He spent hours standing behind his sister's back watching her play patience, reprimanding himself whenever he gave bad advice and groaning when it was good. He entered quite naturally into this Boisrosé nirvana, a sort of suspension of any future, of permanent peace and quiet in which Time resembled a reel of film that has come to a sudden stop due to a power cut.

That evening, Bonne de Boisrosé, with her milky-coffee wig perched on her receding hairline, her Bourbon nose, her perch-in-a-court-bouillon lips, emerged earlier and more actively than usual from her somnolent state to play her part in this barbaric and childish campsite that was the Boisrosés' family life.

"Do you know a Pierre Niox, an antique dealer?" she asked her brother excitedly.

"By name… and by reputation," mumbled Monsieur de Rocheflamme sourly.

"He's bought the Mas Vieux."

"Congratulations. So is he very wealthy, this swindler?"

"He didn't strike me as a swindler in the least," said Hedwige.

Monsieur de Rocheflamme's spitefulness was not merely the distaste of a second-hand goods dealer for a licensed colleague, or that of an old man for a younger one—in short, that natural antagonism that arises from the confrontation of two opposing situations; it was also his passive yet heartfelt antipathy for anything he didn't know and that did not concern his family.

"Uncle André, have some cold leg of lamb; there's still a bit of meat left on it."

Uncle André stopped talking, forgot about Pierre, whom he knew nothing about in any case, and continued to gnaw away at the leg of lamb.

CHAPTER VIII

Pierre's stay in brussels went on long enough to arouse the anxiety of the Boisrosés even though they had no notion of time. Hedwige, in particular, was rather more impatient than her sisters, who never stopped teasing her about her very successful initiative.

Finally, very early one morning, that is to say at about eleven o'clock, the dairywoman who normally provided their telephone link came to tell them that Hedwige was wanted on the phone.

"It's Hédiard, the mangoes have arrived!" cried Madame de Boisrosé, a gluttonous expression on her face.

"It's Monsieur Pierre Niox!" yelled Fromentine simultaneously, with a gleam in her eyes. "Hurry up, Hedwige!"

Hedwige descended the stairs at the nonchalant pace of a goddess. A moment later she came back upstairs.

"It was indeed Monsieur Pierre Niox. He's inviting us to dinner at a restaurant and to the cinema afterwards."

"What," said Madame de Boisrosé, "he's inviting the

entire family? And why to the cinema? That's a weird idea. Why not to his office since it's a business matter?"

Hedwige explained not without some difficulty that, from Pierre's point of view, it was a way in which to establish a connection, to initiate future conversations in order to clarify—

"What a curious language you're speaking in, Hedwige. Where did you pick up these expressions? It sounds like an official announcement," Angélique interrupted. "At last we're to see this famous Monsieur Niox!"

"Not you, Angélique," said Hedwige. "Only Fromentine and I are invited."

Pierre called at Saint-Germain to collect Hedwige and Fromentine in his small car. Being seldom invited out, they had made a great fuss about the occasion and had begun to get themselves ready immediately after lunch. Hedwige had foregone her siesta, and at three o'clock Fromentine had started to do her hair; she was now trying on her few little dresses before deciding on her elder sister's evening dress (clothes, stockings and shoes were interchangeable in the Boisrosé family).

As he drove up the hill to Saint-Germain, Pierre repeated Hedwige's remark to himself: "We shall try not to keep you waiting." "I hope they're going to keep their promise," he thought. "For my part, I want to respond to this effort to be punctual, not by being punctual myself, I always am, but by restraining and controlling myself should they not be. It's just too absurd to turn pleasure into suffering."

Pierre drew up his car in front of the Boisrosés' house. Those were his instructions. Since, however, it had gone half past seven and Hedwige had advised him not to come up, "given that the entrance to their house was via a dark alleyway and badly lit by old lights buried in the ivy, there was no concierge and he would certainly get lost", he started to sound his horn, gently at first, then very loudly.

Pierre began to feel distressed and was not very proud of the fact. He liked to cope with things. He felt cold beneath the hood and the canvas material was vibrating. Beads of mist were forming on the windows. A smell of damp leaves and grass seeped in through the doors. "After all," he thought, "waiting for one woman is not unpleasant; waiting for two is even better."

Cats could be heard mewing. Diligently, Pierre kept himself busy by smoking, dipping the headlights on and off, then the sidelights. He thought about his appointments for the following day, and the day after, he checked his diary.

"Being a chauffeur is the last thing in the world I'd want to do, especially a chauffeur to a Parisienne. I'd rather drive a bus in the country with suitcases that need tying onto the roof rack."

He took a bet with himself that the Boisrosé girls would be there by ten to eight, lost his bet, risked another fortune and got nothing for his money.

"One ought to have a collection of books in the car pocket. For years I haven't found the time to reread my classics. Nowadays they print lengthy masterpieces on India paper... I feel like bounding up the steps four at a time, but I risk going through the wrong door and then causing them to wait, which would be a disaster... I should have brought Placide along. It's true the car can only fit three and it's raining so hard I couldn't ask him to sit in the dickey-seat."

Two shadows passed by in the gleam of the lamplights. Pierre gave a start: "Here they are." No, it was servant girls on their way to the cinema.

"My waiting is a sacrifice," he said. "May the smoke be pure, at least, and the aroma pleasing to the gods. It is good for me to be here, to be hanging around (an odd expression for a man who is seated) and widening the range of my connections, because if my tendency to hurry increases, I shall need to surround myself with new friends, friends who can forewarn me as it were, who are not yet used to me and can give the alarm call.

"If I did not desire what are conventionally termed pleasures, it would be simple; I would obtain them on my own. But I want something else; I want to feel myself being projected forward through my own will; I long for Russian mountains, to be out of breath, to have an empty stomach, for a life gulped down in a trice. I shall kick the bucket one fine day if someone doesn't hold me back, but if anyone does I should prefer, much prefer, that it should be the pretty arm of a woman doing so rather than a sermon from Dr Regencrantz."

"Watch out!" whispered Pierre's liberating angel to him, "you're setting out today on an unfamiliar path, in which you will meet with only troubles and disappointments; you've received an attractive gift from me and it could be a wonderful one if you had an ounce of genius (that ounce of genius that you lack). That noble instinct that singles you out from the throng of mankind, that practical ability to move quickly and alone amid the general mêlée, you're going to lose all that if you become interested in ladies."

These angelic comments tempted Pierre, for one is never tempted quite so dangerously as one is by angels. He struggled with difficulty against the unpleasant thoughts that beset those who are impatient. Thus it was that he happened to see the image of his alluring bed pass by, thus it was that it occurred to him he could very well dine on his own. It would be a good trick to play on these girls. He drummed his fingers nervously on the window pane and traced esoteric monograms in the condensation on the windscreen.

"I hope we're not late," said a voice suddenly from deep inside an upturned collar.

Hedwige pressed her face to the window.

"Absolutely not," Pierre replied politely.

At the restaurant Pierre sat opposite the two sisters, the better to enjoy that glamour women have that reaches its apogee within the first two minutes.

Hedwige placed her elbows on the table in a manner that emphasized the sturdy shape of her shoulders. Impossible not to admire the power of the neck that supported her fine head, whose austereness was softened by her nonchalant gaze and her flecting, quickly removed smile. Hedwige spoke very little, that was her way. More alert, more of a chatterbox, more respectful of fashion, with her plucked eyebrows and the neat set of her reddish hair, it was Fromentine who caught the eye more; her slender figure with its hint of fieriness was dazzling. Fromentine gossiped and cooed, her lips scarcely moving, like those awkward young girls who are starting out in society. Pierre was amazed that the small town of Saint-Germain should have been able to keep such beauties to itself and he congratulated himself on his discovery. Once more he experienced that sedative feeling he had already encountered on his first meeting with Hedwige. The great wave of sweetness, her inner warmth and her muted voice made this impatient man want to slow down, to put his feet on the ground, to breathe freely at last.

"The film doesn't begin until half past ten. Let's not hurry," said Pierre. "We have plenty of time. Ah! How good it is to relax…"

"I can arrive whenever I want at the cinema," said Fromentine confidently, "I always understand."

"I never understand," Pierre replied. "I'm not saying that in order to appear more intelligent than you, but because that's the way it is."

Seeing Hedwige's astonishment, Pierre did not press the point. He realized that he had just made the kind of remark used in his circles that these young creatures would be unable to understand, being far too natural and unused to such sophisticated simplicity. Among some of Pierre's customers and friends, there were people of proverbial preciousness and subtlety who, either because it was the fashion or because it was tactically astute, pretended to be naive, simple, gauche, to imitate Abbot and Costello, to read large-print books or be whipping boys. "We take pot luck when we entertain," boasted the *marquises*; "I'm a peasant," a certain painter used to say who took care to conceal his devilish cunning; "I write in my sleep," proclaimed the most far-seeing critics; "What a clumsy oaf I am," announced an elderly witch; and all the *vicomtes* who buy their shoes from Hellstern & Sons and the millionaires dressed in sackcloth at 200 francs a metre, who awkwardly dunk bread in their coffee, who read aloud the serialized novels of Jean de La Hire, who assert that one should arrive at the theatre "before the lights are dimmed" and who peel oranges in the boxes, the boxes at the Châtelet, because the Châtelet is a thousand times "more attractive" than the Salzburg Festival.

"I don't like," Pierre went on, "being shut up for three hours in a large, dark room criss-crossed by beams that are meant to be projecting onto a screen endless frames showing the most stunning sights in the universe, but which only succeed in making me, unwillingly, the lazy accomplice of vulgar sentiments, foul manners, and actors who are paid so highly that they don't even do you the favour of blinking an eyelid. At the cinema, I always expect the unexplored, some powerful incantation, I want to be drained of myself by the originality of the show. And then… nothing at all!… What are we going to eat? Oysters? How long does it take to open thirty-six oysters?"

The *maître d'hôtel* came out with the customary misleading estimates. Without listening to him, Pierre calculated: "They'll need a good ten seconds per oyster; the man who opens them is on his own; if he uses a serrated knife, they'll have to allow fifteen seconds; for three dozen that's about ten minutes!"

"We'll have whatever you have," said Fromentine, who was stunned by the elegance of the room and whose wide-open eyes resembled those of a Negro being taken to the circus.

"I'm a *petite marmite* man myself; there are five ingredients in the *petite marmite*: soup, bread, boiled meat, vegetables and cheese."

"Let's have that then," said Hedwige in a placatory manner.

"The *petite marmite* is finished," replied the *maître d'hôtel*.

Pierre was not sorry about this, for the soups are always scalding-hot and it would be awkward for him in front of the uninitiated to ask for several cups into which to pour the soup and so cool it more quickly; you don't display your bad habits straight away.

The *maître d'hôtel* fiddled around impatiently with his blank notepad. The Boisrosés contemplated their menus without saying a word. Pierre took the matter in hand since, with women, you could be in the restaurant all night.

"It's late already to offer you a sumptuous dinner, so let's all have the *plat du jour*."

"Yes, yes," Hedwige exclaimed, "never mind the sumptuous dinner."

"Bravo," said Pierre.

"What an electric man!" said Fromentine with a laugh as she exchanged glances with Hedwige.

Pierre realized that both the sisters had already discussed his hastiness and had laughed about it between themselves. This pained him; he promised himself to be more alert.

"We'll make up the time with the wines. Let's wait a little and order a soufflé beforehand. *Maître d'hôtel*, how long would a soufflé take?"

"Twenty minutes, monsieur."

"We'll have it."

"And while you wait?" said the *maître d'hôtel*, who was beginning to wilt.

"But mademoiselle has told you that we are having the *plat du jour!*"

"The *plat du jour* takes ten minutes, monsieur. Nothing beforehand?"

"Why do we have to wait ten minutes longer for the *plat du jour* than for the other dishes?" sighed Pierre. He sensed that he would appear far too unpleasant, or too ridiculous, or too insane were he to get angry over such a minor matter.

"Waiter! Pass us that bowl of crayfish," he said, half leaning over the table and pointing to the crayfish on the nearby trolley. "That bowl there, and not any other, do you understand! And right away!"

"And the wine?"

"Some good champagne as long as it's chilled and ready to drink."

"We'll put it on ice for you," said the wine waiter.

"Which means that you're going to give us warm champagne beforehand."

"We can't chill the champagne beforehand, monsieur, it will ruin it."

"And you prefer to ruin me!" moaned Pierre, cracking his metacarpal joints impatiently.

The peeling, cleaning and sucking of the crayfish tails made Pierre miss the oysters which, after all, can be opened immediately with a good knife and an expert hand.

"How lovely it is," said Hedwige, a very gentle and very happy expression in her eyes, "to eat food one hasn't prepared oneself!"

Pierre looked at her, admiring once more the beauty of her face and that silent melody that emanated from her. She was wearing a turban made of very hairy fur that called to mind something from sixteenth-century Poland and made one want her to wear (which she was not wearing) a slightly orange-red dolman. Pierre felt quite affectionate when he recalled that she had not laughed when Fromentine had started to tease him, and that on the contrary she had seemed saddened. No doubt Fromentine combined the natural maliciousness of redheads with the innocent sadism of girls who suffer and enjoy making others suffer because they are unhappy themselves.

The waiter came to present the *plat du jour*: duck with peas.

"It's very nice, very nice," said Pierre, "but just leave the duck on our table. Dishes that are presented to one ceremoniously only to be spirited away immediately afterwards drive me to despair."

"But I'm about to bring it back to you, monsieur!" said the waiter, half turning around.

Pierre grabbed him by the apron.

"No, no, my friend, bring the chopping board and tell the *maître d'hôtel* to carve it here, in front of us. I'm fed up with waiting!"

Fromentine squirmed. Hedwige smiled in embarrassment. In this way did Pierre gradually ruin an evening that had begun so well. There he was sitting opposite two beautiful, undiscovered girls, at a well-attended table, in a warm restaurant, where everything was progressing normally, according to ritual, with that quiet sophistication and smooth good manners that generations of Parisians had perfected. And yet he had only one desire, one longing, which was to create panic and commotion there. "What a boor I am!" he told himself. "If all these delectable things collapse on me one day, I shall be sorry, but I shall have brought it upon myself."

Pierre had already wolfed down his duck before the waiter had even begun to reheat the legs over the burner. At a nearby table, a woman was shelling some fresh nuts.

"Let's hope they're not planning to offer us any of those!" sighed Pierre as he stole an apple from the passing trolley, which he ate without peeling it.

Fortunately, the soufflé did not take long and the Boisrosé girls did not take coffee, which put a smile back on the face of their host.

"We only drink what we make ourselves; away from home they only ever have Costa Rican. The family coffee comes from Anse à Banane."

"Anse à Banane! What is this wonderful place?"

"It's the Boisrosés' house, in the West Indies," said Fromentine. "I've never been there, nor to the Trou Dauphin, the sugar cane plantation that belongs to us through our mother's side."

"If you don't accept a glass of rum after that, mademoiselle!"

THE MAN IN A HURRY

"When I was little, my nanny used to give me baths in rum. It's put me off rum for good," said Hedwige.

"I'm sorry," said Pierre. "They only have glasses here. I hadn't anticipated baths."

Hedwige's voice had a strong accent when she pronounced the word rum: the initial *r* was slightly suppressed, in the Creole way, followed by a low nasal sound that made the whole of her palate tremble like an echoing chamber and then fade away behind her teeth as the final *m* died on her sealed lips.

"I've heard it said that the smell of molasses hovers over the Antilles just as the scent of the maquis does over Corsica," said Pierre.

"Molasses, do you think that's a nice smell? It stinks of old leather!" cried Fromentine, bursting out laughing.

"Used you to take tafia baths or just rum?" asked Pierre, who was trying desperately to make Hedwige pronounce the *r* again that had enchanted him.

Pierre had forgotten it was time to leave, but all of a sudden he stood up, remembering that it was past ten o'clock.

"You gave me a fright," said Hedwige.

"A fright?"

"The Boisrosé family are carefree and wonderfully indolent and are not used to being aroused with a start," said Fromentine. "Where we come from, the Negresses wake you up by pressing their hands on the soles of your feet. It's the place that's farthest from the heart. You don't feel any shock."

They rose from the table. Pierre threw his overcoat over his shoulders, while the Boisrosé girls disappeared behind that mysterious cloakroom door where all women go never to be seen again, a ceremony that normally made him despair, but which he endured this evening without hopping from one foot to another too much.

They crossed over the Champs-Elysées. The cinema was showing an absurd film, full of well-known stars, all prominently displayed, with faces exposing teeth as large as flagstones and black lips in which every crevice could be seen, with twenty-year-old skins revealing to the audience wrinkles deeper and closer than the Colorado Grand Canyon seen through a telescope. Not a single eyelash or hair was spared. Pierre was right: what passivity of feeling, what lacklustre incidents! One would never have thought that this story had been commissioned by an intelligent human being.

"It's unbearable," Pierre said. "Suppose we went somewhere else?"

"But where can we go at this time?"

"To the Excelsior. They show very good documentaries."

Scarcely had he uttered these words than he dashed off. They tore after him, but he had gone ahead to find his car and drive it out of its parking space. He was back a moment later. Hedwige and Fromentine had scarcely closed their doors before Pierre sped off and pulled up on the Rond-Point, outside the Excelsior. There, he drummed his fingers fruitlessly at the kiosk window, for it was late and the woman at the cash desk had already closed her till, and leapt back into the driver's seat brandishing a box ticket.

When they got to their seats the interval was coming to an end and the bell was already ringing. Pierre settled himself in between these two perfect bodies. He felt totally happy now. He had had his outburst. The evening was going in the right direction. The moment of difficulty had passed. He shared his smile between his two companions. They arranged a future meeting.

"We do need to see each other again to talk business," said Pierre.

"You must come to dinner in Saint-Germain. Mother would be glad to meet you," said Hedwige.

"There'll just be one course, and we promise that you won't have to wait," added Fromentine.

The lights were dimmed. Pierre was hoping that a healthy dose of current affairs would fill them with a surge of impulsive vitality, what with the shouts of the crowd, the sporting activities and the cavalry charges—in short, the whole ebb and flow of contemporary beauty in action.

"Now we'll have fun!" he said playfully, rubbing his hands together.

The glare of the advertisements disappeared. After the orchestra had dragged its way through a Johann Strauss waltz, the screen, alas, announced a slow-motion documentary:

THE DIGESTION OF THE BOA

"There are days when nothing succeeds," sighed Pierre.

"Have you had enough?" asked Hedwige sympathetically.

"Well, I mean… Saint-Germain's a long way. I suggest we go back."

After Pierre had dropped them home, Fromentine undressed in her bedroom and then came and sat on her sister's bed.

"He's a weird fellow, your friend."

"Anyway, he's not boring," Hedwige replied. "Do you think he had fun?"

"To begin with, yes, but he seemed to be in a great hurry, in a hurry to leave us. He must have had another rendezvous," she insinuated.

"Not necessarily."

"Of course he did," Fromentine went on, teasing her.

"I think he probably wanted to be on his own," said Hedwige. "He's an eccentric."

"Is he really an eccentric? I've never heard of a man wanting to be alone. I don't believe in men's solitude."

"What experience you have!"

"He may just be a man who's only allowed to stay out until midnight and who's frightened of missing the call?" added Fromentine casually, as she brushed her red hair.

CHAPTER IX

"HERE I AM, I've rushed over, what is it? What's happened?"

Placide, his scarf knotted beneath a beard that had bristles harder than the back of an irritable porcupine, his hair awry, his trousers around his ankles, has arrived at Pierre Niox's home and finds him extremely calm for once, sprawled in an armchair, a book in his hands.

"Nothing at all," says Pierre calmly.

"What? You're not even ill! It's too bad. So why did you drag me out of bed? So that you can read to me?... And yet more Michelet!"

"He does make some good points," said Pierre.

"A historian shouldn't make points," replied the Chartist. "In any case, Michelet's *Histoire de France* is so confused that you close it having forgotten all your history. But that doesn't explain why you called me urgently. What a pain..."

Placide's dishevelled head and his confusion are so funny that Pierre, keen to prolong the teasing, continues his remarks in the tone of someone giving a lecture.

"Bit by bit, I have drawn up a small gallery of well-known geniuses, a portable pantheon of brilliant men. I give preference to impulsive heroes, to those who are geniuses at the first attempt, to leaders of military forays, to famous raiders. The contemplation of these supermen is as stimulating as listening to a military march. They are my patron saints."

Placide could feel his temper rising.

"I know of only one patron saint for you, and it's St Guy."

"Caesar deserves the first place," Pierre went on imperturbably. "One cannot but praise his crossing of the Rubicon, and also his armies that are dispatched suddenly right into the heart of Germany, and his lightning descents on Rome, from where he immediately set off again to the furthest boundaries of the Empire. Let's read this page again where he relates how he comes to take a stand in deepest Illyria; there, he learns that little Brittany has risen up; ready to lend a helping hand, he shakes off his provincial encampment, hops over the Alps, delivers a right hook to the Armoricans while simultaneously stunning the Germans, who had also risen up, with a left cut..."

"Brutus murdered Caesar because his frenetic behaviour was getting on his nerves and the Senate supported him... and so do I!" yelled Placide.

"Compared to Caesar, the most celebrated conquerors seem to be asleep on their feet," continued Pierre, not listening to him. "Charlemagne, for example, and his forty-year wars that dragged on like his beard! And those dull Crusader knights who got bogged down in arguments about etiquette, in lawsuits about common ownership, and romantic novels; and those dreary tournaments with sermons one after the other from the heralds-at-arms…"

"You're not equipped to understand the sturdy and steadfast beauty of armour," Placide cut in tersely.

"Let us prefer to them, ladies and gentlemen, Henri IV conquering his kingdom unawares, Gustavus Adolphus devouring Europe in a gulp, Condé and his strategic inspiration…"

"Thank you for this brief lesson about famous restless men," Placide interrupted. "Now, tell me why—"

"—Why the greatest par excellence is Napoleon? Ah, Placide, what frantic pursuits amid the bell-towers and the cannon those Empire wars were! Those volte-faces, those perilous leaps, those pugilist's counter-attacks that took advantage of the enemy's slightest loss of equilibrium! The Italian campaign, I tell you, I know it by heart: the dazzling reversal at Montenotte, the scramble at Roveredo, the lightning raid at Bassano, the stunning victory of Marengo, the crossing of the Alps at a canter! Caesar or

Napoleon, it's the same triumph of resourcefulness. They always break out from impossible positions where the old strategy was not expected."

"Enough!" Placide cries. "For once, I'm the one asking you to be brief…"

"And the French campaign in which the old lion, exhausted, out of breath, his muscles failing, suddenly rediscovers his form, his old determination, that way he had of spinning round that still used to terrify visitors to St Helena who came to ogle at him through the bars of the cage!"

Placide came and stood in front of Pierre and, with a malevolent smile, said:

"These leaders were better at winning battles than hearts: you're rather like them in that respect."

"Don't you like me any more, Placide?"

"No."

"Are you sulking?"

"The word is poorly chosen, as is everything you choose to do, what's more," cried Placide in exasperation.

"I've got some good news to give you, however. Aren't you interested? Listen all the same: the two fourth-century urns and the casket from Oslo with gold coils that you didn't approve of me buying, well, Baltimore Museum is buying them back from us at a hundred per cent profit."

"And that's why you asked me to come here," moaned Placide, who was beside himself with rage.

"Yes, that's why I sent for you. And also to tell you that I'm doubling your percentage on it. And also all your percentages on all our business deals, so satisfied am I with the smooth running of our partnership."

Placide remained speechless, blushing and turning pale alternately.

"What, you're not pleased?" asked Pierre with a smile.

"No, I am certainly not!" said Placide irritably. "The way you behave is killing me. Do you realize that I almost fainted from surprise! I'm terrified of shocks. Whenever you do something kind for me, you do it so suddenly that it makes me feel angrier than I am when I get a fine! You wake me up with a jolt! You don't allow me time to get dressed. Not even the time to sleep, or so little that you prevent me from sleeping properly. You don't actually give me time for anything! I'm your scapegoat. I feel I'm always trying to catch up with you. I need to live normally and not feel cooped up at the back of the train in the role of brakeman. And since I'm here this morning against my wishes, I'm taking the opportunity to tell you that I'm breaking off our partnership and that I'm setting up on my own."

"Are you serious?" asked Pierre.

He gazed in astonishment at this friend of fifteen years' standing, in whom he had noticed nothing more than an incomprehensible hostility. He felt like saying: "But what have I done to you?" since he was unable to understand that a mere difference in their respective tempos could fill Placide's soul with such resentment.

He tried to see things from Placide's standpoint, to view his own self impartially; what could he be blamed for? A little too much hastiness, verging occasionally—very rarely—on feverish activity. It was a fault, a shortcoming rather, a delightful shortcoming; so many people are lethargic, dead weights who are impossible to shift. In his case, everything was dynamism and lightness. People should, on the contrary, be grateful to him for speeding things up and bringing them to a satisfactory conclusion so quickly.

Placide had calmed down somewhat; he continued dispassionately:

"I need a more temperate climate than yours; you roast, while I need to simmer. Ever since I left the École des Chartes, you've been my evil genius…"

"Come now, I've been your salvation! I've broken you in, I've given you a flick of the whip when you needed it. Without me, would you have ever left your Mama for a single meal?"

"You're right there, you've disrupted my dearest habits; you've jostled me, you've hypnotized me! You were never in the least grateful for the lessons you attended at my school, because the good antique dealer, the artistic antique dealer, is me and not you; you've got a nose, that's all."

"My dear Placide, I've never disputed any of your great virtues, but you do have a few small faults: you're meticulous, fussy, cautious, circumspect; admit that without me you would have daydreamed your life away... don't you think?"

"I don't intend to continue this discussion," said Placide very curtly, "let's just say that we're divorcing due to incompatibility of temperaments. At Saint-Vallier, when we had that accident and after you had almost killed me, you left me on my own all night in your abandoned car by the banks of the Rhône; I was already so furious that I'd decided never to see you again. I felt sorry for you and I changed my mind, but since then your frantic express-train frenzy has only got worse. As in the meantime an international association of antique dealers has been set up in Rome and I have been asked to join as an expert on Gothic art, I've accepted. Does that vex you?"

Pierre considered the matter:

"No," he said. "Better that than you blaming me later on for not allowing you to try your luck."

"As you can see, I am delighted by this ready agreement," said Placide, who was feeling both offended and consoled, for he had feared rather more resistance. "No hard feelings, dear fellow, no hard feelings, my slippery old eel!"

And he went out giving an affected little wave.

Pierre was left alone gazing at the ceiling for a while. He was thinking of the way in which he would reorganize his business, without a partner. A great deal of boring work in prospect, assets to be shared out, further funds to be found. He would have to get down to it straight away. For once, his "straight away" did not signify "immediately", since Pierre did not stir; he even sat down again in his armchair and reflected.

"That idiot has ruined my day!"

His bad mood filled him with unpleasant images. In his mind's eye he thought about the evening before last with the two girls that had begun so happily and ended so gloomily. What could have cast such a spell on him?

He kicked his chair away and rang for Chantepie, who did not come. He rang again. The sound of the bell, which failed to activate the late, limping arrival of the elderly servant, grew mournful. It was like a stone falling into a well. Pierre opened the doors and shouted:

"Chantepie!"

He looked around to see whether one of those notes was not lying around that Chantepie left whenever he went out shopping to inform or ask questions of his master: "Has monsieur thought about tomorrow's dinner?" or "The shirts have not come back, there was no word from the laundryman: monsieur must not scold me".

Lying on top of the kitchen scales, Pierre found an envelope addressed to him:

Monsieur,

I want to respectfully say to monsieur that I no longer wish to serve him and that I'm off and that's that. I've been to see Doctor Abraham the same one who cancels monsieur's fines for me becoz he is the town councillor and who also gives me free consultations without making me pay even though he's Jewish. "Chantepie you must calm down, you're the delicate sort and cannot endure for long the heavy work that is put upon you, you're killing yourself Chantepie." "Monsieur Abraham," I replied to him, "I would be happy to die on the job for I have no children and nothing but disappointments and no money."

It's not the muscles shrinking it's the nerves that are killing me and I can't stand monsieur any longer I'm fed up with rushing around for him all the time without a break and

THE MAN IN A HURRY

always at the double I can't wait to slow down I swallow my tears but I'm going after so many years without whingeing I'm not angry with monsieur who was always honest with me and good and who often picked me up when I was feeling gloomy and when I couldn't stand up on account of my rheumatism, monsieur is not stupid monsieur will understand.

Sincerely yours.

Chantepie (Gasparin)

"So Chantepie's leaving too!" said Pierre mockingly. "Here I am twice cuckolded, and in the rarest manner, cuckold without a wife. Chantepie and Placide both agreeing to blame me for excessive speed. It's comical!

"Meanwhile, here I am alone. Alone, alone," he repeated as he paced up and down the hall. "If this continues I shall soon have no one to speak to. I shall think aloud like the polar explorers.

"Alone! In fact, it's only right. What is speed if not a race that is won, the prize for which is loneliness. We sow what we reap... we sow in the hope that the seed will not grow again," Pierre concluded angrily. "I'm the champion of adversity. I've endured that invisible pressure that infiltrates us and is known as slowness better than others. I am a sporting spectacle," he concluded proudly.

"Yes, but what about when I'm old? When I'll have lost my spurt (it's the spurt that loses its edge first), and then my starting speed, when my pace has slowed down, when I start to look like everyone else, what will become of me?

"No, I'll never be old. The day that slowness gets the better of me I shall die of asphyxiation. Death is probably nothing more than a difference of pressure between our outer and our inner beings. When the outer one becomes the stronger, we die.

"Nevertheless, I won't always be able to pass through people like a ray, without clinging on to any of them. Human beings have a reality, a volume, movement: what a shock there'll be when we meet one another! Or what they call meeting! That is to say exchange faithfulness, warmth, vitality, and all part of an intimacy that I have never known until now. In short, the day I fall in love with a woman, when there will be someone else close to me apart from colleagues or servants, from people I lunch, dine, sleep with, paddle or pedal with—the day when I shall have to split a part of myself in two, hoping that that part also splits into new sections which will be my children…

"It's strange that with other people, all this should happen smoothly, without their even seeming to notice it; they must have an instinct that's lacking in me and that operates differently. They bond together somehow…

haphazardly… but it's happiness all the same. What's more," he added to comfort himself, "it's not without its difficulties: the pieces function and get stuck and even break up… at the law courts. But since the universal mechanism encompasses specific cogs, the world continues to roll along. Therefore I don't have to worry about it.

"It's me I ought to worry about. I'm frightened of not being normal, of being unnatural. I'm not sure that an understanding between me and other people is possible. The proof: Placide and Chantepie.

"Love is a dangerous territory for athletes. During the wars, the clearest skies were those in which the greatest number of aviators were killed. What will happen to me when I experience love?

"For I'm ready for love just as I am for death, or for poverty; I'm not the kind to tiptoe his way around the elemental forces and the great affairs of life. I shall pay cash on the nail when the time comes for me to become involved and commit myself.

"To do so you need to know yourself well, know who you are, what you're worth. I believed myself to be a man like any other man, one merely endowed with a little more liveliness. Is this liveliness that I'm so proud of speed? Or is it a way of dissembling and dragging one's feet, a delaying tactic, a way of avoiding the real answers, of substituting the great leap that every man must make into the unknown with a series of small hops? But Chantepie has left me. My cat has left me. Placide is leaving me. I have no friends. (He always dwelt on this.) Were I to ransack my bottom drawer, all I would come up with are relatives or colleagues. Am I a monster? My pulse is regular and my blood pressure is about normal. I know of no physical defects, my family background is excellent, my spinal cord would be the envy of a tightrope-walker. So why do people avoid me? Why am I left on my own? I thought of myself as a ball of fire; perhaps I'm just burnt out."

Pierre had reached that point where he was no longer capable of expressing himself in sentences. Or else he no longer dared to.

He remembered something Regencrantz had said: "By moving so quickly, are you fleeing or pursuing?" "If I am fleeing," he said to himself, "what exactly am I fleeing from?"

When he began to tackle this riddle, the fugitive found himself surrounded by question marks that held him back like hooks.

CHAPTER X

"ONE BEHIND MY NECK, really hot… One behind my left leg. This one's cold and is freezing my right leg!"

Bonne de Boisrosé is surrounded by rubber hot-water bottles. She looks like a horse wading through a river on wineskins.

The table has been placed at the foot of the bed, a pretty little hexagonal chess table, lent by the uncle, on which the glasses touch one another, with a place laid at each of the six sides. The Boisrosé girls are serving at table, for the maid only comes in the morning. Maids have been solicited on several occasions by means of advertisements, but the concierge had painted such a colourful picture of the Boisrosé household beforehand that they never got beyond the entrance hall.

Fromentine has placed a white lotus flower in a celadon full of water in the centre of the table. Hedwige is putting the plates on top of the oven to warm. They have washed, for once discarding the bathrobes, morning coats, dressing gowns and other indoor clothes which they live in. Hedwige is wearing white: it's Angélique's dress. Angélique is in black: it's Fromentine's dress. Fromentine is in black and white: she has borrowed the dress from her elder sister and the tunic from her younger one; the gold necklaces are from her mother. Bonne de Boisrosé is wearing guipure, her bust resting on sheets trimmed with Valenciennes lacework, looking like a hairdresser's model on a pedestal covered with ruffled material.

Pierre Niox is coming to dinner. He has been invited, ostensibly to thank him for his flowers, but in reality to discuss the sale of the Mas Vieux. Madame de Boisrosé had decided that this time it should be Angélique who would raise the subject, Hedwige not having proved up to the mark since she had allowed two opportunities to pass without reaching a conclusion.

Pierre rings the bell. It's almost as if he is there already. He doesn't open doors, it's as though he were forcing his way in. He dashes through, striding past the entrance hall and the ritual introductions and into the drawing room where he is awaited, not without ceremony, since the presence of a stranger is fairly rare at Saint-Germain. Fromentine, who had opened the landing door to him, followed at a run, hoping, quite wrongly, that she would reach the drawing room at the same time as him. As soon as enters the room, Pierre exclaims:

"So much finery and so much beauty just for me!"

"In this way you are sure of being favoured," Fromentine replied playfully. "Excuse me one moment, I'm going to find Hedwige."

Pierre was left in private conversation with Angélique. She headed astutely straight for the Mas Vieux. Pierre gave her an enthusiastic description of it in a few words.

"I don't know the house, unfortunately," Angélique replied. "Father bought it when he was separated from Mamicha and he sold it without informing us. Poor Papa was very ill and was probably badly advised. So were we, we don't have anyone to help us, we're four women on our own who know nothing about business matters."

Pierre interrupted her:

"I know what's bothering you, but believe me, don't worry. I have an idea… still unformed, but achievable. Your sister Fromentine teases me about my haste; this time, you see, I am taking my time."

"Can I not know beforehand?" asked Angélique.

"Why do such beautiful women concern themselves with all this language of business and money? It's for men like me to free them from their worries."

He was so unaccustomed to these phrases of gentlemanly chivalry that he was astonished to hear himself utter them.

Fromentine returned, bringing Hedwige with her.

"Come and say hello to my mother. Forgive her for receiving you lying in bed, she's not feeling very well today."

Pierre feared disturbing Madame de Boisrosé and resisted; he resisted badly, because he was watching Hedwige as she spoke. He was mesmerized by women's lips; he saw little else, initially. It was through their lips that he began to puzzle them out; it was the first real effect they made on him. Just as a deaf man uses the lips of the person he is conversing with to understand the words he is unable to hear, so it was from their lips that he interpreted their distinctive features, their affectations, the truths about them. It is the mouth, first of all, that gives her away. Pierre had had his fill of pretty, foolish mouths that never shut; despondent mouths that try to cheer themselves up by applying lipstick, but whose muscles slacken and droop; elastic, hysterical mouths that shoot off in every direction; restless mouths that muddle up the words to be spoken; tragic mouths, on stage and in speeches, looking rather like a black hole in Melpomene's mask; fashionable mouths, advertisements for toothpaste; busy, harsh mouths that hold the purse strings; mouths that have disintegrated due to illness.

But Hedwige had a firm, well-balanced mouth that radiated serenity and contemplation; a mouth that was in harmony with her eyes and with every part of her face and her soul.

Fromentine was growing restless:

"Yes, yes, you must come and see Mother," she said. "You will be obliged to go in there since we are having dinner at the foot of her bed. It's what we call the little dining table."

And she opened the bedroom door with a great shriek of laughter, pushing Pierre closer to the bed.

"I must compliment you on your daughters, madame," he said with a bow.

"Three daughters, it's a disaster. Don't remind me, monsieur, that I have three daughters."

"They're very beautiful."

"As far as that's concerned, yes, they're beautiful and they're good," said Madame de Boisrosé with such natural pride that it could no longer be termed pride. And with a wave of her hand she sought the agreement of her son-in-law Amyot and Monsieur de Rocheflamme, who were keeping her company.

Pierre thought it was charming to have dinner in the bedroom. He was fascinated by this intimacy of women in its purest state, without any affectation, cunning or social concerns. The cooking resembled some sort of leisure activity, the cutlery something of a conjuring trick; saucepans, plates, bottles protruded from every corner and they lent this tea party an atmosphere of make-believe and entertainment. Pierre was on the point of saying: "How much quicker it is than in a restaurant!", but he preferred not to remind them of that disastrous first evening.

Vincent Amyot, Angélique's husband, was a witty mind inside a ninety-kilo body. Although extremely intelligent in private, as soon as he wished to shine and make himself attractive to a stranger he lost his natural wit and expressed himself like a book, like a boring book. This former *poly-technicien*[5] wrote articles on economic affairs for the weeklies that were brimming with authority and facile pessimism. He had tried his hand at writing detective novels and historical essays, and he wrote too much; but unlike the work of artists, musicians and orators, who overwhelm their friends and relations with exhibitions, concerts and conferences, the creations of a friend who's a writer are always avoidable. And so no one was familiar with Amyot's output. Apart, that is, from a few ministers of finance who, with the sensitivity peculiar to all politicians, did not absorb the lessons that he delivered with theoretical infallibility from on high, and which resulted, in practice, in a forecast of banking disasters. Pierre listened to the conversation, stock-still.

Pierre stock-still, what an amazing sight! As motionless as a quivering arrow, as a missile in an arsenal. Pierre wasting his time, but feeling and giving the impression that he was benefiting in every respect. Pierre lethargic, Pierre munching; munching his apple tart instead of choking on it, not unscrewing the sugar sprinkler, not eating everything from the same plate, not covering his cake with salt instead of sugar. Pierre polishing his rough edges, making the most of his evening and thoroughly immersing himself in every second of it. Could it last?

It did last, however. They savoured their food. They sipped their drinks. The ladies dipped sugar lumps in their coffee. Pierre listened to Madame de Boisrosé expressing various complaints about the present age and her daughters countering her moans with timid objections and deferential approval. They also listened to the wind howling and the red oven crackling. He listened to the *polytechnicien*, his thesis about the gyratory movement of long-term investments and his paradoxes that concluded with a QED. And when, in turn, Uncle Rocheflamme spoke, Pierre was quite pleased to listen to him grinding his coffee and making banal remarks, the former in between his legs, the others through gritted teeth.

"Even so, France…" Amyot began, joining in with this very French phrase.

"We are letting ourselves be led by circumstances," groused Monsieur de Rocheflamme, sounding as idiotic as the radio. "It's one of our misfortunes not to have any leaders. We have men of distinction, but no characters. Now Poincaré, he was a leader."

"Poincaré had substance," said Pierre, glad to cling instinctively in this deluge of generalizations onto an actual name.

"Yes, but he carried no conviction: I'm going to fill you in on the problem with France. All things being equal…"

And to start with, backing his argument up with anecdotes and a few drawn-out metaphors, Amyot explained that what was lacking in the Treaty of Versailles "was heart".

Interspersed with peerless notions on the art of leading nations, the evening had reached its highest degree of dreariness when Pierre, benumbed and anaesthetized, suddenly felt his evil genius rising to the surface. With a firm but gentle nudge, this familiar phantom was pointing him towards the door.

Pierre looked at the door, a large, handsome door with three panels and a gleaming doorknob that only required a hand to turn it.

"I can't just leave like that," he thought, steeling himself. "It's impossible."

"What the Treaty of Versailles could have been…" Amyot was expanding.

The door appeared to open onto a magical staircase that led up a gentle slope to the street. Often, as he was falling asleep, the man in a hurry imagined a model house, a house which one would leave via gradients as speedy as toboggan runs, where a lift would transport you in your car up to the drawing room; a house from which you could send your letters and parcels straight from the window giving onto the street along spiralling chutes, as in the large stores; in which, as in the dining rooms of Ludwig II of Bavaria, the table would rise ready-laid from under the floor through a trapdoor; in which one's clothes, by means of a system of pulleys, would dress you instantly; in which visitors, triggered by a clock, would arrive at the stated time in armchairs pulled by trolleys and would depart again on rails as soon as the most important words had been spoken, leaving the conversations recorded on wax walls.

"Always peripheral to events, our statesmen…" Amyot was still dragging on.

Monsieur de Rocheflamme, who was no longer even responding to his nephew by marriage, was now admiring his sister's success. The three girls were talking among themselves. Pierre awoke with a start. He had been asleep. Nobody appeared to have noticed. For how long had he been asleep?

"… a more sincere outlook," Amyot continued.

By piecing both ends of the sentence together, Pierre concluded that he had only been asleep for three words.

He now felt a great weight upon his shoulders, as overburdened as he did when he jumped out of bed on a day crammed with anxieties and meetings. And yet, five minutes earlier, he had been happy. But his familiar and demanding phantom was continuing to lead him towards the door. He absolutely had to get a breath of air.

"I've no more tobacco," he said. "Would you mind if I went to buy some?"

"The tobacconist's is a long way away," Bonne de Boisrosé pointed out.

"We have some Virginia," Fromentine offered.

"Do you want some Caporal?" said Monsieur de Rocheflamme.

"Forgive me. I'm used to a Turkish tobacco from the Levant. I'll be back. It will only take a moment."

Pierre dashed down the stairs four at a time. In the street, he took a deep breath. Hundred-year-old street lamps were making circles through the mist. The avenue was deserted, the city indifferent. Pierre took to his heels. He breathed the air deep into his lungs. Never in his life had he felt so happy. His rubberized soles held the road well, his arms flew in the air, his long, well-built legs gave him total freedom. What a pleasure the party had been! He felt no qualms about causing a disturbance in a sleeping neighbourhood where the guard dogs were all barking.

He walked past the tobacconist's shop without going in because he had Turkish tobacco in his pocket.

He stopped, he felt better. A clock chimed ten o'clock. His swiftness had kept him sane. He felt more inclined to be polite now and he even thought that he might enjoy going back to his hosts. He retraced his steps.

"I had to go on foot. My car wouldn't start," he said by way of excuse. "You must think me extremely rude?"

Hedwige smiled. Pierre could see that she had not been taken in, but was grateful for the effort he had made. He rejoined the group. On seeing him, Uncle Rocheflamme rushed over.

"I'm not well established," he said, "and you would search in vain for the name of Rocheflamme in the directory of antique dealers: it's not there. I'm a maverick; I put independence above everything else… Look, my dear fellow, here's something that will interest you," he said, opening his wallet, "read this card from Waldeck-Rousseau. Yes, I had some correspondence with him. Good God, it wasn't exactly yesterday, this was in 1901… listen."

He read in a very loud voice: "'I can only approve, sir, the title of your forthcoming newspaper and I wish long life to the *Indépendant*. Independence means setting oneself free from other people, that is to say true freedom,

freedom that a subsidy from the Ministry of the Interior might compromise'... mmm... mmm... The rest is of no importance," Monsieur de Rocheflamme muttered.

"Nice letter," said Pierre, embarrassed.

"I've lots of others," the uncle went on, having rediscovered his self-assurance. "My contemporaries have been pleased to pay tribute to my public-spirited activities as well as to my professional ones. I spent the war as pennant-bearer to General Hély d'Oissel, despite my age. But take a look at my commendation."

He produced a folded and torn shred of paper and handed it to Pierre.

"Did you read it? 'Proud and independent character...'"

"That's really nice," said Pierre.

"One day you must come to my home and I'll show you the pearls of my collection: I've got letters from the poet Edmond Rostand, from Baron Édouard de Rothschild, from the novelist Paul Hervieu and even from Rockefeller; all acknowledge my artistic ability and my natural pride; all congratulate me on never having been a slave to fashion, never tied to any one party, never dependent on anything or anyone else. Me, a servant, nay! Neither slavery, nor compromise. That's how I am, to put it bluntly!"

"It's unusual," said Pierre.

"That's the way I am. If ever we do business together..."

"The centuries divide us, alas," Pierre replied with deference and suspicion. "You deal in the eighteenth century, whilst I…"

"I can take a step backwards, and you a step forwards. And we shall meet halfway; amid the Gothic, for example. By the way, I've heard of an exceptional opportunity: it's an ivory casket…"

Pierre thought it wise to bring him down a peg.

"Stick to marquetry, it's safer, and let me bury myself in barbarism on my own; for me, a language becomes decadent as soon as it is written down, and a Riesener chest is the ultimate in written style… Whereas a bronze from Luristan or a Mycenaean cup is a spoken legend."

"I've never ever seen any!" exclaimed Fromentine. "Oh, Monsieur Niox, do show me one."

"With pleasure," said Pierre, relieved to be rid of the uncle. "I'll take you to the Louvre one morning… all three of you."

The rest of the evening was extremely pleasant as the Boisrosé girls frolicked among themselves, without resorting to any scheming or underhand approach towards the outsider, each of them with her own particular looks, her way of moving, her grace and her warmth, while the blending of voices, the entwining of gestures and the succession of these individual melodies built up into a musical drone, into an assortment of continuously picturesque colours. Angélique, argumentative, full of ready answers, her wit restrained. Fromentine, emitting wild shrieks and shaking the corkscrew out of her frizzled hair. Hedwige, enigmatic, contained, controlling them from on high.

It was midnight. The stove had been replenished several times. Pierre had settled in, unable to free himself from the spell, to quit this vanilla-flavoured empire where time did not infiltrate, and where he would have remained until dawn had Monsieur de Rocheflamme, among other idiotic remarks and Gallicisms, not spoken of "returning to his Penates".

Pierre was the last to leave.

"The staircase is Fromentine's handiwork," announced Madame de Boisrosé, whose old-fashioned manner matched her brother's.

But Fromentine, having been squeezing lemons, was rinsing her hands and so it was Hedwige who came down to open the gate.

"Take my overcoat," said Pierre. "I can just as easily throw it over your shoulders as over mine."

There was no time switch to light up the staircase. It was lit only by the lamplight on the ground floor, through the stairwell; thus it was the staircase railings that first cast their shadows on the walls and the steps, followed by

Hedwige's tall, slanting shadow, which looked as though it were descending into some caged tomb. "Everything this girl does is wonderful, the entire effect she has on me is astonishing," Pierre mused.

Once she was downstairs, she threw off the overcoat. What style there was in this provincial ground-floor hall, tiled in black and white, with its Pompeian starkness, and with Hedwige clad in ancient garb, wearing black and white as well, like a steel engraving!

"Let us sit for a moment on this bench"—age unknown, ebony, moth-eaten red velvet—"I feel happy in your house, Hedwige. What tranquillity. Ever since I have known you, I've had solemn thoughts."

"Sad thoughts?"

"Oh no! But I've been reflecting. For some time things have been taking a strange turn for me and all paths seem to be steering me towards marriage. And you are the only woman who appeals to me. Give the word 'appeal' its most intense meaning."

He looked at her; she was rubbing her lovely, slender hands together.

"Hedwige, aren't you going to answer me?"

"I'd like to wait," she said hesitantly. "I'm not just being flirtatious, you know, but since I feel totally happy here with my mother and my sisters, the moment doesn't seem right."

Pierre interrupted her impatiently.

"What moment? I don't understand; give me a clear answer. Don't you love me?"

"I don't know," she said in the same tone of uncertainty. "I just know that it would upset something were I to love you straight away. Wait."

"No, I can't wait! When a beautiful object attracts me in a shop window, I walk in and I take it away with me immediately. I know only too well that it won't be there the following day."

Hedwige said nothing and was gazing down at the ground. She was listening attentively to her inner self formulating the reply she would give to Pierre. When she looked up he had disappeared, having performed one of those instant, invisible and silent vanishing acts for which he had the untransmittable secret.

CHAPTER XI

"WELL, TOO BAD. Wait? No. No woman is worth waiting for."

Waiting was burdensome to Pierre. To him slowness always felt like kilograms, like tons. Whenever he had to slow his pace in the street in order to allow the companion to whom he was talking to catch up, who had dropped a hundred yards behind without Pierre realizing, he felt as though he had suddenly been transformed into a donkey collapsing beneath a packsaddle. Love, too, is a great weight in men's lives; it's a handicap. There's nothing so weighty as the imponderable. The heart is a leaden organ. When a man and a woman meet, they don't study one another so much as weigh each other up; they know that the day will come when one of them will have to carry the other on his or her shoulders. For a couple is not a lateral bonding, it's a vertical assembly.

"And now, enough of this business. Let's get a grip on ourselves. We shall think of something else."

Pierre considered what his most urgent project was. The

Mas Vieux. Take ten days of holiday, go down to the South of France, get the repair works under way…

"Well, it turns out that at a certain moment I did consider marriage; I cast the net: Hedwige happened to be inside it. If the notion of marriage returns at some later date, all I'll have to do is cast out again. Tomorrow morning, I'll dash down to the Mas Vieux."

At the Mas Vieux, for the past four days they have been trellising, mixing cement, repairing the roof, loosening bricks, drilling holes, knocking down ceilings. A stone quarry has been cleared in the forest, where a sawyer and a polisher are cutting up blocks, carving slabs and restoring bits of missing corners, chipped window sills and doorsteps. The embellishments, the handrails, the mouldings have been destroyed; the fountain has been done away with. The garden has given up trying to be an attractive square, relinquished its geranium beds, lost its bower that was the pride of the trellis-maker, sacrificed its lawns for the sake of style, and under the gaze of its new owner is returning to forest. Fences and windbreaks made from roots of heather now cut a dark violet line through the rosemary and wild mimosa. The house looks younger, or rather it grows a century older by the day.

Pierre is doing demolition work; he's never had so much fun; all day long he hammers, beats, wears out his muscles, and it's a voluptuous pleasure for him to see the rubble crumbling and watch effect succeed cause immediately. In Paris, hemmed in between four walls with thoughts that were not always pleasant, he had accumulated a potential for bad moods, which he is unburdening himself of here. He is taking out his nervous tension on the house; he uses his pickaxe as a dog uses its fangs. He forgets to have lunch, he spends his life on the scaffolding, he saws against the grain, he holds his hammer the wrong way round, he blunts the axes, he uses the chisel to bring down bits of old wattle that collapse like flaky pastry beneath his blows. When he is exhausted, he stops, adds a few finishing touches to his labours, then, having recovered his breath, he hurls himself at the clay once more and the plaster dust is blown away in a white cloud by the mistral. He treats demolition work as a physical exercise, as a brawl, as an acrobatic act.

He had decided to pull down the old farmyard, which has no animals apart from a horse and three hens and which merely spoils the view. This yard, which adjoins the chapel, was built on the edge of a spur and consisted of four sides around which the outbuildings were situated: hayloft, garage, stable, pantry, hen house and pressing shed. All these had to be "blown up"; what's more it was "southern" work: bamboo covered with clay and straw mortar, and nothing held firm; a prod with a stick was enough to poke a hole through it. Only the four inner walls of the courtyard still remained standing.

That morning, Pierre was tackling the pointing in the wall by the gable; pickaxe in hand, using three times as much force as was needed, he brought the crumbling plaster down; suddenly he heard the noise of something hard beneath the iron bar.

"Hey! There's stone down there."

Some instinct made him dig more gently; throwing down his pickaxe, he began to scrape in small thrusts with a chisel; something black appeared: an old foundation stone? Pierre put his hand down, felt the cold, polished granite surface; his heart beating, he started to dig, clawing away at a crazy speed, his cheek pressed close to the ground, refusing to step back in order to see the whole thing, not allowing himself any conjecture for fear of disappointment.

No, there was no longer any mistake: what was appearing was a granite tambour bursting out of its battered clay plinth. There was the shaft of the column, the top of the shaft, the stone volute that surrounded it and finally the pink marble capital with its sculpted decorations, heads of men or animals that were still intact and most authentically Roman.

Pierre could scarcely believe it. He had been on excavations before, but he had never had anything jump out at him, in a leap of eight centuries, emerging quite untouched, still partly immured, but very much alive. His head was spinning beneath the winter sun and, because he had been staring so intently, his eyes saw nothing but darkness and red stars. Large blisters of water were bursting in the palms of his burning hands, preventing him from taking up his pickaxe again; he spat on his hands, hoisted up his trousers and called to his labourers so loudly that they broke off drinking from their wineskins and ran over to him, convinced that he had discovered treasure.

"Look at what I've found! A Roman column; while I was digging. There must be others!"

His enthusiasm was so obvious that the workers, who were disappointed, but who were moved and felt for him, eagerly took part in the search. The hatchet revealed a further column, supporting a fine stone arch and the beginnings of another; very gradually the continuous festoons of the arcatures were laid bare.

By the end of the day, two-thirds of a Roman cloister, freed of its layers of plaster, stood out against the sky.

Pierre no longer felt weary; alone now, standing in the midst of his newly discovered little basilica, he continued to contemplate the details; within each arch a picture had been formed in the landscape, with either a pine cone blown there by the mistral, a wisp of white foam from the sea, or the branch of a fig tree. Dusk was gradually falling, shadows and a scattering of stars filled the arches, and Pierre could still see the pure movement within them.

Cloîtres silencieux, voûtes des monastères,
C'est vous, sombres caveaux, vous, qui savez aimer.[6]

"If only Hedwige were here!" he murmured.

How he should love to live here with her, observing the monastic rule—and he the frenetic man! Together they would walk and shelter beneath the vaults; these angles and approaches would shatter their lethargy, divide their meditations into four cardinal points. A cloister, that was what had always been lacking in his life originally, an enclosed space; once they were enclosed within this square, their movements shaped by the collapsed decay of the arches, they would enter into the perfect rhythm.

Two kilometres from the Mas Vieux perched the village of La Penne. A minor road transformed into the bed of a stream ran down to it, spewing out schist and flint stones in torrents. Half a century previously, there were no inhabitants left in this village; fig trees grew freely, loosening the foundations of the houses that were still standing. Amid the collapsed roofs, gypsies and unemployed agricultural workers sometimes dossed down there, making their fires among the broken tiles. One of these nomads, a young Genoese man (who looked like Gambetta, what's more), had set up camp there. He was a handsome wild bull of a creature, as tall as the Farnese Bull, with a craggy, hairy chest; he had gradually seduced the girls in this land where there was a paucity of men, had introduced some Ligurian blood into these French deserts, and had repopulated the region. He was known as Magali. A tribe of Magalis had been sired biblically among the crevices of these old walls, keeping themselves alive by burning sticks, vine shoots, beams and shutters, poaching, collecting chestnuts, repruning abandoned vines, dynamiting sea bream and sucking goats' udders like vipers.

Nowadays a hundred or so people lived in the village, all either legitimately or illegitimately Magalis. From being a beggar, the eighty-year-old Magali had become a village worthy; from being a vagabond, the god Terminus. He had married the most successful, the best-endowed of his grandsons to the daughter of an estate agent from Grimaud, a Mademoiselle Estramuri, a parishioner who subscribed to fashion magazines, was imperious by nature and wise in business matters, and who ran an ancient little al fresco restaurant that she had restored, which served snacks and drinks beneath the bamboo awnings to cart drivers, seasonal workers and cork-strippers.

The Magalis rarely left La Penne; they could be seen in the autumn when they came down to the wine-growers' co-operative in Bormes to tamper with the grapes, or at Le Lavandou station where they caught the train to Toulon. They did not live at all badly, they frequently ate meat, did some fishing for the local lords of the manor, worked listlessly, and were so lazy that they did not even bother to pick up their figs. It was only in September that they became a little busier, during the *vendange*, when they put a real effort into picking the grapes and producing their alcohol; they all had a fondness for drink. The father especially, puffy and red-faced, was always at the bottle. As his beard grew whiter, old Magali had exchanged his sexual vitality for political influence: a freemason and a bigwig who was listened to, for he made all his tribe vote, he had set up one of his daughters as postmistress at Hyères. With official approval, he kept a watch on neighbouring landowners and made their lives impossible unless an understanding was reached. From deep in the valley at La Penne, he scanned the horizon like a wrecked sailor; in the holiday season he found positions for his granddaughters and great-granddaughters who had not yet found jobs as maids at the summer visitors' homes;

in the winter, thanks to information they had gleaned, and with a deft Latin lightness of touch, he discreetly robbed those houses that had not been entrusted to his care. An innate malevolence, democratic impunity, and the friendliness of the police meant that the Magalis were formidable creators of myths; the girls spread slander as far as Saint-Raphaël, they listened to telephone conversations, read letters by holding them up to the light, and extended the area of their anonymous denunciations as far away as Marseille.

Scarcely had the little cloister of the Mas Vieux seen— or rather, seen anew—the light of day, than the Magalis were alerted by one of their own kin who worked there as a labourer. Madame Magali, *née* Estramuri, immediately summoned the Magali tribe to a sort of council meeting and gave an outline of the situation. While those best equipped took the hint, the more ignorant ones listened to her respectfully as she emphasized the importance of the discovery and listed all the benefits that could accrue to the village as a result: the cloister would attract crowds of tourists; petrol stations would open surrounded by shops selling postcards and local souvenirs; guides and interpreters would be seen coming to and from La Penne: all this would benefit the Magalis, and the little snack bar that had become the Magali Restaurant would feature on the gastronomic pages of the *Guide Michelin*. A road suitable for motor cars would have to be built, of course; two kilometres from the Mas Vieux to La Penne, 500 metres from La Penne to the main road. Not a great deal in actual fact; Monsieur Niox, the Parisian millionaire, would put up the money and would make a profit from it. Without further ado, Madame Magali dispatched her husband to the Mas Vieux. Forty minutes later, he had already returned.

"Well?"

"Well, to put it simply, he sent me packing. And he wasn't even polite. As far as I can see, he doesn't want to pay for the road."

The following day and the day after that, the missions and delegations gathered pace. The Magalis offered their work free of charge, then did their best to obtain a departmental grant. Infuriated, Pierre refused to let them in.

Whereupon the pirate-patriarch Magali, a serpent coiled round his staff, turned up in person. Wearing an Alpine hunter's beret over his grimy locks, his belly squeezed in by an orange-coloured leather cartridge belt that was always empty, his gun slung over his shoulder, and reeking of wine, the elderly tramp, these days as plump as a sow but still a pirate at heart, forced his way in.

From the back of the chicken-run, Pierre was astonished to see this Silenus disguised as Tartarin[7] loom up;

he wished he could have shut the door, but the Mas Vieux in its state of demolition no longer had any. Magali had already launched into a lengthy utterance that contained everything: welcoming greetings, descriptions of the beauties of the landscape and its hidden dangers, offers of protection against the natives whom Magali knew better than anyone since he was one himself, all embellished with local legends.

"You're very lucky, Monsieur Niox, to have this lovely little chapel, *aquelle poulido picholo capello*, which is famous hereabouts, *dans lou païs!* When you come here at Christmas, you will get a surprise! *serès étouna!* And I promise you, a great *paour*, a fright. At midnight, some Capuchin friars come to sing the Mass here, *maï les verras pas, perqué ésiston pas!* But you won't see them, 'cos they don't exist!"

"Is my chapel haunted?" asked Pierre in amusement.

"Haunted, I didn't say that," protested the old mountebank, superficially enlightened but innately superstitious. "It's the people from these parts that tell a tale from the year one thousand: of a little monk who got bored at the cloister, right in the *plaço*, the very place, where you are. He poisoned his abbot and took the crozier and the ring and the wife and *lou resto*, all the rest! The other monks got married the same day and then they all ran away with the vases and the chasubles and the relics and they became robbers on the road to the Alps. These brigands were friends of the devil, but they weren't *fâchas avec lou Boun Diou,* they weren't angry with God and every Sunday they came back to their chapel—your one, eh!—to say Mass. Finally, the Bishop of Digne, he expelled them and he brought back order and *gentilezza dans lou païs,* but they poisoned him too, put some *veneno* in his ciborium, and started up their hellish practices again, *un vido d'inferi.*"

At this point the old man winked with his little red eye and he implied in a few enticing words that it was Pierre's responsibility to recreate equally alluring debauchery in these deserted locations. As for the road, Magali would take care of that. In a fit of inspiration, he pointed out the site for the future Grand Hôtel du Cloître on a ridge not far away, with its tennis court, its garage and its swimming pool where the lovely tourist ladies would frolic.

Pierre listened in total dismay.

"*Maï!* You've done a good deal, Monsieur Niox, God knows. Your land must be worth gold! And then the building sites, they're gold in bars."

In a flash, Pierre saw this five-act tragedy unfolding:

LE MAS VIEUX

Centre for Tourist Attractions

In a voice strangled with rage, he said:

"My house is my own. No one shall set foot here, you least of all. You will kindly get the hell out of here!"

"But Monsieur Niox, you haven't understood a thing— *rein comprès*," said the astonished old man indignantly. "Perhaps you think *que van vous vola* that your view is going to be stolen from you? Magali does not steal views, he's an artist! He admires your cloister, reckons it's a building of public utility! A national treasure! You'll be awarded a decoration, monsieur, as a reward for *vostre descouverto*, your discovery!"

"Now listen to me, Magali," said Pierre, foaming with rage, "Do you see this gate? By this evening it will have a door and a padlock, and tomorrow, behind this door, there will be a pair of mastiffs and not a single human being is going to go near them, if he values his life."

"Then *que prétendès?* What are your intentions?" said the old man, who had gone pale.

"My intentions are to keep my cloister to myself alone, yes."

Magali burst into a paroxysm of fury and poured out a hail of Niçois invective that came to an abrupt stop; an unctuous smile spread over his face.

"*Fassès errour*, you're making a mistake, Monsieur Niox, your cloister is *la proprietà dé la Francé*. It's French property, and if what you say is true you could have the Commission for Historical Monuments on to you." He paused for a moment and added in a meaningful tone: "The Commission for Historical Monuments is on friendly terms with our lawyer, Maître Caressa."

And, removing his beret in the sort of grand gesture of mock politeness associated with declarations of war, Magali shuffled away.

Pierre did not even have the choice between conceding and resisting; conceding meant three stars in the Guide Joanne,[8] wardens in caps parading through his olive trees, coaches from Marseille, shrieks of delight from tourists; resisting meant enduring daily and multifaceted persecution, both spiteful and relentless. But resistance would become impossible if Caressa and the Beaux-Arts people got involved. Pierre had no choice but to leave… leave, yes, but taking his cloister with him (he wasn't going to surrender it to this gang if it was the last thing he did), and doing so quickly, for he risked being listed.

Within a few minutes he had drawn up his battle plan.

He paid and dismissed his workers after he had made them put up a temporary door, which he locked tightly. At three o'clock in the morning, he left by car for Ventimiglia;

at eight o'clock he employed some Italian builders; he hired a coach, filled it with his workers and provisions, took his entire staff to the Mas Vieux under the supervision of an energetic foreman whose silence he bought, and within a few days he had dismantled his cloister piece by piece like a clock. He himself ran around, telephoned, gabbled away in Italian, operated the roller and the hoist and distributed tips. Once the work was well under way and while the stones, all numbered and sorted, were being lined up one behind the other on the ground, Pierre rushed off to Cannes, dashed around Toulon, and went as far as Marseille. Ten-ton trucks hired by him toiled up to the Mas Vieux during the night, through woods, amid avalanches of gravel. Throughout the day they were filled with small columns, foundation stones, arches, capitals and tiles. The following night, a night with no moon, the convoy hurried down from the hills, escaped to the coast and unloaded material at different points; at Golfe Juan into a tartane, at Cannes into an old yacht, at Salins d'Hyères a trawler took the cargo on board. In the evening this fleet cast off and transported the charming little monument, which had not moved for ten centuries and which was now sailing the high seas, to Port-Vendres, and from there, two days later, to Barcelona with all the papers in order, the blessing of the customs, and a certificate of origin.

CHAPTER XII

"HELLO, is that Monsieur Niox? Is that Quick Silver?" said a woman's voice over the telephone.

And because he groaned, not answering with either a yes or a no, the twittering interspersed with giggles of laughter allowed him to recognize Fromentine's voice. She scolded him for having forgotten them and reminded him of his promise to take them to the Louvre. She suggested a rendezvous the following day, which Pierre accepted, delighted at the prospect of seeing Hedwige again. They agreed to meet at two o'clock at the square du Carrousel.

"The museum is only open until four o'clock," said Pierre. "Try to arrive a little before closing time."

He was waiting for them in front of the Pavillon Mollien, in the coldest spot in Paris. They approached him head-on, asserting their full height. Pierre saw six marvellous legs coming towards him, walking with an imperious spirit and sparkle. He was dazzled, horrified. "If these girls were determined enough and followed up their ideas, nothing could withstand them. They've got an amazingly powerful presence. Everything grows dim once they take charge."

As they came up to him, the troupe of Mademoiselles Boisrosé detached themselves and surrounded him, all talking at the same time, then shortly afterwards individually, each doing their best to attract his attention. How could he possibly cope with three of them? "But lack of concentration and the inability to persevere will be their downfall," he added to reassure himself. "They will remain children and will never generate anything."

They began at the beginning, with the fifty-ton objects that were impossible to lift, with the granite sphinxes doomed to remain for all eternity amid the dampness of the ground floor, with the stone Molochs, with all the simulated gods that would never reach a higher floor in any gallery and that would break the floorboards were they to be moved upstairs. Pierre Niox and his flock walked at a goodly pace and the noise of the women's heels echoed on the stone slabs. Angélique wanted to stop, saying that she "adored" these monsters, their solitariness and their impotence, and that she could understand lovers arranging to meet in their shade. She emphasized this point eagerly, which surprised Pierre.

They inspected the ranks of obsolete gods, arranged by the Beaux-Arts in an eternal and administrative symmetry.

"Whose idea was it to collect all this?" asked Hedwige.

"The Renaissance, the Convention and the Second Empire," Pierre replied. "The Louvre owes everything to them. It's the poor periods that make the best collections."

Followed by his three Graces, he strode past the antique sculpture, made his way through the Middle Ages, talking a great deal all the while. Angélique thanked him for "adding so much to her artistic knowledge", which irritated Pierre because she was hopeless, mistaking Trajan's column for the Vendôme column, the Bols for the Rembrandts, and going into raptures over the plaster casts as though they were original work. To please her guide, Angélique exaggerated her enthusiasm, not wishing to miss a single drawing.

"There are forty-eight thousand of them," said Pierre.

Angélique adopted a studiously stooping attitude and pretended to ponder over the masterpieces, which got on Pierre's nerves, particularly as the only things she called masterpieces were either under glass or those immediately in front of the benches. She discovered resemblances in every painting: a Frans Hals reminded her of Uncle Rocheflamme; Guercino's *Faith, Hope and Charity at the Feet of God* represented herself and her sisters grouped around Mamicha.

Pierre, beside himself, dropped her off at the Clock Pavilion counter.

Pierre preferred the other two sisters because of their passivity. He snatched them away as though they were succulent prey and began to pace through the Apollo Gallery. The Venuses, the Hercules, the marbles and the bronzes, the pots and the vases did their best to solicit them as they passed, but their charms were to no avail. Pierre would not tolerate anyone liking what he disliked. He scanned the room with his eagle eye, trusting in his own dazzling good taste, and led his companions directly to the rare or perfect object. Hedwige followed, feeling rather irritated herself; firstly because she was not the object of any particular attention on Pierre's part, and also because her foot was painful, due to a new inner sole. Her head was spinning. She had the feeling she was falling down a precipice of colours and draperies, into a pit of gilt frames writhing with school mythologies.

Pierre dismissed the minor Dutch masters and the effete Italians with all the disrespect due to them.

"Straight to the summits!" he cried, and despite Hedwige's timid attempt to confess a liking for the Primitives, he dragged her off to the Spanish and French eighteenth-century schools. Scarcely had he reached Goya than she begged for mercy.

"Pierre Niox is the devil in person!" said Fromentine to Hedwige, laughing as she spoke.

"It was the devil who took Jesus Christ up the mountain and showed him the view," replied Pierre, who had overheard.

Hedwige was not joking. She was in such pain that she felt she was being burnt on a slow flame. She would have preferred not to leave Pierre alone with Fromentine, who was following him at a brisk pace, having adopted his long stride. But her longing to take her shoes off was more powerful. She left them on their own. It was agreed they should meet in the Salon Carré, at closing time.

Fromentine glanced over her shoulder frequently: she could glimpse Hedwige in the distance, growing smaller and smaller, looking initially like a moving portrait, then like a character in an indoor painting, then like a miniature; eventually she disappeared entirely. Pierre and Fromentine set off together. The girl was determined to inflict unintelligible chatter on her companion, her gibberish spouting from a mouth buried in her fur, but he gazed only at her bottle-green eyes and the reddish curls trapped in between the silver-fox on her hat and that on her collar. The most spacious galleries opened up before them now like paths replete with gold and allegories. The Sabine women reached out their arms to them and the shipwrecked survivors of the

Raft of the Medusa their fists; athletically, they sped past them. Pierre had finally met someone who could keep up with him; he led the way, but without walking ahead of Fromentine, who easily kept pace with him. She moved freely, proud of her conquest and happy to have the man entirely to herself and to be rid at last of all his paintings and statues, about which she understood nothing; it suited her youthfulness that this Louvre, intended for the study of fine arts, should be transformed into a playground; it struck her as normal to be the only working masterpiece there, the only living statue.

Pierre was fully aware of the attractions of this adaptable and supple companion, who followed him with obedient ease and wore low rubberized heels. Fromentine indulged his weaknesses.

"This is the way I like to visit museums," she said, "you really do know how to see!"

"And choose," Pierre replied.

She looked at him with a radiant and firm gaze, trying to give the verb that he had uttered without any ulterior motive a romantic, fateful meaning.

"You have to know a great deal to be able to choose," she added with schoolgirl admiration. "You probably have to have loved a great deal and suffered a great deal."

"I'm a good coach."

"Most of all, you're a good teacher. And not in the least weird, whatever people say. I pretend to move slowly because that's how the family moves, but I never get tired. In the mountains, I scatter the hordes. Phew! I'm so hot!"

"Let me take your bag and your silver-fox."

"I'd never allow a man to carry anything."

She joked teasingly about gentlemen who offer to take your clothing and who, when you hand it to them, don't forgive you.

They were now striding through the schools, the countries, the glories, the centuries. It was becoming a race, a splendid competition that left art-lovers astonished and wardens amazed. The partitions of the Louvre were turning into hedges and the polished staircases into rivers.

They were hardly speaking to one another any more, they were aiming purely to outdo each other, they "justified themselves through distance", to use Fromentine's words. She admired this tall fellow, who was energetic and efficient, as calm in his activities as he was sitting in an armchair; from time to time she asked him the odd opinion as she would a true friend, and when he gave it to her she would respond simply with pious silence and an earnest, thoughtful demeanour.

She certainly had a hold on him, this man in a hurry. With a sure instinct, she had seen through his weaknesses, and she was entering into his lively, perverse game with the innocent dishonesty of virgins.

"I'm not like Angélique," she would say, "I don't enjoy painting at all. All I enjoy is exercise. I seek whatever delights me, whatever uplifts me, what transports me!"

With that complete lack of discernment characteristic of men whose quirks are encouraged, Pierre considered Fromentine to be loyal, honest and natural.

"Do you know that you would make an excellent secretary?" he said.

This frantic canter through the necropolis of art, the sudden absence of her sisters, the irritating cries of "We're closing, we're closing", this "marvellous" proposal that had just been made to her all had a dazzling effect on Fromentine. She, in turn, felt a childish need to provoke and astonish. She leant over to Pierre and told him in all seriousness:

"You are prolific."

They found themselves in the Salon Carré just at the moment when the wardens were shutting up shop. The closing bell was ringing. The immortal masterpieces, warm, well protected and sure of a good night, would now be able to cohabit without any admirers other than firemen on their rounds.

Angélique, looking pale and weary, and Hedwige,

hobbling like Ribera's *Clubfoot*, were waiting for their sister, who arrived with five minutes to spare, the sole representative of the family left in the company of the space-gobbler. Pierre was very pleased to have loosened the Boisrosés' ties. Fromentine looked radiant.

"Monsieur Niox has taken me on as a secretary!" she exclaimed.

"Now all you need is to learn how to spell," said Angélique.

CHAPTER XIII

MADAME DE BOISROSÉ was shuffling cards as she waited for her daughters.

For some time now, she was occasionally on her own. In this bedroom, where four female existences used to unfold harmoniously, something had changed. Bonne felt it as an almost physical sensation, as though a strong draught from outside had blown away the warmth and the aroma of family virtues. She even gave this draught its proper name; but although she had figured everything out, she apportioned no blame, she said nothing and pretended she had not noticed anything, for, as monarch of this small state, she possessed that essential quality that monarchs have, that of not intervening until the last moment. This did not prevent her from getting dreadfully bored. And so, when the cleaning lady came to announce Madame de La Chaufournerie, she was delighted to welcome her.

Madame de La Chaufournerie was a tiny tinted and painted old lady, who scurried about in a self-effacing way, and who only took centre stage at tragic moments, just as the chorus occupies the proscenium arch while kings and queens are murdering one another in Mycenaean palaces. Bonne suspected her of having the evil eye and only proffered two fingers in the shape of a horn to greet her, but she happily put up with her because she could pour out her feelings freely in her presence, which is the only pleasant form of conversation; this confidante's deafness and failing memory guaranteed discretion. Bonne treated her with disdainful indulgence; she simultaneously despised her and felt sorry for her for having married off her two daughters to officers who hadn't a penny, which—though irritating in the circumstances—made them perfectly happy, since it meant being far away from their mother.

Madame de La Chaufournerie, though lifeless to herself, had not finished sacrificing herself for her children, bequeathing them virtually her entire pension, doing without everything for their sake, wearing herself out doing their shopping and considering herself happy if her daily advice—which she lavished on them by letter (even though she lived in the same neighbourhood) and which covered the full range of a woman's existence, from the shape of her hairstyle to what precautions to take against microbes—was, if not exactly followed, received without impatience. Her life was like a perpetual battle in which, claws splayed and holding her breath, she was ready to pounce on any dangers that might threaten her daughters. She had the heart of a soldier in the heat of battle, paying no attention to hunger, thirst, exhaustion, fear or what was impossible; in the heroic atmosphere in which she immersed herself, the amenities of life—pleasure, comfort, respect, politeness—played no part and even had no meaning; this fragile little old lady was tough as a trooper, she attacked and surmounted whatever obstacle lay in her path and made herself unbearable wherever she went. As a result, she had no friends, which did not matter to her since she had no need of them, and the only person she saw was Bonne de Boisrosé in whom she believed, quite incorrectly, she recognized a motherly love that resembled her own.

Barely had she entered the room than Madame de La Chaufournerie came, as was her wont, straight to the point.

"I no longer see your daughters," she said, "or rather I no longer see them from my window. Fromentine, in particular. Where are they rushing off to like that?"

"What, Herminie," Bonne drawled, "What! Didn't you know that Fromentine has become secretary to a well-known antique dealer?"

Herminie, who, once she had asked her questions, was not bothered about the answers, launched into a long speech that had not the least connection with the Boisrosé girls. She jumbled her sentences together in a uniform vocal register that prevented one from remembering any of them. This monotonous verbiage plunged Madame de Boisrosé into an extremely pleasant sort of hypnotized doze in which she poured out her feelings aloud.

"You're right," she said, "we don't see Fromentine any more. As soon as she comes home, she locks herself away in her bedroom. She is, of course, sorting out her clothes and basing everything around this one central purpose: 'a man to take her out'. Wouldn't she be better off reading my *Figaro* to me? And the airs she puts on! She continually annoys her sisters. Hedwige sulks. It's understandable, the younger one is trespassing on her preserve... she'll return empty-handed; I've seen only too clearly that if *he* is chatting to Fromentine, he's only really looking at Hedwige; but Angélique, I do rather wonder what's biting her? She's bored; did she get bored before? To think that I was counting on this man to restore some order to my affairs and all he has done is to sew disorder in my household! He's indecisive, a dawdler," she concluded in a caustic tone that pierced Madame de La Chaufournerie's sluggish eardrum. "Yes, a dawdler!"

"But of whom are you talking, my dear?" the latter replied. And since Bonne looked vague and did not answer: "Would it be about a good catch for your girls?" (Herminie was prone to the sort of insights which, along with her exceptional inquisitorial ability, would have taken her far

174

as an examining magistrate…) "And of course, all three are in love with him?"

Bonne gave a start.

"In love! My girls in love! Well, that would be the last straw!"

She drew her heavy jade-green Ottoman morning coat over her bosom (any allusions to love aroused these reflexes of threatened modesty in her) and cast a resentful glance at her friend.

"Love, love, that's all you ever think about!" she said severely. "Should a woman of your age be meddling in such filth! Men ought to disgust you, just as they do me! You do make me laugh."

But she wasn't laughing; it was Madame de La Chaufournerie, her face like that of a scrawny overworked nag, who broke into an extremely rare fit of laughter.

"It's you with your horror of men who's the comical one! So have you decided never to marry your daughters?" she said.

"Yes, men are repugnant, but my daughters ought to get married," said Bonne peremptorily.

The new secretary was extremely useful: since she knew neither shorthand nor typing, Pierre was obliged to learn them himself; since she did not know Paris very well, he did his own shopping and because she organized her own time badly, he also did Fromentine's. She was aware of this and she laughed.

"I've never been so well waited upon," she would say, "as I have since I've been employed."

The girl answered the telephone and kept an eye on the house. Reclining on the sofa in the empty office, she leafed through illustrated magazines. To begin with, this office had disappointed her.

"But where's your antique shop then?" she asked Pierre.

To her astonishment, he showed her his safe.

"There," he said.

"And here was I thinking you had a very dark shop piled with collections of crocodiles up to the ceiling, with ticketed prices hanging on the end of their tails, and pretty little tea sets, and dalmatic vestments embroidered in gold, all lit by lantern fish! What a disappointment! Are you going out? Be kind, Pierre, bring me back some American cigarettes."

He came back loaded with supplies.

"How quick you've been! I'm flabbergasted. You really are an electric man. It's wonderful. Where do find the time?"

"Did anyone phone?"

"Yes. A foreign gentleman. I couldn't catch his name."

"Try to remember…"

"It was something like Stravinsky… Striesky… something with 'ski' in it."

"It wasn't Erckmann by any chance?"

"Yes, Erckmann, exactly."

"He's the keeper of the Ethnology Museum in Stockholm. I was waiting for him to call."

"Oh? I rang off. I always ring off, for that matter, when I don't understand."

"And what have you done in my absence, Fromentine?"

"I've made a mess."

And she laughed as she pointed to the magazines on the floor and the papers that were scattered around.

"You would make a very poor cleaning lady; a jumble shop cleaner, at best."

After a week, Pierre re-engaged his former secretary and kept Fromentine for trips to rue Masseran to play tennis on a covered court.

He no longer talked about Hedwige. He was indifferent to Angélique. He never mentioned the Boisrosés. To think that he had almost thrown in the towel. "And now I'm turning over a new leaf," he often said. Had he done so this time, turned a page without leaving a bookmark, without leaving a dried flower as a memory?

"I loathe things that have been papered over," he sometimes exclaimed. Regencrantz, who had watched him rushing eagerly for a drink when he wasn't thirsty, would have said that he had also thrown himself into this business without having the least desire to do so. He had vanished from the Boisrosés' home just as he always did everywhere, as if through a trapdoor. In the blink of an eyelid he was no longer there; he melted into the crowd like sugar in water; walls absorbed him; he slipped away as people do in dreams; dreams are apartments without doors that one enters through walls.

Pierre had passed through many a milieu in this way without pausing there, doing whatever business he had to do quickly and never coming back. At the casino, he walked into the gaming room and shouted "*banco!*" over everyone's heads; before they had had time to look round, he had grabbed his winnings and disappeared. Disappeared for the season too, for he detested the game and only played it in order to test his luck.

"What a card you are, Quick Silver!" Fromentine said as she passed him the two racquets, which he tucked under his arm. "The things you teach me!" she added with apparent ecstasy.

Pierre was in the habit of leaving Fromentine in the street or in his car, waiting for him like a small dog. She was furthermore wonderfully passive and easily distracted, with, at the same time, a great facility for not doing or thinking of anything for hours on end, like a becalmed sailing ship. When, a moment later, Pierre returned, ready to set off at full tilt, she would follow him with the same easy manner, keeping up the same absolutely neutral appearance, never complaining, and with that marvellous temperament that frivolous, selfish people have.

Coming back from rue Masseran, Pierre stopped in boulevard de Grenelle in front of a shop which, even as a child, used to fascinate him. They had made clocks there since the eighteenth century and the wrought-iron sign hanging outside represented a belfry. Dials in the shop window informed passing travellers from the *métro* what the time was in every language. The time in Stamboul was in Turkish letters, the time in Calcutta in Bengali, the time in Suez in Arabic, the time in Peking in Chinese characters.

"How many minutes these dials must have ticked off over one hundred and fifty years!" Pierre exclaimed. "Think of it… what human impetus could compete against them? What diastoles and systoles will ever match their range and their mechanism?"

"You're a philosopher in your own way," replied Fromentine with shrewd simplicity, "the philosopher of the quarter-second."

"I'm not a philosophic person," replied Pierre drily. "I'm a tragic person. You don't understand a thing."

"Talk to me more about yourself," sighed Fromentine as she reapplied some rouge, "it's fascinating."

Pierre had not been back to Saint-Germain since the visit to the Louvre. But he would have liked to talk to Fromentine about her sisters. Each time, she found an excuse for not responding to him. And when he was with her, he felt increasingly more alone than he had done beforehand. He would have liked to know how the Boisrosés reacted to Fromentine's absence, to her returning home late at night, to the presents he gave her—in short, to that sort of artificial household atmosphere brought about by the relationship of a pretty secretary with her employer, where thoughts are dictated on notepads, where the trousseau is replaced by files, the jam cupboards by metal cabinets, kisses by licked envelopes and cradles by desk trays.

Yet this beautiful girl, at his side all day long, did not imply a presence, however. She brought him no relief in his isolation. Even Chantepie, even Placide radiated more warmth. Even the cat did. With everyone else, Pierre felt some resistance and thus some warmth (from the friction). With Fromentine, he felt none at all. She gave way to him on everything.

It was worse than ever.

Since she now brought up his post when she arrived in the morning, he did not even have a relationship with the concierge. When he was with Fromentine, Pierre sometimes thought of Angélique and Hedwige, rather as the owner of a Houdon plaster cast must think of the original; Fromentine was less of a Boisrosé and more a plaster cast of the other Boisrosé girls. He thought of her sisters in the way that one might want to reread a classic in the original, having developed a liking for it from the early pages of a translation. He remembered the little tea party at Saint-Germain, and the more he visualized the polished drawing room, the bedroom with its canopied bed and the black stove with its little red light, the lonelier he felt.

As lonely as if he were in the desert.

The less he was invited the more he felt the attraction of that little provincial place so far away, of that precipitous little town to which Fromentine returned every evening: the side plates stacked inside the larger ones, the financial and economic chatter of the dismal Vincent; the tall figure of Hedwige, reticent, but fiery deep down because of that very reticence, and passionate; their first loving words at the foot of the staircase; Angélique and her attentiveness (when she passed a plate to you, it was more like a caress).

Pierre did, after all, owe her a response. Had he not told her she need not worry, that he had an "idea", that he would sort out their Mas Vieux business?

"As for the Mas Vieux, I told you that I had an idea. If I have not mentioned it to you again, it's because that promise…"

Pierre had taken it upon himself to write to Angélique and to go and see her, at a time when Fromentine was not there.

"You don't owe us anything," Angélique said simply, as she shook her lovely raffia-coloured hair.

"… It's just that in my mind that promise happened to be the natural sequel to my undertaking to Hedwige. Perhaps you didn't know that I asked her to marry me?"

"I do know."

"Perhaps you didn't know that she refused?"

"No, she didn't refuse. She told you to wait, which is not the same thing."

"I longed for her too much for it not to be the same thing."

"Why did you employ Fromentine as a secretary?"

"To tell you the truth, dear Angélique, it has been a very foolish venture, more and more absurd, and all I want is to be free of it."

Pierre stood up, set off with his neck outstretched, like a wild duck on a direct flight, stopped because of lack of space, and returned to Angélique.

"Will you talk to me about Hedwige instead?"

"You'll have to keep still if you want me to explain Hedwige to you," Angélique began. "She's someone who is totally honest and very loyal. You showed great human understanding in choosing her: I admire you for that and I like you even more because of it. The family want Hedwige to be happy, but I want you to be happy together and at the same time. For a start, Hedwige is far more intelligent than all of us put together (it's true that when we're all together, we're silly and frivolous). Of course, she's not very cultured (my methodical and scientific Vincent often says that in the Boisrosés' home books are only used to prop up table legs), but you yourself have enough culture and erudition to manage without a learned wife. Then Hedwige is exceptionally honest: as a child, she was the one out of all of us who lied the least readily. All right, you know all this only too well and you would prefer to see me revealing Hedwige's faults? Very well. You are not unaware that there are two kinds of human beings: the givers and the takers. Hedwige clearly belongs to the former. But like all givers, her nerves are frail; her sensitivity is exceptional. She is impressionable; she can be easily discouraged; the slightest thing exhausts her and when she's worn out, you may find her unsure of herself; no, it's not that… how can I put it… you may find her… a little changeable; anyway, you won't find her like that! I'm warning you so that you don't get upset; avoid using force with her; listen: Hedwige always gives in. Hedwige is someone who's both calm and good. Take care of her, give her the time to breathe and she will repay everything in long years of happiness because she loves you and she wants to be your wife."

"Has she told you so?"

"Amongst ourselves, we don't tell each other things. There's no point. Everything has been said long before we talk about it."

"When may I see her?" asked Pierre.

"Come to the house tomorrow."

Thus did Pierre set off again to Saint-Germain. He, who has never taken a backward step, is once again climbing the steep road that leads him to the Boisrosés' home. He, for whom instantaneity is dogma and for whom haste is second nature, is patiently retracing the path already trod.

In love as in everything else, he behaved ardently. But saying "in love" is to exclude love. One might as well describe love affairs as delights. Pierre wolfed down ladies in the twinkling of an eye. He enlivened them, he swept them off their feet, he pushed them into corners, he found something to dislike about them and, all of a sudden, he broke up with them. Their unimportance, the pride they experienced in seeing themselves transformed into a burning bush, their inviting sighs, the passiveness with which they resisted did the rest. Particularly since no one could be kinder than he was. This starving wolf who rushed out with gaping and fiery jaws had never frightened a single lamb; the lambs actually ran towards him, not being in the habit of remaining terror-stricken for long. Pierre upset the objects of his attention graciously and irked them just as much as was necessary with his restless behaviour; he hugged and kissed openly, his mouth was fresh, his skin was warm. He strung words together well, he threw himself at women, devoured them without digesting them, and vanished before they had the time to say "phew", not that a woman would ever utter such a sound. He telescoped situations, returning to the classical unities of time, place and action. He readily confused the declaration of love with ravishment in the taxi, the taxi with the enclosed theatre box, the staircase with the sofa, the squeezed hand with the arm around the waist, the handkerchief with the brassiere, the first date with the last, and the tact and consideration of the early stages with the ecstasies of the ending. All this with so little space between the point of departure and the destination that women believed they were being offered an initial token of gratitude when he was already giving them a farewell present.

He would make plans to die rather than be trapped into wedding preparations every time. The looser the women were, the more fickle they found him. The entire vocabulary that was once used for artillerymen and lovers could equally apply to him: Pierre prepared for action, he unmasked, he struck, he dismantled. It was charming because it was what the young did and, apart from a few tears, it actually suited everyone. He could count on his fingers, the sprightly lad, the girls whom he had made cry, or who had slapped him, or with whom he had genuinely fallen out. He was born like that, belonging to an age when love brought no shame on anyone, when one deprived oneself of nothing, when duties and obligations were by common consent reduced to the minimum. "There's no reason," Pierre used to say, "why a pleasure ride by rail should not also be an express train." His train was always full and he had never had to complain about a derailment.

But Pierre had just reached his thirty-fifth birthday. Not having discovered love, he began to treat it with respect. "The day I find a woman whom I don't throw myself at," he told himself, "I shall have arrived at my destination." He sensed that when that day came, it would not be he who would have to give up his bad habits, it would be they that would give him up.

Hedwige was waiting for him in the drawing room. The tea stood steaming on the tray; an indoor dress, red like that of the old silks of the Orient, flowed down her firm body in lovely folds, like a waterfall over a rock. This scenario immediately made him want to be outside.

"Let's go out," he said, "take a coat. I won't be able to speak unless I have fresh air."

They went for a walk on the nearby terrace, in the winter twilight, with the early evening lights of Paris below them and the tall forest trees that stopped in a straight line at the edge of the lawn.

Hedwige agreed to accompany him without making any fuss. She found it natural that a hand other than hers should record her fate. She relied on God to take good care of her. Following Pierre in this park did not bother her. She is serene, sensible and brave. The geese are keeping watch.

Pierre was also very self-possessed, very calm. With gravitation causing them to lean towards one another, their fingers became entwined and they were able to reach a deeper understanding of a situation that distinguished them from other people and yet made them similar to everyone else.

This coral-red and sulphur-yellow dusk, this garden filled with naked statues beneath the snow-filled sky, these dark oak trees swaying in the breeze—all these romantic incantations, far from exciting Pierre, cautioned him to exercise modesty and restraint. He felt an expectation growing inside him and he was trying hard to fill it because it was leading him beyond, not just his desires, but what he felt himself capable of. Just as a Christian hopes for a holy death, he was hoping for a real life. His respect for what was happening to him and for the person who was causing it to happen—since Hedwige is innocent and spotless in every respect—preclude him from making any aggressive move.

For the first time ever he is taking his time and he is doing so with infinite pleasure, for he has his life in front of him and he is moving, at a natural pace, along the widest and best-known of roads; a road whose surroundings he does not recognize and whose name he is even unfamiliar with, since he has never been along it; it's a road designed for pedestrians, where fast cars cannot go. He is going to knock at the oracle's door, like peasants at the door of the Blessed Virgin, to ask whether their land will be fertile. He is leaving daily life behind and is entering a dream in which children, inventors, madmen and those who draw the jackpot live, a dream conducive to the fulfilment of grand designs, not of petty desires. That is why he moves with the heaviness of a man asleep, at the slow pace of a deep-sea diver.

Hedwige regards this immemorial man as a man of today. Every generation of young women has its particular type of man just as every generation has one author and every author is only ever loyal to one hero.

Night has fallen. Pierre no longer knows how long he has been sitting on this bench without uncrossing his legs; beside him, Hedwige has not stirred, she whose pliant movements are so beautiful. The ground at their feet, ravaged by winter, is arid and skeletal and the frozen pebbles by the balusters shatter into splinters.

Up above, the Milky Way resembles a caravan trail worn away by ancient suns.

"Before God or before any other maker of the stars," Pierre said suddenly, "I am ready to wait for you as long as is needed, and I have made up my mind not to marry anyone else but you."

Hedwige drew closer to him and laid her head on his shoulder.

PART TWO

The Price of Time

CHAPTER XIV

PIERRE AND HEDWIGE were married at the end of the month and went to live in Neuilly in an apartment that Picrre had hastily furnished and one that suited his wife's nonchalant habits; in this way domestic problems were reduced to choosing common parts and drawing up demarcations of which drawers and wardrobe space were whose.

The layout of an apartment is often indicative of the layout of the heart. Pierre and Hedwige had adjoining but separate bedrooms. Pierre had wanted this partition; between him and his wife there was this enormous structure, this mountain of plaster which for two weeks had divided what the law had brought together. The two parties spoke to one another through it from their beds at night and were woken merrily each morning by knockings on the wall; and from each side of this equator, like poles apart, they kept away from each other for the night.

This was what Pierre had wanted (and Hedwige, both serious and prudish, had not appeared surprised, quite the contrary), not that he had not desired her immediately, for he was in love, youthful and deeply moved by her feelings for him. But he experienced a sharp and bitter pleasure in disciplining himself and starting life as though he had been married for thirty years. He was put off by the notion of throwing himself at Hedwige and taking her by surprise or by legal agreement. Firstly, the fulfilment of conjugal rights had something ridiculous and bestial, judicial and Louis Philippe-like about it. Undressing a woman, tearing off her dress and displaying the wife's nightgown at the window to neighbours gathered in the street, as in certain Jewish rites, is not really the greatest homage you can pay her. Pierre had sworn to himself not to cast Hedwige all of a sudden into a new universe, that of the senses. And so it was that they lived so chastely that they might have been mistaken for campsite friends, for one of those couples innocently introduced to one another through the small ads at the Touring Club de France. Pierre had used all his strength as a man to stop himself from violating Hedwige as he violated everything else. It was the finest gift he could give her, the greatest proof of his love and respect he could pay her. He had had to make a colossal effort; proceeding slowly is not easy when you are not used to it. And, of course, he also forbade himself that sexual chemistry, those kitchen recipes for voluptuous pleasure invented over the idle centuries. No love in the saddle, no touching-up in the gods, but none of that intimate touching-up that our fathers resorted to either, none of that figure-skating beneath the mirrors of the canopy, none of those breaks at billiards that only entertain old men while they still have the means.

It was between himself and his passion for Hedwige, rather than between Hedwige and him, that Pierre had erected this partition. He had wanted to put himself to the test: "If I can restrain myself in this matter, I will be able to control myself in all other respects. Other successes will come easily to me, I shall have disassociated love with gluttony and I shall have triumphed over my demon for good."

He could be accused of coldness, of indifference; he did not mind because all that concerned him was this haste that had until now spoilt love for him. Only Hedwige mattered; he was concerned purely for her, he cared for her alone, and he wanted to be good and humane with her. If she moved too slowly for him, he would wait for her; if he succeeded in taking her in hand, in urging her on without rushing her, he would raise her to his own speed, but by degrees. By taking her time, nature managed to transform reptiles into creatures that flew. Without risking Hedwige stumbling, he would teach her to fly. The plundering of a besieged body, the conquering caresses, the honourable wounds are a thing and a pleasure of the moment, but when what is at stake is an entire lifetime, one must set one's watch by eternity.

Hedwige was waiting: it was certainly her turn. She watched respectfully, with all her solicitous strength, this future that she was embarking upon, this moment that society and novels trumpeted, one that she had not craved and which had crept up on her unawares. A new life was beginning for her under the gaze of this man who was a stranger, a gentle savage and a person of such terrible rapidity who would descend on her in a torrent and, with masterly precision and elemental ardour, sweep her away to goodness knows where.

Her heart beating behind the white partition, she was waiting and it seemed a long time to her, as long as boredom, toothache, insomnia and all those machines that whiled away the hours. Why did lightning not strike? "I should like it to be all over already," she thought.

One evening, she tiptoed into Pierre's bedroom to watch him sleeping, hoping that his stillness would betray him and reveal the secret of his strength or his weakness. The mystery of a person asleep behind that closed door seemed deeper to her than ever and it frightened her. She watched him curled up into a ball, his thumbs tucked into the palms of his hands like a small child, tangled up in his sheets, no longer knocking anything down as he passed, no longer whirling around except in dreams from which she was excluded. For the first time ever, she wondered who Pierre was and why he loved her, and she realized that what she had exchanged with him were vows, not secrets, and rings that were merely bands and not keys.

Since she was straightforward and direct, she put the question to him first thing the following morning:

"Who are you, Pierre?"

He opened his eyes in astonishment; we are always surprised when others are not satisfied with the image we present to them.

"I am the person I am to be," he said, laughing.

But Hedwige was frowning and peering at him searchingly.

"Do you realize that I know nothing at all about you, your parents, your friends, your past life, your family history, your character?"

"I have neither parents nor friends; my character is as easy to fathom as the nose on my face, and I've forgotten my past because you were not part of it; in any case everything to do with yesterday bores me, I've only ever written one sonnet and that was in praise of tomorrow."

"Oh Pierre," said Hedwige, "you're not taking me seriously!"

She looked so upset that he relented immediately.

"Well, I do have one friend, an old pal named Placide who knows me so well that he fell out with me; but we made up later. He even sent me a beautiful silver and crocodile sponge bag for my wedding. I'll bring him to meet you for lunch. You can ask him all the questions you please. Pretend to make some unpleasant remarks, the normal number of treacherous things that figure in what's called 'a perceptive friendship', and you'll learn more about me than I know myself."

"I need Roustoutzeff's book on *Animal Style in South Russia and China* (Princeton, 1926); it should be there; could you find it for me, dear Placide, while I finish this monograph?"

"I'll come and help you," said Hedwige.

They had finished lunch and were taking coffee in Pierre's study.

"A monograph?" asked Placide.

"Yes," said Pierre, "and it would actually be of interest to both of you. I'm writing something about the cloister, which after all I owe in part to both of you. It's come from the United States."

Placide and Hedwige were on their knees, picking up large volumes, knocking down stacks of books and arranging them any old how.

"Ah! Here it is," said Hedwige, laying her hands on the copy and, extremely pleased with herself, taking it to Pierre.

"Thank you, my love," answered Pierre distractedly, for he was already stuck into Gourhan's *Bestiary of Chinese Bronze*. "It's been superseded."

"Ah, now that's typical of your husband," exclaimed Placide. "'Superseded'. It's one of his favourite expressions. He asks you for something, you go to great lengths to find it and then when you give it to him, he's already found something better. I can't recall one single occasion when I've been able to do a favour for him in time. 'Superseded'," he repeated, shrugging his shoulders. "I know some people who mean a lot to you and who say: it's been surpassed. But your way of going farther back is to go farther away."

"Yes, it's true," said Hedwige, "he's marvellous. He's a magician."

"I don't share that view," Placide replied. "He's fairly successful, but not in his chosen career. He was made to be an office runner, a motorcycle delivery man, an arbitrager, a screenwriter, a switchboard operator, anything you like, but not a collector of period objects. Period pieces have true values and true values pay no heed to haste. 'Time does not respect what is done without it.' You can be sure that objects like this, which have endured for three thousand years, have been created gradually."

He showed Hedwige a shapeless block of mouldy stone, a lump of excavated jade depicting a wild boar.

"Is that a period piece?" asked Hedwige, intrigued. "It doesn't look like a work of art."

"You don't have to have taste to recognize the art of the Middle Ages," replied Pierre, who had finished writing and was stretched out on his sofa, blowing the smoke from his cigar up to the ceiling. "But I must respond to Placide… in actual fact, a primitive work of art represents count-less hours of work and that is what makes it priceless for me. I think of the ordinary man who has put his heart and his strength into it, of the woman, of the family who have sacrificed their eyes to embroider that chasuble or this shroud. But please believe me when I say that those people worked quickly, the time element was not wasted. It's just that their sense of speed was not ours. A fine piece of material, of gold or silverware, it's the equivalent of a thousand ploughed and sowed fields, of more than a hundred forests that have been cleared, it accounts for more hardship and time expended than the longest illness. And what wretched tools they used! When I contemplate a piece of ivory or enamelware, it's as if I were reaching out my hand to all those who made it, owned it and sold it again and again over the centuries: I can hear them, they speak to me. The initial shock you get from a work of art is a psychic one, next comes the technical examination, the patina, the holes caused by woodworm, and other absurdities. The first thing a work of art does is yell at you from afar that it has lived. It projects its own aura before it."

Placide gave an ironic smile:

"I was a student at the École des Chartes. I have a magnifying glass for an eye and always will have. But in your case, we know you have a hawk's eye assisted by the sensibility of a clairvoyant."

"It's simply that I don't have the guts to go round in circles, as you all do, without becoming seasick. For you, life is a cycle; for me it's a flat spiral, Goethe's spiral; you don't get out of it by turning back; the backwards gallop is a false revolution, a curators' revolution; you have to run speedily to the end of each period in order to rise higher. In France (a land that was quick once), we have become prolix and apathetic; the day we rediscover our traditional pace, in a new Middle Ages period, we shall produce more *Princesses de Clèves* and *Manon Lescauts*, we shall discover Molières who will churn out their plays, Pascals who will dash off their pamphlets. It's not through eighteen-volume novels by Madame de Charrière that France will make her mark on posterity, it's through small portable bombs such as *Candide* or *Atala*."

He stopped to catch his breath.

"What was I saying? I've forgotten."

"You're losing your ideas along the way," Placide sniggered.

"I remember. Napoleon is not concise because he is the emperor, he's the emperor because he is concise. If I hadn't been concise, I wouldn't have got the Mas Vieux or Hedwige. Placide, I'm leaving her with you, I have to go out. You must explain to her in what ways I resemble Napoleon."

Sitting in her armchair, her hands crossed like a little girl waiting to be told a lovely story, Hedwige looked questioningly at Placide.

"Well, madame," said Placide, "are you waiting for me to discuss the antique dealer with the nimble feet with you? It's a joke. You know him better than I do!"

"I don't know him," said Hedwige simply. "Who can know Pierre?"

"Then why do you come to me?"

"Because you've followed his career for a long time and you can tell me about his life."

The subject did not inspire Placide greatly, but he liked to hold forth and he could not have found a better audience. Already fascinated, she lapped up his words. He began in a light-hearted tone, mannered and slightly mocking, running through the school years, the successful exam results and the early days in what he called "business".

"In art," he said, "Pierre delved back in time with the same frenzy with which he approached everyday life. From the Gothic, which was his speciality, he hopped over, God knows why, to the Merovingian and from the Merovingian he dashed over to Iranian sources."

With a condescendingly forgiving smile, he explained how Pierre had gained ground on everyone else and discovered, sometimes at excavation sites, sometimes in private collections, objects that were ten or fifteen centuries older than the steel trains or duralumin planes aboard which he took them away, and how this "treasure-hunt" satisfied his need for "irrational trips away". He acknowledged generously, nevertheless, that Pierre, before any of his colleagues in either the old or the new world, had taken the trouble to study ethnography, popular art, linguistics, archaeology and aerial photography, helped by an aptitude and a prodigious memory, which enabled him to take part in excavations and to discover trails with a flair that tended to irritate the specialists.

"Ah! How many sleepless nights must this dabbler Pierre have cost the collectors!" exclaimed Placide.

He began to discourse on the subject, which for him was inexhaustible.

"The great collections are not forbidding piles of trinkets or featureless graveyards of remains as those who attend the famous auction houses imagine. They live, die, are reborn, they improve, they deteriorate. Some of them disintegrate in a day, like a theory. For the art of vanished ages, and especially the most ancient ones, is as inventive in renewing itself as is the brain of a man of genius; living in the earth and even at the bottom of the seas, buried deep down all over the globe, it bubbles upwards, emerges from the darkness, bursts forth, disconcerts people, shakes them up. It's a constant revolution, a continuous refining. Each discovery is a provocation that demands a response. Such and such a top-quality Sassanid piece will be greeted in New York harbour like a diva; and it will have been enough for it to appear, not merely because of the pleasure it gives, but in order to downgrade what had given pleasure up till then. Solomon's temple is rebuilt every day, and taste, which we have wrongly made synonymous with talent, is in a state of perpetual imbalance. It only takes a new site in the civilization of the Indus, or a tear in the centuries-old curtain that conceals the Hittite Empire from us, for a museum, until then highly regarded, to be relegated to the rank of an old second-hand dealer. It only needs a tomb opening up near Pretoria and for the small statue of a sleeping rhinoceros alongside a Bantu skeleton to emerge for telegrams to fly and for chapters of art history and market prices to fluctuate in Buenos Aires, London or Budapest. And, as it happens, Pierre was there in Pretoria," Placide concluded as he stood up to drink a glass of water.

"Go on, go on," begged Hedwige.

"But I'm thrilled to continue, madame. I am desirous of pleasing you. Would I not be making myself unworthy of your trust if I failed to retrace the stream of my memory as you have invited me to do?"

Placide listened to himself speaking with as much pleasure as he was listened to. Begun in a tone of amiable nonchalance, the biography was attaining epic status. Placide became so suitably aroused that he eventually managed to paint a portrait of Pierre designed to kindle an imagination that only required a spark. A portrait he regretted because he was jealous of Pierre, but, for once, truth was stronger than malice.

He paused again, but Hedwige pressed him with questions; Pierre had taken part in excavations; had he taken any risks?

"No more than the other archaeologists," said Placide, screwing up his face. "Of course, in Tse-Kiang, for example, when he was working on the excavation of the famous city built of pieces of Sung pottery that had misfired—imagine that, a city built entirely of Sung vases! A band of Chinese generals captured Pierre and stole his bags of silver dollars. Those are some of the minor misfortunes of a profession that has many high points. In Luristan, for example, at the opening of a Neolithic tomb, when they discovered a funeral cart surrounded by a pack of hunting dogs and forty horses, all intact; a marvellous vision, but a fleeting one, because on contact with the air everything that was made of wood or bone turned to dust, leaving only the bits and pieces, the small bells, the wheel hub—in short, the metal... I also love his story of the skull. Do you know it?"

"No."

"In a desert in Mongolia he discovered the huge skull of a horse—that of Genghis Khan's horse, he immediately claimed—a malevolent skull that wreaked ruin and death and which eventually caused their plane to crash. That lucky Pierre was the only survivor of the accident."

Hedwige shuddered. Delighted to have had such an effect, Placide continued:

"I should also like to tell you of another of our excellent Pierre's juicy adventures: his forced landing in a district of

Baluchistan on a day in Ramadan when any foreigner found out of doors was immediately butchered. Did Pierre know this or had he guessed it?—he doesn't lack for intuition at times—in any case he walked through the entire town, bolt upright, staring straight ahead and as though turned in on himself, with such determination not to be seen or above all lynched, that he passed *unnoticed*!"

Placide stopped talking, his job was done; Hedwige was no longer listening to him, she was waiting for Pierre.

He entered the room in a whirlwind.

"Quick, Hedwige, I'm taking you with me."

"What time is it?" asked Hedwige.

"Thanks to you, it's four o'clock," replied Pierre, proudly pointing to his watch.

Hedwige had given him as a wedding present a magnificent stopwatch chronometer, with nineteen markers for every hundredth of a second and with adjustable repeaters. It was a symbolic present that was not so much a reward as a good lesson.

Pierre placed a fur-trimmed hat on his wife's head, wrapped her up in an ocelot fur coat that he had just bought her and that made her look like a maenad (a maenad with her entire head), and whisked her outside.

"Fancy not knowing how to go downstairs on the banister at your age, Hedwige! What, not even on your stomach?"

He lifted her up, making her jump from one landing to another. Hedwige deliberately pressed herself heavily against him. She admired him for always being out in the open, free, daring, tall and quick.

"When I was little, I learnt a La Fontaine fable," she said. "An eagle that was carrying a tortoise through the air... I remember it very well: the tortoise falls and is about to smash into someone's skull which the eagle, from up above, took for a pebble."

"Yes, the skull was that of Aeschylus if I remember correctly. Having a tortoise land on your head! Yet another who would have been killed by slowness," Pierre sighed.

He hugged Hedwige passionately, much more tightly than was necessary. But Hedwige did not notice, she thought that without him she would fall. In the arms of her husband, it seemed to her that she was flying as in dreams. As she went down the steps, at that very moment, she was dreaming... The eagle in the fable was Pierre; he was taking her, in his talons, on a long hunting trip; she was a poor, bleeding creature beneath his wingspan; he, in a high, audacious, sustained flight, was drawing spirals above the earth, similar to the curves of the labyrinth.

Through the windows of the stairwell, she could see the ground very far away in the distance and the pavement, very far below. She snuggled against him in joyful silence, anticipating some scratches from his royal bird's claws; she was happy. All she lacked was an injury. Once more the bloody image returned, and remained with her until the foot of the stairs.

CHAPTER XV

T HE MAN IN A HURRY had decided to hurry up at last. He would have Hedwige that very night. For almost six weeks he had been deferring the moment. It was over. He would descend onto that fertile plain. He would talk as a prince does; he would help himself to the harvest; he would control, with the full span of his domination, with all the power of his possession, that huge treasure that was Hedwige herself.

Pierre had chosen his moment, chosen it well. The timing was not merely lawful, but legitimate. Hedwige was not only contracted, but bound to him; she appeared loving and willing. She would certainly give of herself entirely: an essential condition of a great friendship, without which marriage is a bedroom as easy of access as prostitution, or a society—a polite society—game.

Pierre was looking forward to this evening, barely a few hours away.

"I'm going to take Hedwige to a restaurant, to a nice restaurant, like the last time. (I hope it will be better than the first time.) Afterwards, we shall go to the theatre. After our unfortunate experience at the cinema, we must give the theatre a chance. There must be some young playwrights who write lively dialogue… Let's see, what's showing?… *Michel Strogoff*… *Le Chapeau de paille d'Italie*… *Tosca*… *Le Bossu*… *Les Burgraves*… Paris is certainly the centre of a great dramatic renaissance! Ah, here's something better: *La Planche à plonger*, at the Mathurins. There must be some activity there. 'Madly energetic', say the adverts."

By seven o'clock, Hedwige had not returned from Saint-Germain.

"She's not used to my car, let's hope she hasn't had an accident. Why do women always confuse the time of departure with the time of arrival? They obey some invisible clock; the proof is that they are consistently late; they keep to psychological time and not to the Observatoire time, that time that comes grating out of the radio, as if through a reed pipe."

Pierre lit cigarettes, one after the other (he sometimes lit several at the same time).

"In actual fact, there are three types of time: exterior time, interior time and organic time, which is that of our body busy getting older, our body that knows, with the dreadful precision of the unconscious, how many heartbeats it has left before the grave. I still have black hair and flexible arteries, but underneath my black hair there must be an impatient white hair that knows that the hour it is to appear will chime."

Pierre looked out of the window.

"Time likes to play a coconut shy game with us," he thought. "It bombards us every second; when we are kids, we recover immediately; then, less and less quickly; the spring wears out, we stagger about more and more until the day that we tumble over for good and when, like an old worn-out doll, we leave an empty space between the nurse and the soldier. Ever since Metchnikoff, doctors have been bending over the human body trying to discover the secret of its longevity: why should a pigeon, which has the same cell structure as a crow, live twenty times less? If time is the same for all organisms, why do we heal at different speeds? If I heal in five days and Hedwige in two, won't we find it difficult to adjust our bodies to the same speed? The years she lives will actually be fifteen or sixteen months long; whereas the years I live shall be of eight or nine months. Therefore Hedwige, having promised to be back by seven o'clock, is not late; even though it's eight o'clock."

She arrived enveloped in a large cape belonging to Angélique. Having set off in violet, she came back in grey. Even in the midst of grieving, she dressed up.

"I have mitigating circumstances…" she began.

"Get dressed quickly, we're dining at the cabaret and we're going to the theatre."

"Will you stay until the end?"

"I promise."

"I'm already dressed," said Hedwige. "Just a little powder, but… why are you making your bed already?"

"Precisely because I intend staying until the end of the show."

While she was powdering herself, Pierre brought in the chair on which he would lay his clothes that evening when he got back, filled the glass from which he would drink water, laid out the nightshirt he would put on, and took out the suit he would wear next day from the cupboard.

"You're exaggerating," said Hedwige affectionately, sadly.

When Pierre thought about the future in her presence, it was nothing much more than a state of mind, but when he lived it, dashing around with orchestrated movements, it induced a manic automatism in him that was really rather tiresome. He opened one drawer, closed the other with his foot, put on a glove with his teeth so that he didn't have to lay down the pen he was using to make notes.

"You need ten hands," she said.

"Get a move on, instead of making fun of me. We're in a hurry…"

"The house is not on fire."

On his hands and knees, Pierre was now spreading out the foam-rubber mat upon which he would do his exercises when he woke up. He went to look for his dressing gown. He sharpened his razor, doing so himself because he worried overly about the servants delaying everything.

"I'm ready."

Hedwige went to her bedroom, sat down at her dressing table and hastily set out a few veils on a pale background so that she could make her choice.

"From the moment a woman says she is ready," thought Pierre, "a great deal of time elapses before she leaves the house, and even when she has left, there is the 'How silly of me, I almost forgot…' that causes her to go back inside."

"I was trying to move too quickly," said Hedwige. "I wanted to please you. One of the buttons of my sleeve has got caught in the netting of the veil. Pierre, don't get impatient. I can't see what I'm doing. Be kind and untangle it for me. It won't come out."

"Hurry up, hurry up!"

"Release me, please don't allow me to be upset any more, dear husband."

When Hedwige put things in this way, tenderly, emphasizing her own incompetence, exaggerating her own foolishness, Pierre immediately relaxed.

"If I'm made the scapegoat, then it will have served you right!" he said. "Anyway, no one's thinking of complaining. And rightly so."

"You haven't invited anyone else, I hope?" said Hedwige affectionately. "Rushing around must be so enjoyable for you that one doesn't really feel guilty for having made you wait," she concluded, tying her hat veil into a knot as if putting a full stop at the end of the sentence.

At the restaurant, Pierre once again skipped the rituals. He refused to put his coat in the cloakroom. He went straight over and raided the cold buffet; he came back, his plate loaded with cold meats, jellied eggs, and with some oranges in his pockets. People used to say that every time he went to a restaurant, Pierre would create a fuss.

"Not so much bread, darling…"

"I can't stand slow table service. I feel I want to eat my neighbour's helping. So I go and serve myself."

"You swallow without chewing. On the fireplace in our dining room I shall have engraved—"

"*You must…?*"

"No. The remark Brillat-Savarin liked most of all and which they used to say to me all the time at boarding school: 'You're eating too quickly.'"

"When I was little, Mother used to say that I didn't suck my feeding bottle, I hurled myself at it. When I was older, I used to go to an automat bar on the boulevards, near the Parisiana. I was never as happy as when I was there. I gobbled everything down; I became dyspeptic (they had to dose me with pigs' gastric juices). It was wonderful, that bar: one click and piles of sandwiches would descend straight into your mouth…"

Hedwige was fiddling nervously with the corner of the tablecloth.

"You don't eat, you swallow your plate! And look at those stains on your tie!"

"Would monsieur like some strawberries? They're the early crop."

The maître d'hôtel presented them to him in their packaging, rather like a nurse presenting you with your appendix after an operation.

"Strawberries in January! They're not the early crop, they're late strawberries from last year!" Pierre replied.

Coffee was brought, together with hygienically wrapped sugar lumps. Pierre tossed them into his cup without unwrapping them.

"You really are impossible, my love! It's as though things didn't belong to you, as though you were stealing them."

"Because the paper will end up floating on top of its own accord!"

At the theatre, Pierre bought two stalls seats, 85 and 87. They set off, following the usherette.

"85 and 87 are already occupied," said the usherette.

"Any more of this and I'll jump onto the stage!"

"Wait on these folding seats until the interval, monsieur. They must have put the people in 185 and 187 in 85 and 87…"

"Then let's sit in 185 and 187," said Pierre peremptorily.

"Unfortunately, 185 and 187 are occupied."

"There's nothing in the world slower and more foolish than an usherette," groaned the man in a hurry.

And supporting himself on the partition of a ground-floor box, he stepped into it, fell inside it with a great deal of noise, and refused to leave. Amid much murmuring, Hedwige came and sat beside him.

La Planche à plonger was by Jean Alavoine, a dashing young playwright who, with his lively dovetailing of situations, his use of effects that had not been attempted before and a few very well-plotted scenes, had made many of those who produced plays for Paris audiences seem outmoded.

"I was very keen on seeing the first act," said Pierre. "I know Alavoine, he gets straight to the point."

This was true of the author's early work, two-act plays staged in an avant-garde theatre where the director, a saintly man, awaited the takings before he could go and eat. But success had come in the past two years and Alavoine now did as his colleagues did: he took his time, did not fritter away his small amount of capital, and stretched out a sketch into a three-act play.

"It's amazing, we can't endure expository scenes any more," Pierre sighed. "The audiences have been primed by film, they have guessed from the third line what they won't be told until three-quarters of an hour later and, as with German grammar, they get bored waiting for the verb."

"I'm not bored. I'm just happy sitting beside you."

Only the stage set looked new. It depicted a camping site in the mountains. But the dialogue, although brilliantly syncopated in the way a tennis championship is, was that of a scribbler.

From the beginning of the second act, the author, having said all he had to say, had turned to the director and given him the task of spinning things out. During a ball, the young male lead is reminded of his former lovers: through a brilliant innovation, the various women he had favoured appear, just as he is naming them, and they descend a staircase, each wearing a mask and hat of the period. In order to fill out this meagre curtain-raiser-cum-fairy tale, a certain number of characters walk to and fro bearing Chinese lanterns.

"This is really intolerable!" moaned Pierre.

This time he did not dare say: "Suppose we went somewhere else?", but he thought it nonetheless.

"I'm enjoying myself," said Hedwige.

"And to think that Aeschylus is so short!"

"Would you like a sweet?" said Hedwige affectionately, offering him one.

"The *Oresteia* fits into the hollow of your hand."

"Suck it. Don't crunch it!"

"Have you ever timed *Agamemnon*? Barely half an hour's reading! What takes up time in Greek theatre is the chorus with its bear-dancing, three steps to the right, three steps to the left. As for the rest, Fate has no sooner been mentioned than it has knocked already and all those famous murderers are already lying rigid without having bothered to justify themselves. Are you really sure that there's no fourth act at least?"

Pierre held on until the middle of the last act. But then things began to take a turn for the worse. In Alavoine's play, an irresolute Fate was unable to bring down its quarry.

And yet he wasn't being asked to make his characters die, merely to make them live.

Pierre suddenly got to his feet, for the image of his warm house, his inviting bed, his pyjamas with their arms laid out in a fan and Hedwige's pink nightdress, its glint of gold lace rolled out on a fur rug and made to look pinker still by the embers of the fire, had suddenly affected him like a finger on a trigger. He pushed open the door of the box, grabbed Hedwige by the arm and gulped in what little fresh air there was in the narrow corridor.

"Hadn't you promised to stay until the end?"

"I made a mistake, that's all."

They went home. Pierre started to get undressed on the stairs. Firstly, his waistcoat; secondly, his tie; thirdly, his braces. When he reached their door, he was holding his clothes miraculously in his hand. And while Hedwige was turning the key in the lock, he took the opportunity to unlace his shoes.

"I'm getting into your bed to warm it," he said.

He was under the blanket before Hedwige had removed her hat. He watched her making her preparations for bed:

a large bag of cotton wool, cream for taking off make-up, skin lotion, tissues, large combs, looking glasses etc. (And she wasn't concerned about her appearance!) Noises of cupboard drawers, of running or gushing water.

It was the hour when the buses run less frequently, when the *métro* amplifies its underground noise by a few seconds, when those who are on their own are mistaken for couples because of the echo in the reverberating streets and the shadows on the walls, when the night belongs to elderly journalists, and to all women, the women who make scenes and the women who are kind and gentle.

While she was tossing pads of cotton wool stained pink by make-up into the waste-paper basket, Hedwige was glancing behind her in the looking glass, like a driver watching the car that is about to overtake him in his rear-view mirror. She had realized that this was the night. She had guessed from a very slight hint of hoarseness in Pierre's voice that he was hungry for her. He was taking up more space, talking far less and gradually settling into the thick wool of the mattress which, in spite of the padding, had adapted to her shape. All she could see was his black hair. The only sign on earth of this world of unsatisfied impulses that he typified was a lock of hair. This restless, over-excitable and intrepid man now lay as stock-still as a post. It was both touching and worrying. Pierre had often romped about on Hedwige's bed in the morning and the evening. He had occasionally slipped beneath her eider-down, but he had never got into her bed. He had never remained there as he was doing now. Was he one of those who like to be tucked in or someone who moves around in the night and pulls up the covers in the morning? She was going to discover all about him, to be able to explain him in straightforward language, to keep him in an enclosed field of linen from which he could not shy away again; she was going to find out whether her seductive powers would cause him to lie still or make him move about; she was going to get to the core of his secret, to discover finally whether Pierre's haste was generated by muscles or just nerves, by strength or weakness.

So intense was her curiosity that she felt none of that sweet shame experienced by girls who have never slept with a man.

CHAPTER XVI

THE BOISROSÉ FAMILY'S wounds healed slowly, and they all maintained a silence about their amputation. Hedwige's marriage which, after all, was natural, even honourable and certainly desirable so long as it was merely a marriage of convenience, became, from the moment it took on the appearance of a love match, an object of scandal, a notion all the more obsessive the more firmly it was swept aside. Contrary to the laws of perspective, Hedwige grew taller once she moved away. No one dared talk about her, at least not "plainly", because they did not refrain from speaking in that sort of coded language that families use without danger of conflict to control their most explosive secrets.

The happiness that a loved one discovers when he or she has left us, after previously having experienced it with us alone, is not merely immoral, but humiliating too, because it forces us to reach difficult conclusions about ourselves and to make admissions of suspicion and distress. Shame is not always the awareness of the harm we do, it is often the awareness of the harm done to us. The Boisrosés felt ashamed because of Hedwige, and even more so in her presence than when away from her, for Hedwige frequently came to Saint-Germain, even though Bonne claimed that "we never see her". (For Bonne, there was never a halfway point between all and nothing, and if she had not spent twenty-four hours with her head on her mother's knees then she had not come at all.) And yet she suffered less from Hedwige's disloyalty than her daughters did because, being more experienced than them and being endowed with a more dependable sixth sense, she had no doubt that the lost sheep would return. For Fromentine and Angélique, the absence of Hedwige was a disaster; their grief was heightened by a sense of impoverishment; in addition to their individual beauty the three sisters had a kind of beauty in togetherness. Like an ancient cellar full of liqueurs in which a clumsy servant had broken one of the three carafes, like a triptych in which one of the three sections had vanished, they were left incomplete and depreciated, having lost ninety per cent of their value.

Although Angélique had also married, and had also gone through her crisis of growing up, her conscience was clear: in her, there was nothing to exorcize. Her sorrow was thus tinged with disapproval. As for Fromentine, she harboured a host of small demons, silly, grimacing

creatures that teased her like a thousand needling irrita-
tions caused by uric acid, and they made her envy, loathe
and adore Hedwige simultaneously. Secretly, she admired
her for becoming self-sufficient and she was half upset and
half delighted at the thought of the wave of melancholy
that had so troubled the Boisrosés. Being a better person
than her, Angélique felt sorry for her mother and she had
settled herself on the chaise-longue at Saint-Germain in
a bedridden attitude entirely in keeping with this disaster.
She looked after Bonne de Boisrosé, massaging her, and
carrying her from one part of her bedroom to another
just as Aeneas carried his father on his shoulders, while
Monsieur de Rocheflamme took his part in the family
grief and jealousy as uncle, old man and antique dealer.

Only Vincent Amyot, intrigued by Pierre's achievement
and dazzled by this inexplicable marvel—a Boisrosé girl
living away from the nest—allowed his delight to show;
disregarding the general inhibition, he mentioned the name
of the missing girl purely for the pleasure of doing what
was forbidden and for the spectacle of a mother-in-law in a
state of distress. He took pleasure in teasing, from which he
derived flimsy revenge, informing Fromentine that Hedwige
was wearing new fox furs and that she would not lend them
to her; telling Angélique that Hedwige had confessed to
making Creole dishes for Pierre; letting Bonne know that

from the moment she was first married her daughter had not once spent a night away, that is to say she had slept with her husband, and that there was therefore no point in keeping her room and her bed untouched unless it was to do so for a beloved person who had died. The family allowed him to drone on; secretly, they had not entirely given up hope of seeing an end to the profligate daughter's lawful vagrancy. But for the time being Hedwige was in love. Hedwige loved someone outside the permitted perimeter, and her love was remarkable for the time it had lasted; Hedwige had disappeared; the family waters had closed over Hedwige's plunge.

The doorbell rang, but the ring was not unfamiliar; that succession of light, delicate trills that was like music, everyone knew that ring, it was *her*. She came in, as tall as the door, with that sumptuous air that all tall women have, even the poorest, wearing a white scarf round her neck like a flag of truce.

"Hedwige!"

She made her way over to her mother's outstretched arms, mounted the steep folds of the eiderdown and the snowfield of drapery, and collapsed onto the beloved breast like someone returning to their homeland. Bonne de Boisrosé, at the risk of spoiling the triumph that was unfolding, took Hedwige's head in her hands and gazed into the velvety white face pitted with golden, dutiful eyes. No blemishes? Yes, two wrinkles, the first, at the corners of her mouth. They were scarcely wrinkles; they began like small lines, but at each side of the small aperture and contracted by the muscles of the mouth, there were the beginnings of a slight furrow, a fissure that no transversal line would stop as it made its way to the crevice and the gully.

At a glance, Madame de Boisrosé had seen all she needed to see: Hedwige was unhappy, Hedwige was pregnant. Two things which often go together, that need to be explained to men so that they understand, but which a mother can decipher like an open book. Her perfect nose had become translucent and taut due to repeated bouts of sickness. Her fine features had softened and faded; skeletal bones were pushing the flesh from behind and stretching it, making her eye sockets hollow and revealing the depths of her soul in the prison of her eyes, which had acquired a distracted, distant expression, a sort of aversion to the outside world, as the eyes of those who are very ill do.

For Bonne, the hour of battle had finally struck; she was going to begin her struggle against this weak and meticulous adversary, so full of ideas that they made him seem foolish, so fearful that he found safety in flight—in a word, her struggle against the man. In snatching his booty from him, Bonne proved to be a surprising and totally immoral bandit, with a speed of execution that Pierre would have admired; but Pierre suspected nothing, had not sensed anything, and anyway, if he had been forewarned, he would not have understood.

"Angélique, your sister looks tired; go and make her bed," ordered a radiant Bonne.

Hedwige would return to the obeisance of Saint-Germain. She could certainly go to Pierre's house, lend him her presence, accept the written rule of conjugal life and even give birth to a child, but it would make no difference. It was now certain that no new law would stipulate attachment to the mother and that an obligation all the more powerful for not being contracted would always bind the child first and foremost to its own family. There would simply be another human being on earth and, if it was a girl, one more Boisrosé.

"I'm fine," Hedwige repeated, without letting her mother go, "I'm absolutely fine…"

She gazed at her mother's bedroom as though she were returning to it after a long journey, just as the traveller who has been all over the world and endured deserts, shipwrecks and revolutions is amazed to see the white porcelain owl still perched on top of its box. She recognized the strong smell of oranges studded with cloves in the Creole manner. She was returning to her native soil, to the body of her mother which, in spite of its shapelessness and caducity, had a strange grandeur about it, blameworthy and comical perhaps when seen from outside, but which had the wild beauty of those passionate landscapes where selfishness is rated so highly that it is impossible to distinguish it from love.

Half past seven. Hedwige is not back.

Pierre, who had arranged to leave work early, is astonished. Nowadays, when he returns to his home, to their home, he hates finding his house empty. When it is said of a parcel that it is "awaiting delivery", no one realizes how painful it is for a parcel to be unclaimed.

Hedwige is not there and it is as if the pictures had been taken down and the furniture sold in her absence. Where can she be? She had set off to visit her mother at about four o'clock and she should have left Saint-Germain to return to Neuilly at about six. The road via Marly is direct: branch off at Abreuvoir, uphill, then down to Saint-Cloud, through Garches. She had done it many a time. Unless she had gone through the forest and had broken down in the woods?

"People will say that I shall always, always, always be waiting! Waiting, hoping. Driven to despair, waiting again. Being on the lookout, yet still within these four walls! How well I understand that caged animals die prematurely! It's appalling to be on your own once you have been a couple. And on one's own at seven in the evening without anyone for company apart from that idiot whose name is 'me'. The lack of imagination of mirrors is astounding. When I was a child, I longed for a looking glass in which I could see movements other than my own."

Pierre presses his nose against the window so that he can see the street better. But his nose creates several large blotches that soon prevent him from seeing a thing. In any case, there is nothing to see other than a view of Paris that looks diminished through the mist. It is pretty chilly. In modern houses, all the benefit of radiators is lost because the walls are so thin. Moping around, feeling gloomy: these words quite appropriately link feeling cold with waiting. Expectancy is a blockage in which all our plans find themselves frozen.

"I actually needed Hedwige this evening, I particularly needed her."

Pierre was quivering with nervousness and disappointment. A woman being late is nothing very much, but as the noises grew more muffled in the fine mist, as the busy elevator came down again empty, a feeling of failure descended on him. All the tortures that are used metaphorically to describe waiting—the mouth in the water, thorns, the grill or burning coals—seemed very minor compared to what he was going through.

Pierre did not normally telephone Saint-Germain often, because it was very complicated to call and make the Boisrosés come down to the dairy. He resigned himself to doing so, however, because the dairy closed at eight o'clock. Fromentine came on the line.

"Is Hedwige with you?"

"Yes, dear Pierre. I was just about to call and tell you."

"Will she be at Saint-Germain for long? Why hasn't she come home?"

"She's in bed."

"In bed? Is she ill?"

"No."

"Then, what's the point?"

"She's lying down and she's resting."

"If anyone goes to bed at seven in the evening, they must be ill."

"Not in our house."

"In my house you do," retorted Pierre curtly.

"But haven't you seen how she looks? You make her do too much."

"Very well. I'm leaving straight away for Saint-Germain."

"I'm telling you, she's not ill. Leave her with us for one night. What difference can it make to you, dear Pierre? It would make us so happy."

"I need her, and particularly today."

"Listen… be reasonable… forcing her to get dressed, making her go out into the night… what time would she arrive? The road's bad, as you well know."

Pierre imagined Hedwige lost in the fog, with a flat tyre, unable to lift up the spare wheel herself. There were two places on her route that he dreaded: the crossroads at Louveciennes and the last bend on the hill at Saint-Germain. Fromentine was still droning on, affectionate, insistent, slightly mocking:

"Do us this little favour, my dear restless, ever-frothy brother-in-law! Tomorrow, at first light, Hedwige will be back with you."

"She has leave until nine o'clock in the morning, then! No later," replied Pierre who, in a hoarse voice that he tried to make softer, did his best to sound like a decent, forgiving fellow.

He hung up in a fury, turned round and saw the empty studio flat, vacated for the entire night. It is ghastly when you were counting on someone not even to have the expectation to keep you company.

He wanted to have supper, but found only a solitary egg at the back of an empty cupboard, like a diplodocus's egg in the Gobi desert; he also found an apple, deader than a still life.

"She's not coming back… it must be my fault if she's not coming back. Am I horrid? Am I boring? The fact is that she doesn't love me as I love her. Why? I've been aware for some time that things haven't been going well, but why?"

Truth to tell, he had not felt anything of the sort until then, but when one is in a poor state of mind it is hard to believe that it has only just occurred and so you pretend you have been in that state for a long time.

Pierre, who lived in the future as a fish takes to water, found it hard to think back on time that had passed. Weary of searching, he resorted to another pastime and opened his *Manual of American Archaeology* at the chapter on Columbian silver vases. To no avail. He always started analysing his marital relationship again.

"I wonder whether, at the start of my relationship with Hedwige, I may not have made a wrong move. I thought I was being clever disguising myself as someone else, I mean as someone who was a slow mover. Whereas Hedwige was expecting me—the *me*, as I am; the 'no sooner said than done' man—and she didn't find me."

On each of the seven floors, the lift had brought back seven husbands to their seven wives, and now it was over. There was no longer the same noise in the building any more. Occasionally, a water pipe vibrated due to air pressure. The concierge had brought up the post. The maids had taken the dogs down to the pavement. Nothing more would happen until the distant hour when the milkman and the dustbins arrived. There would just be Pierre consulting his *Archaeology*. Through the wisps of smoke from all the cigarettes consumed, Pierre caught sight of his bed, the bed of a solitary man. This reminded him of his fiery, unpredictable life as a bachelor when he only went out when love summoned him. Out of habit, he got into bed, with nothing else to look at apart from the ceiling, which showed patches of damp. Above the ceiling was the terrace, with the summer garden. Every time they watered the flower beds in this garden, the water ran through the cement and also watered the furniture in his bedroom. So much for modern comfort.

"Hedwige must be having great fun right now with her mother and her sisters. This boarding-school atmosphere is ridiculous. They whisper secrets to each other from one bed to the other. What can they be talking about? What secrets? Are they at my expense? No, Hedwige probably isn't having great fun: for her to leave me alone here, it must be something important. Let's see: could I have taken marriage too seriously? I don't believe in penning people in, of course, but that doesn't mean to say I condone pick-pocketing when it's a matter of bringing two people together. I told myself marriage was not a game, but a difficult and beautiful task to accomplish. Perhaps it's not difficult; perhaps I made it so by imagining it to be so."

Pierre waited a moment to fall asleep; the brass handles of the chest of drawers gleamed softly, the telephone stood outlined in black against the white wall as usual. The wickerwork pattern on the chair was so regular that merely looking at the cane latticework induced a drowsiness that made sleep very imminent. A slight nervous tremor kept Pierre on that gentle slope. He picked up his Beuchat: "*The plateau of Bogota was the scene of an open struggle among the caciques. At the time when Belalcazar was exploring Columbia...*" He switched off the light. Then the loneliness grew until it became intolerable. In the darkness, the suspension of time became appalling. Hedwige's absence took on a huge importance.

"She's had enough of me, it's obvious. How was I not aware of it earlier?"

And Pierre, hurling his book away (he never put books down, he threw them across the room), started to delve into the problem once more.

"For after all, since I can't be accused of hurrying or pestering Hedwige, since I wooed her stealthily... docilely, since I caused her no shock, since I approached her at the same pace she approached me and since nothing could have come between us given our perfect understanding, then it's because I made a mistake in not hurrying her. Perhaps she was expecting to be taken straightforwardly and immediately; girls these days know very well what awaits them and that it's not very pleasant the first time, and that it becomes more agreeable later on. It is we who persist in believing, through our foolishness, vanity and sadism, that we are going to hold in our arms shivering, terrified virgins who will get all worked up over this business.

"I must have been rather ridiculous and seemed fairly silly with my strategy of sitting there like a patient tom, night after night, in front of his pussycat! She thought me impotent, of that there can be no doubt. And my self-control must have won her over, I mean lost her."

Pierre switched on the light again. He saw his shadow on the wall: it was a dispossessed, excommunicated shadow, a shadow embarrassed to be in the light, a shadow that would have preferred the shade. An unpleasant memory and one he always avoided came back to him and would not go away.

"And then… and then there was my wedding night."

Pierre paused: he had smoked so much, and the tobacco was so hot that his tongue was burning. He searched in vain for a carafe of water; it irritated him to have to get up and see that lonely shadow on the white wall: he drank water that tasted like burnt rubber straight from his hot-water bottle. The bad memory came back to plague him: he recalled his failed evening a fortnight ago, the absurd Alavoine play, the hurried return home before the end of the last act, the sudden, premeditated and certainly clumsy way he had dived into Hedwige's bed.

"Hedwige resisted me, why? To begin with, she was willing, no doubt about that; she wanted and was eager to know me. And I, I… well, I hesitated for ages. I was in awe of her; through her nakedness, I could see her fully dressed, proud, demure and beautiful, too beautiful.

"So I feared the worst and plunged into the water so as not to be left on the shore for good. She tensed up violently, recalcitrant, stubborn, frigid."

He tossed and turned. Even normally, lying in a horizontal position infuriated and exhausted him; he only felt at ease when he was standing up; as soon as he lay down, unlike all other men, he could feel the weight of his body, his head heavier than a paving stone, his back sinking into the blanket, his pelvis and even his heels which hurt when they came into contact with the mattress. And he longed for the morning, to be getting up, to be upright, for the earth to be like a springboard on which he would at last regain the lightness that was his strength. He had chosen a bed that was so wide in order that he could do the scissors, possibly a cartwheel, and even pretend to himself that he was running, that he was swimming; but at the slightest nightmare he once again felt trapped in his sheets and dreamt that he was being thrown into some dark Bosphorus, sewn into a sack and powerless.

Through tossing and turning in his bed, Pierre has allowed the cold, satin bedspread to slip onto the floor; he is lying on frozen peaks, his sheets eventually fall off too, goodness knows where.

"I plunged into her as if she were some difficult obstacle, something forbidden that infuriated me; something that contradicted everything that I had originally loved and found passionate and sensitive about her. I can see her that evening in her bed, clad in white as though in mourning…

"I was insistent, I was aware of my clumsiness, but my overexcitement got the better of me. This Lucretia-like resistance infuriated me. I behaved like a hustling bully. I rushed things at the end… and what did I achieve? Total disharmony."

And Pierre could still see his solitary, hasty self lying beside this tight-lipped woman looking as beautiful as she would in death.

"And there I was thinking I could create a work of art with my own hands: a fine outcome!"

Pierre fell back heavily on his pillow.

"Yet God is my witness that in all of this I acted sincerely and in good faith! I thought only of her! I should have been like all men and thought only of myself; you can't save other people without saving yourself first. Sincere in my embarrassment, in my determination to act slowly, in my zealousness to keep still… then suddenly shooting off in one direction and behaving with a brutality that was unacceptable, I must certainly have struck her as loathsome, distorted and ridiculous.

"Conclusion: here I am this evening, victorious, holding my ground, but holding it alone."

CHAPTER XVII

Pierre woke up in the morning feeling refreshed, rested and calmer; he felt ashamed of his nocturnal alarms. Would he not have done better just to have accepted Fromentine's simple explanation: Hedwige was tired and it was past the time to return home, that was all…

But what had she done yesterday that was so exhausting? At eight o'clock in the morning they had gone skating at Molitor; at half past nine they had gulped down a hot chocolate at Prévost's; at ten o'clock they had chosen fabrics for a coat (Pierre, let loose among the samples, went straight to the prettiest material, depriving himself of the pleasure of making up his mind); at half past ten they went to buy some American corned beef from a charcuterie at Les Halles; from there he had taken her to the Doucet Library where he needed to make a sketch (very quickly, without even getting down from the librarian's ladder), then to the Cernuschi Museum; after that, she had waited for him in the car while he negotiated a deal with Gulbenkian; since the time for lunch was well past, they made do with a few sandwiches soaked in beer in a bar on the Champs-Elysées. At three o'clock, while he took part in the committee meeting of the Musées Nationaux, he had sent Hedwige to try on her dresses, with instructions to collect him at four o'clock at the printers of an art magazine he owned and to drop him at the Arts of Benin exhibition in the avenue Matignon, from where she had driven back to Saint-Germain. Well? What was so tiring about that? An absolutely normal day. But her indolent sisters must have persuaded her that she needed to rest.

Pierre stretched exultantly. How good it was in the morning, ideas had clarity, things were back in their proper place, seen in their true proportions and in their natural colours; in the morning they had the transparency of crystal whereas in the evening the sun had stained them yellow like a bad Venetian painter, and at night it was the fakes that proliferated! Pierre had rediscovered sanity and reason and clear common sense, those "very French" virtues.

But nothing is so blinding as complete clarity; mirages are a diurnal phenomenon. It's during the dark hours of insomnia, the hours of pessimism par excellence, that the heart probes deepest and attains the truth.

*

Nine o'clock and Hedwige is not there.

When you arrange a time with a woman, you do so without believing she will keep it, it's inclined to be a time you arrange with yourself: you tell yourself that it's only after that time that you will have to suffer. That is the consolatory virtue of the rendezvous, the rendezvous at which they do not turn up.

Half past nine. Pierre is still waiting and time is flowing by. People talk of time flowing by as though it were tumbling from a spring and as though this spring were situated somewhere uphill. When Pierre looks up, it is as if he were searching for the fountain that marks the beginning of this great stream.

"It must be a salt-water source," he sighs, "heavy with all the tears of those who have waited."

At ten o'clock, Pierre was due to meet the director of the Bremen Museum of Ethnography. He rings the Hôtel Bradford to cancel the meeting. Then, since his morning has been wasted and the weather is fine, and because he is very much on edge, not having slept, and because he needs to keep himself busy, he climbs up to the terrace to do a little gardening, for it's the right moment, one needs to be ready for the arrival of spring.

It is not the right moment, mid-February is too early.

"February or March, aren't they more or less the same?"

No, the great frosts are the worry; they're even obligatory. But the weather is as it is in April, it's so still this morning. All of a sudden the west wind, while staying loyal to its traditions of warmth, no longer carries its cargo of large Atlantic clouds—there has been an inexplicable delay in the arrival of the tide—and it has left the sky completely blue, completely empty, like its colleague the east wind, but without the cold.

Pierre climbs up the spiral staircase and reaches the terrace. He is very proud of his garden, which measures barely ten by thirty metres and which only has three sides, being enclosed on the fourth by a wall from which three of the building's chimneys protrude, quickly transforming any visitors into chimney sweeps. In the middle of the three trimmed box hedges that protect the little garden there are small ovals through which you can see Paris, her distinctive monuments, her layers of variously coloured smoke with, in the centre, the basilica of Montmartre ready to ring out like the President's bell, before he takes the floor.

"There's the west, and over there, it's the north-east…"

When Pierre brings his friends up here, they are as lost as they would be at sea.

At the foot of each section of box hedge there is a small flower bed where Pierre grows common flowers that bloom in about mid-June: flax, poppies, foxgloves, lupins. In the centre there is a larger bed containing early fruit and vegetables, consisting of two cold frames and lit with neon lighting, which he is not a little proud of and which soothes all the disappointments that somnolent nature inflicts on him.

"And above all, give me something that grows quickly!" Pierre exclaims to Monsieur Priapet when he calls at Le Bon Cultivateur on the Quai de la Mégisserie to place his horticultural order.

Imperturbable, having retained his florid countryman's complexion in the heart of the city, Monsieur Priapet, the god of gardens, believes only in the established order of gardening traditions and in the celestial code. But since chemical products make a good profit, he happily yields to the impatient fervour of his Parisian and suburban customers.

"Give me something that grows quickly! Why do we have to wait till June when we have sown seeds in March?" asks Pierre, hopping from foot to foot.

"Because the earth is cold, monsieur."

"Let's warm it. What have you got in here?"

"Some *Subitosa*. Keep to the proportions of one spoonful to five litres of water. I know what you're like, Monsieur Niox, don't go and do what you did last year and put five spoonfuls to one litre. Remember that you burned all your spindle trees. Eh, do you remember?"

"And what does this sack contain?"

"Some *Précipital*."

"What a beautiful name! Vilmorin has a genius for neologisms. How do you use it?"

Monsieur Priapet winks and brings out a Molière-like syringe.

"You apply injections."

"A good crack of the whip on nature's behind, that'll teach her!" said Pierre. "Then give me some *Activitte* too. And add some *Superroburella*, one kilo, ten kilos!"

"Be careful. It's a very stimulating product! Try some of our selected seeds instead," advised Monsieur Priapet as he rubbed his bright red cheeks.

"Really? Are they guaranteed? Are they quick?"

"I wouldn't just recommend them to anyone, except to a gardener like you! Look, you'll get some 'interesting' results with the *Bursting tomato* and with the *Lightning chervil*. Do you know the extra-early *Express* sweet peas from Suttons?"

"Give me twenty packets. And put a sack of arsenic mash in my car; and another of *Sulphuretted Prefoliate*."

"That's hyperactive, Monsieur Niox. Watch out! I'll do as you ask, but for a truly reinforced fertilizer that's anti-cryptogamic and that will really benefit you, there's nothing like *Prematurol* from Truffaut's. Have you seen their *Begonias semperflorens* on the Cours-la-Reine when they've been watered with that? They're huge."

And Pierre departs straight away, his pockets filled with the *Horticulturalist's Diary*, the *Manual of Floriculture*, eager to start planting and transplanting.

Once back home, he will increase his efforts, naturally, and fill his flower beds with stimulating substances and ashes that are so blazingly hot that they still burn the feet at the moment of planting.

"Here, I plant my clematis; behind them, the scabious; above, the pyrethrums. My delphiniums and my columbines are already in place: for two years I haven't had to bother about them… My galloping wisteria has died from phthisis. I'm going to replace it with those nice things that are sturdy and that always grow before anything else: nasturtiums and runner beans. What a huge comfort runner beans are for the wretched amateur! They grow tall, they knock down walls, they explode, they cover everything, they get completely out of hand and they don't give you any trouble."

The man in a hurry pours on the nitrogen; he is unrestrained with the potassium phosphate, he shoves on ammoniac citrate at fever pitch. His ideal solution is to be rid of the sad geraniums and begonias his forefathers grew, to achieve those herbaceous borders they have in

England where the flowerings follow one another on the same ground; from week to week, a blue flower bed gives way to a yellow one, then pink, then white, like a series of fireworks, with luminous fountains sending up rockets.

There is nothing else he needs; the one thing he lacks is land; but nothing is harder than finding land to buy in Paris. Horticulturists sell everything, except land!

In the gazebo, Pierre arranges his tools around a crate that is the last remnant of an unfortunate attempt to grow crops in catalysed water the previous year; with the aid of phosphoric salts, Monsieur Priapet had promised him instant canna, early anemones and a plethora of radishes: it was a flop.

Alongside spades in the shape of a swan's neck, hoeing forks and harrows, there were scarifying claws and shears for cutting the lawn that stood rusting, while a tiny, toothless rake lay among the labels, with shards of broken pots and bits of vegetable cloches that cracked when you walked over them. A box of *Armenian specifica* for speeding up the laying of hens' eggs provided the final evidence of an attempt to fatten up chickens that was abandoned at an earlier period amid corpses of one-day-old chicks that had died from white diarrhoea.

Pierre uses sulphated mulch and screens to protect his irises and primroses.

"Let us consult my *Amateur Gardener* calendar. 'February…
prepare your soil…' Done that. 'Beware cutting lilac too
soon…' These people really do lack any enthusiasm. Why
not protect rose bushes from greenfly now? (But the greenfly are also late)… 'Sow foxgloves in March.' Who cares!
Let's try and sow them in February and we shall see…"

Thus does Pierre interfere with the flowering and overtax
the vegetation. Every morning he will come, nose to the
ground and with wet knees, to keep an eye on the new
growths. He'll scratch with a blackened nail in order
to encourage the little tip of the tulip, he'll raise up the
wilting hyacinth (even though he has had them sent over
from Scotland, so that on finding themselves in Paris, they
might get a good southern surprise). He watches the hole.
He sprinkles, he soaks, he splashes rather than waters. No
matter what, no matter when. The water leaks through
the ceiling (he waters so early in the year that there are
sometimes stalactites down below, in his study).

"Nature needs to be tamed, to be given an example
of vigour!"

Pierre mops his forehead, glistening with beads of sweat
unknown in the Garden of Eden. He turns round: Hedwige
is there, looking at him, simultaneously severe and smiling.

"Sorry for keeping you waiting," says Pierre ironically.
"You see: I lingered in the garden."

She stands there in formal black clothes (an afternoon dress with only a small length of skunk fur fitted snugly round her neck) silhouetted against a very pale blue sky, high above the horizon, a horizon that barely reaches halfway up her legs, as in portraits of the Spanish School.

"Don't make fun of me," she says. "I got up late."

Having made up his mind not to criticize her, Pierre continues in the same tone of voice:

"It's like my tulips. This year, nothing is getting up."

"Nature has eternity ahead of her," Hedwige replies.

"Yes, alas! With nature one always has the impression that autumn is missing the summer and that winter never seriously settles in until the moment when you might rightly expect spring to be arriving. So when will these tulips, which are a particularly tough variety from the north of the Zuider Zee, reveal their colours? They're white ones; I chose them with you in mind, you who like white flowers, with a border of black tulips, to show them at their best."

"I wonder, restless gardener, how you would manage if you had to wait nine months for a child? I mean, of course, wait for a woman who would be expecting... Indeed, perhaps you wouldn't wait?"

Pierre went back to put on his leather coat, which he had hung on a nail so that he could do the gardening, wiped his muddy hands on the back of his dungarees and looked at his wife. Her face was a pale, parchment-like colour.

"Firstly, there can be no birth without union, no union without love and no love without excitement. A child, therefore, is something sudden, something that doesn't wait. It's a surprise that is the result of a collision. It's the fruit of a sleepless night. It doesn't settle at its mother's breast as though it were at a picnic, it's hurled out when you're flat on your back like a seed about to burst. It starts by waking everybody up in the middle of the night, by causing the doctor and midwife to come running. It's new wine which can't bear being put in a bottle."

"Seriously, what would you do?"

"You've caught me unawares. I've never thought about the question much. I think my reaction would be like anyone else's."

"I'm not sure about that."

"Think of this tiny prospective creature, compressed in this narrow box; it has just one idea, which is to get out, to be born and to spin out its days in the lovely sunshine. Tiny things yearn for the gigantic; the bud craves the leaf; assets require interest: everything that lives aspires to growing taller, becoming larger and multiplying."

"You see yourself as a grandfather already!" said Hedwige, bursting out laughing.

Pierre laughs too, happy at his wife's gaiety, but he suddenly becomes thoughtful.

"So why are you telling me all this... today?"

"Only because I think it's useful to think about things before doing them... so as not to regret them afterwards."

"Regret them? Me, regret having a child? You're joking."

"I'm very serious."

"Regret having something that would have its source in you! I think I would overflow with joy, I would celebrate it everywhere, it would be more important than anything! A child of yours, goodness me: what an acceleration of our existence!"

"I'm pregnant," Hedwige replied quietly.

No sound, no lights shining near them. They were alone in this suspended garden, high above the ground, totally alone, facing one another and both of them suddenly feeling very lonely, doing their best to transform this new notion into a series of conventional settings (the belly, the outfit, the nursing home, the pram, etc.).

"Well," Pierre said simply in a very low voice.

"Are you pleased?"

"I don't know whether it's pleasure, it's... it feels strange."

"Do you understand why I felt so weary yesterday? When I arrived at Saint-Germain I actually fainted."

"Sorry!"

Pierre pulled himself together; he brought out a large red handkerchief and took his wife in his arms.

"Thank you," he said, with tears in his eyes.

"Now, I'm going to ask you just one thing, Pierre…"

"What is it?"

"I beg you to be patient."

"But of course, I'm bound to be! I'll be stoical."

"You swear?"

"I swear."

"No stamping about, no shouting if I'm late, or inundating police stations with phone calls."

"All right."

"No behaving like a compass that's lost its bearings."

"Very well."

"No losing me in the street and walking miles in front of me, hunched up like a racing cyclist."

"OK."

"No lighting the fire just to make toast."

"Agreed."

"No getting angry when the starter doesn't work."

"It goes without saying."

"No smashing up things when they don't give way."

"Is that all?"

"Yes."

"Anyone would think it was a business agreement."

Hedwige burst out laughing.

"No, a peace treaty and a pact... for months, dear Pierre, I'm going to be lethargic, a slowcoach, frequently disheartened, clumsy and shapeless. You'll have to give me credit..."

"Unlimited credit!"

"You're going to try to live properly, by which I mean respect the present moment. In that way, we'll manage to..."

"It's not me who's speaking in the future, this time, it's you. You'll see, Hedwige, I am curable, I'm going to start all over again, I'm going to slow down, I'll dawdle; you'll be amazed. Come and sit beside me."

"Suppose we go down first of all? I'm feeling a bit cold."

They sat side by side on the sofa. Wanting to be useful, Pierre threw some coal into the fireplace, lay flat on his tummy to use the bellows, and was obliged to open the windows wide to get rid of the smoke. They felt even colder, but gradually everything improved. Hedwige snuggled up. Pierre jumped up and down, buzzed about and made a lot of noise.

"What's happened to us is wonderful! I was so nervous just now, so far from realizing what awaited me, Hedwige, that I haven't thanked you properly. My dearest one! What variety there is in our marriage! No one day is like another. It's like a mad canter through life. I'm totally overwhelmed with happiness!"

"Don't stride about the flat like that, Pierre, or I'm going to feel ill."

"Already? It's even sweeter cherishing plans than it is cherishing a woman. Let's see: if it's a girl, we'll call her Laurentine… or Micheline…"

"Still this need to act quickly!"

"… or Gervaise."

"And if it's a boy?"

"I'll call him Rustique," said Pierre immediately. "I like Rustique."

"How ghastly!"

The lunch hour had long passed and they were still musing about the future, mortgaging it. Pierre was talking nonsense and daydreaming, while Hedwige was, even now, having some difficulty in trying to follow him.

At two o'clock, they felt hungry. Pierre rang Prunier's, interspersing his order with his plans.

"Hello! Passy 17-87?… Where will you give birth?… Could you send me a lobster?… I'll be the one who rocks it in the cradle."

"At least wait until you have rung off. Prunier's are likely to send you a pair of baby-scales."

"Will you let me cradle it?"

"Oh no! You would demolish it!"

"We shall have a nickel-plated pram with mudguards. I shall push it myself."

"You'd race with it."

"Wait for me. I'm going down to get some champagne from the cellar. I'll be back up in a jiffy."

Pierre opened the door abruptly without bothering to close it, leapt down two flights of stairs and came back up again.

"Hedwige, I love you."

Once again, he was out of the room. Once again, the stairs could be heard creaking beneath his weight. He retraced his steps and, taking Hedwige by the wrists, said:

"All I have to give you is my time: it's entirely yours."

Returning from the cellar, he seized Hedwige, he made her dance, he lifted her into the air, he ripped her blouse and messed up her hair. He hummed "Blanche-Neige" and sang "Les Dragons de Villars" at the top of his voice, while at the same time juggling with the plates and laying the tablecloth, making jerky and comic movements, as they do in the music halls.

"Hedwige," he said solemnly, brandishing a large loaf of bread, "you have given me what I want most in the world!"

"A child?"

"Better than that, some prospects."

CHAPTER XVIII

O NE MORNING, on waking, Pierre received a letter from Doctor Regencrantz:

Monsieur Velocipedist,

The last time I saw you, I informed of you of my imminent departure for Palestine. I was only waiting for a visa for Honduras. Honduras refused me one. Your regulations having forbidden me to practise medicine in France, in order to earn my living, I joined a woollen broker's firm in Roubaix. Since then, I have been hopping from one job to another, as the hamadryad jumps from branch to branch, but like it I am sure of reaching the end of the forest.

For the time being, I am up to my neck in marmalade during the daytime, and at night I continue my scientific work in France's third largest city, which is Bordeaux. What made me choose this city is that I know the Korean consul there, who has hopes of obtaining a Korean visa for me so that I can leave your beautiful country. I shall arrive in Paris a week on Saturday in order to put my affairs in order with your administrative authorities. May I call in to see you… if you are not rushing around too much? I have often thought of you. Have you displayed any fine symptoms of overexcitement recently? I wish you much happiness, by which I mean the quickest thing in the world, which is the Idea.

With my sincere good wishes, Monsieur Velocipedist.

Regencrantz.

PS The fakirs, who are motionless by definition, chose as a yardstick for the greatest speed imaginable the Idea, which they call *mano-java*. *Mano-java* goes around the planet far more quickly than the Hertzian wave: that is why I hope you go faster than the *mano-java*. R

"That good old Regencrantz!" said Pierre aloud.

"What?" Hedwige, still sleepy, murmured lazily. She turned her head towards her husband without opening her eyes. She was prolonging that moment of bliss when, like those goddesses in tapestries supported by cupids, she was hovering in the sky borne on the interwoven arms of all those whom she loved: Mamicha, Pierre, Angélique, Fromentine.

How happy she had been during the past fortnight! How delightful Pierre had become! How those momentarily closed hearts at Saint-Germain had reopened for her, the ungrateful but repentant daughter who had thought she could lead her life without motherly help… A mother wise and good, an omniscient mother, Mamicha had smoothed out everything, resolved everything. One night was all she needed. Having arrived the previous day, exhausted, disappointed and drained, Hedwige had set off again the next morning fortified and equipped once more with that surprising sense of security she felt when she was with her mother; it even seemed that, from a distance, Bonne had exerted her magical effect on Pierre, for he was transformed.

"What?" said Hedwige once more, without moving, so that she did not have to wake up completely.

Pierre handed Regencrantz's letter to her.

"I'll invite him to lunch," he said.

"Who?"

"Regencrantz. He's a Jewish doctor."

"Did he look after you?"

"No, but I interest him."

"Then he's the one who needs to be looked after," said Hedwige, making a charming expression.

"Thank you very much. I met him, dearest Hedwige, at a time when I was of no interest to anyone."

"So were you feeling sad?"

"No."

Hedwige considered this response for a moment.

"Tell me," she went on, "would you feel sad now, Pierre, if I weren't interested in you?"

"Yes."

"So you think you need me?"

"Utterly."

"Ut-ter-ly," Hedwige repeated. "Are you sure about it? Explain yourself…"

"No, I won't explain. Go to sleep."

"Why don't you want to explain?"

"Because it's *my* business."

"It's mine too, and I need to know."

Pierre sat down on the bed, pressing his face to that of his wife, and gently nibbled the base of her nose. She pushed him away.

"Be serious," she said, "talk to me."

"Hedwige," said Pierre, "for me you are the present."

Since she did not understand, he tried to make himself clearer.

"A present that I can live in, do you see, in which I can breathe, that has space… a present that's truly present and no longer that evolving future I used to inhabit."

Hedwige had got out of bed, put on a pink dressing gown like her mother's and was laying the table for breakfast, an old Boisrosé custom she was unable to cast off; she opened a jar of sweet lemon jam she had brought back from Saint-Germain and started to dip into it.

"But all the same," she said, "one can't smell the future. It's in the present that there are all the sensations: heat, cold, aromas, this coffee that you're drinking, well everything!"

"Well, exactly, I couldn't smell them. All those things you have just mentioned had no reality for me. My only reality was the future, and I firmly believed in this gaseous substance, open to billions and billions of formations and an infinite number of combinations!"

"And now?"

"Now that you're mine, really and truly, and getting heavier, now that I can hear your fifty-five kilos causing the floorboards to bend, I have settled into the present day as I would into a padded armchair, I am bound by all sorts of exact needs and precise pleasures, I know that it is ten o'clock, that the hyacinth is white and fragrant, that the sun is pouring in, as huge as a Louis XIV brass, and that Hedwige has broken a cup trying to dry it…"

"Sorry," she said.

"I was living on my own in the future; ever since you have been here, I'm no longer lonely and odd, I confront everything, and everything is straightforward, Hedwige, everything is suddenly so clear-cut, so calm. How lovely the home is when one doesn't have to be making preparations for departure! How beautiful Paris is when you realize that you were born there… And all that, because *you are*. By giving you to me, God made me a present: the present. Admire the fact that the French language should have just one word for the two things!"

Doctor Regencrantz arrived on the stroke of one, a crafty look in his eyes, his ears full of angora hair, his bony, rabbinical nose set between two large bagpiper's cheeks, very pink, very chubby, constantly looking as though he were rejoicing in the midst of the greatest difficulties, simultaneously discussing pathology, a detailed study of the French language, plans for departure and the making of marmalade.

To hit the right note, Pierre welcomed him with an embrace.

"Dear doctor," he said, "I've missed you. Will you admit that you've missed me just as much and that you haven't found many characters as interesting as me for taking what you call replicas?"

"What conceit! I file my index cards between two barrels of jams and I already have as many as I have visas on my passport!"

"I hope they will take you further."

Hedwige came in wearing a long, flowing dress the

same shade as her skin. Regencrantz looked at her without concealing his admiration.

"And so, gracious madame, you have married Monsieur Velocipedist," he said.

"Velocipedist?" Hedwige repeated, intrigued.

"I reckon that suits him well. It was Goethe who coined the word. He spoke of a velocipedist future. He even added that we would die of it."

"Do you hear that, Pierre?" said Hedwige.

"And at a time when the *Weimar Gazette* only came out once a week, Goethe was already forecasting an iron age when newspapers would appear three times a day."

"The world has always moved quickly," said Pierre with a shrug of his shoulders, "yet people no more know how to recognize speed than they know how to detect past beauty and former love affairs on the wrinkled faces of old women. 'By taking the train too frequently from Paris to Saint-Germain,' said Thiers in the 1840s, 'one risks detaching the retina, so rapid will the succession of images be.' I may add that my wife rather shares Monsieur Thiers' view. Will you have an aperitif?"

"One only has to set eyes on madame," said Regencrantz, "to realize that she is exactly the wife you need. Madame is a human character. Furthermore, madame is young and athletic, she won't have any trouble keeping up with you."

"Even though I have taken a thousandth of a second to give her a child and she's going to take nine months…"

"Pierre!" screeched Hedwige, blushing furiously, "please…"

"Believe me, Monsieur Niox, adjust yourself to madame. I can tell from her aura that she has a good influence on you. Otherwise, you'll go back to your bad habits. Pfft! Lost like a meteorite in astral space!"

"I can assure you I'm looking after myself, doctor."

"Good, very good. You're not alone on our terrestrial globe, you should think of others, of those who do not have your openness of judgement. You're an intelligent man and you're letting yourself get caught in the oldest, best-known trap of all: tomorrow, pigs may fly."

Hedwige wore an inscrutable smile. Regencrantz gave her a crafty look.

"A doctor is allowed to be indiscreet," he said. "Does Monsieur Niox make you happy? Dare tell me in his presence."

"You are not indiscreet," she replied, "and I make no secret of my happiness."

"I see," said Regencrantz solemnly. "He makes you happy, but he makes you feel seasick. If I were President of France, I would punish you, Monsieur Niox."

"Presidents don't punish, they reprieve."

"I would sentence you to stand still."

"Under arrest," Pierre corrected him.

"No, no! I know your interesting language very well, I said 'to stand still, to several days not moving'."[9]

"Why not for an entire life, like a fakir?"

"That would be a fair punishment. It's the one St Simeon Stylites inflicted on himself. I've got a leaflet about him that I'll show you. The case of this saint is a curious one."

"Do you also take replicas of saints?"

The doctor had a good appetite: he made sure he got not just his lunch, but his dinner too. He polished off his third chop, the half-kilo of sautéed potatoes that Pierre piled on his plate, and he droned on knowledgeably:

"Before climbing up his pillar, Simeon was a successful man."

"A runner… a womaniser," laughed Pierre.

"Ha, ha, very good![10] Yes, a runner who was admired and very popular. He resolved everything in Rome. Princes came from the far ends of the earth to consult him, and kings used to disguise themselves so that they were not seen asking his advice; all they then had to do was to make use of this advice in order to keep their people happy. His fame spread even to the Persians and the Scythians. Since he was modest and wanted to avoid all those bores who were preventing him from concentrating on his salvation, he dedicated himself to solitude and hoisted himself up onto a pillar six cubits high, then onto another of twenty-two cubits, and finally onto a third that rose thirty-two cubits above the crowd."

"For someone who didn't care for fame…" Pierre intervened.

"They sent up his food by a rope. He remained night and day, stuck up there, not moving, in the same position, because his platform was too narrow for him to stretch out on it."

"Were there railings?" asked Hedwige, who felt giddy listening to this story.

"That's much debated… I also have a leaflet about a Lombard deacon who tried to imitate the Stylite in Dresden. The cold caused his toenails to fall out and the bishops convened to make him come down from his pillar. Do you understand, my dear fellow, the lesson these sages are giving you?"

"Regencrantz, you bore me with your sermons, which are outdated in any case. You're out of touch; you'd do better to ask Hedwige questions and, above all, to eat. Another slice of foie gras?"

Pierre emptied the entire dish onto his guest's plate.

"With pleasure. So, madame, your husband is no longer a velocipedist? Have you cured him? Ha! ha!"

Hedwige held out both hands, palms up, in a gesture of charming modesty; her supple fingers reached outwards like a cornucopia, and only her golden eyes were laughing while, out of politeness, her expression remained serious, for she found the little doctor excessively comical. He looked less like a little doctor, she thought, than a large microbe.

"I am cured, as you say," Pierre continued, "even though this word does not mean anything since I was never ill—a drop of red wine, doctor?—I am cured or, rather, I have adopted a new approach. You remember, Regencrantz, I often spoke to you about this bath of slowness in which France wallows. We continue to think of ourselves as light-footed and speedy without noticing that every other country has overtaken us. At the Olympic Games, I suffered a mar-tyr's death watching those whom we persist in calling 'clumsy Germans', as in eighteenth-century fairy tales, outperform us in the preliminary heats. Nowadays, it's we who churn out copious one-thousand-page theses and they who turn everything upside down with the *Essay on Relativity*, which has three pages. Here people reckon that's not being serious. The French think only of their own centre of gravity; they have positioned it so low (left of centre) that they haven't any spurt left. Our army is nothing but a load of office scribblers on wheels; we have put springs everywhere to deaden the shock; but where has anyone seen a racing vehicle that has springs? The sprinter would be killed at the first bend. In any case, we don't make sprinters; we are artists, we build statues of sprinters... a shot of brandy, Regencrantz?"

"With pleasure... and then?"

"Well, afterwards... I met Hedwige, daughter of the slow-paced Boisrosé family, and she taught me to love slowness. There can be no question that speed is a dead end: the ambassadors who used carriages brought peace with them, while ministers who travel by air bring war. Just go to the cinema and watch an accident in slow motion, as God might have arranged it: it's just a succession of caresses; the plane skims the ground; the ground smashes the aircraft to pieces with more delicacy than the gourmet peels his fig, and the flames that are about to send the passengers up in smoke resemble a fire that has not been lit properly. It is speed, which by bringing two people intimately closer together, produces the deadly shock... All this, my good friend, has made me reflect and it has occurred to me that by rushing about too quickly I could be well on the way to affecting my feelings for my wife and my most precious concerns might become like hard corks."

Thoughtful all of a sudden, Pierre looked at Hedwige.

"One question, Regencrantz..." he said briskly.

"I'm listening."

Pierre reconsidered:

"No. Pretend I said nothing."

They moved to the café. Pierre took the doctor to one side. And very hurriedly, in a low voice:

"This is what I wanted to ask you: Hedwige will have her baby in October. Just imagine that, not till October! I feel as though I could never wait that long. Isn't there a way…"

"What way? What do you mean?" asked Regencrantz stiffly. "Nature moves at her own pace. Be like her."

"Ah!" said Pierre, disappointed, as he turned his head towards Hedwige to make sure she wasn't listening. "Forgive my ignorance, doctor, I wanted so much to save time… I'm longing to know what sex it is… The fortune tellers always get it wrong. Might there not be some scientific procedure…"

"At four months, some Americans dye the mother's cells and those of the child at the same time, and as a result, know its sex."

"That's wonderful! In less than two months, I could know!"

"Yes, but I have to tell you that it's not recommended at all. In Europe, you won't find any doctor who is prepared to do it. You'll have to make do with fortune tellers."

"Too bad," Pierre sighed, resigned to the fact. "I'll do as I always do, I'll wait."

*

Pierre went downstairs with Regencrantz, having offered to drop him by car in the centre of town if, in exchange, he would agree to accompany him beforehand for a brief walk in the Bois de Boulogne.

"Let's go quickly, doctor, quickly, what they call presto."

"Quickly, Monsieur Niox? I thought you were cured?"

"Basically, you're right," Pierre replied, laughing. "Why quickly? My meeting is not until four o'clock."

Which did not prevent them from setting off at full tilt down to the Bois.

"Looking at these police lights, flashing red and green alternately," Regencrantz continued, carrying on with his theme and hanging onto the door handle, "you will observe that we do not advance at a regular pace, but rather in a series of leaps interrupted by stops. This is how nature and genius behave."

"Let's get out and walk now," said Pierre, interrupting him.

The doctor did his best to follow; he ran after him with very short steps, on his heels, taking care not to slip, as though on ice. After a quarter of an hour he could go no farther and spoke in a panting voice:

"One day... I met... a man... the fastest in the world, a famous record-holder..."

"Commodore Swift, perhaps?" asked Pierre respectfully.

"The very man.

"You must hear this anecdote. It's made for you even in its moral aspect. But let's stop here, please. I am, as you say, exhausted."

Struggling for breath, Regencrantz collapsed onto a bench.

"Give me time to tell you my story…"

"I'm listening to you patiently," said Pierre.

"I had discovered during a trip to the United States that Commodore Swift happened to be at a country club to the north of Salt Lake and it struck me as a unique opportunity to encounter the record-holder. Some friends arranged it all for me. Shortly beforehand, Swift had reached a speed of eight hundred and eighty-two kilometres per hour, that's two hundred and forty-five metres per second. He had not only brought the earth closer to the air and the car to the aeroplane, and to sound, and to light, and to all the ethereal things that are transmitted and propelled with greater freedom, but he had also gained sovereign rights over all sportsmen and also over all those men in a hurry in the world who, like you, Monsieur Pierre Niox, should recognize him as king."

"Speed like that, it's the infinite," sighed Pierre admiringly.

"Whereas I find that a number, no matter which one, even a record-breaking number, restricts and stifles the infinite," replied the doctor. "When I walked into the lounge of the country club, it appeared to me to be empty. One man, just one, was there, slumped in an armchair. His legs were stretched out on the table and you could see the thick soles of his shoes, his arms hung down, his eyes were half closed, and he stared at me without blinking; he looked like a piece of furniture or, rather, a building, so rooted to the spot did he seem. Outside, through the thick bay windows of the monastic room, I noticed the beach, extending over a glassy surface which it prolonged, differing from it only in its paler shade of colour. Low, grey clouds sped by.

"At this hour of the morning, in America, everybody has left for work. Men and women were bustling about, people were running to their place of employment, the suburban trains were hurtling over the points bringing businessmen to more business meetings. I was shocked to see this man, on his own, lying motionless in an armchair in the empty lounge of a club.

'I'm sorry I'm late,' I ventured.

'You're actually early.'

'Are you sure that I shouldn't have waited and that the commodore will still be able to see me?'

'Doctor Regencrantz,' he said, 'the commodore has nothing to do. I am the commodore.'

He held out the empty palms of his enormous hands, useless machine tools. He also pointed to his inactive feet, hanging in the air as though on pedals.

'Lousy climate, it really is,' he sighed.

I looked at him in astonishment, so amazed that I could not utter a word.

'Does it surprise you that I should have nothing to do? All winter, I've been tuning up *Fireflash*. In the wind-tunnel workshop I had to alter the rear compression tanks which were producing too much resistance, reduce the heavy tubing of the radiator, because *Fireflash* was nose-diving, then rebuild it in light metal because the water was boiling too quickly. The car's ready now and all I can do is wait.'

'And what are you waiting for, commodore?' I asked with interest.

'A favourable day, and during that day, a propitious hour, and during that hour, the few necessary seconds.'

'What!' I exclaimed, 'Is it possible that since the winter…'

'That's right. What do you expect, adverse winds were blowing up until April; in May the ground became clayey; at the beginning of July the first tornadoes arrived. In short, I've been waiting for the right moment for four months, for one hundred and seventeen days exactly,' he groaned angrily.

I risked a joke:

'Is there a great deal of slack season in a racing driver's job?' I said.

'Yes. I can say that for eight months I haven't progressed an inch.'

Commodore Swift crossed his legs wearily; he sucked at his tobacco-less pipe. He sighed and looked around him like a paralysed man waiting for the nurse to come by so that he could have his vegetable broth. His innocent face, covered with patches of red, turned towards me, imploring, gentle and without hope. He stood up slowly, somewhat unsure of his movements, his muscles limp, his centre of gravity unsteady, uncertain in his gait and in the future of all progress on foot.

'We can always go to the garage,' he said to me, 'that will keep us busy for a while. You'll see *Fireflash*. *Fireflash* has been around a long time, but she's a beautiful piece of machinery all the same.'

Once the car had been found and the tarpaulin removed, I caught sight of a mass of crimson-red curved sheet metal which, due to it having been designed for speed, no longer had any shape. The eye slipped over her like the wind. She was not slender like the petrel or spindly like a torpedo; from a forty-five-degree angle, she resembled a plate, in profile a pear, and from the front a large soup tureen. She lay heavily on the sand, plump, pot-bellied and dormant.

'What!' I thought, 'Can this be the machine that the fastest things have difficulty grasping hold of and whose striated, elongated and egg-shaped image is transmitted to us by belinograph all over the globe?'

The commodore started her up and, through a narrow neck, slid down into the single seat. It was as if the flesh of a lobster were returning with difficulty into the shell of the claw. He pumped the throttle, switched on the ignition, released the compressed air and obtained a few splutters.

'Is this for a test run?' I asked, delighted already.

'I'd be surprised. What's the wind speed this morning?'

'Thirty-two metres per second,' replied an assistant.

'What did we have yesterday? At the same time?'

'Twenty-seven metres per second.'

'Above eighteen metres per second, there's no point in attempting anything,' the commodore sighed resignedly. 'I'm not starting up just to amuse you, doctor.'

The American's head disappeared into the sheet metal and his voice was drowned out by the thunder of quadruple exhaust pipes. The mechanics were bustling about already, but with a motion of his hand he indicated to them not to move. Installed like a worm inside his pear, the record-breaker sat motionless in the midst of his 600 horsepower, his machine that was unable to take off, the sixty-four cylinders that strove to no purpose, his sixteen carburettors which, through the static, exuded petrol that at any moment could be transformed into energy."

"It's fascinating," Pierre broke in. "And then?"

"That was all," Regencrantz continued. "The commodore switched off the ignition and remained there, absolutely unwilling to move, sitting there solemnly, affected in turn by the lethargy that *Fireflash* seemed to have communicated to him; an eternal silence fell over the salty beach.

"The powder must be wet, that's why *Fireflash* hasn't set off," I thought. "Speed must be a strange sort of fairy for everything to be sacrificed because of it, even time! Here is a great man who, in one hundred and seventeen consecutive days, has not managed to travel one mile. He's really a saint, a patient hero, a victim of slowness. The commodore deserves fame, but not of the kind he's searching for. It would be better for him to be famous under another name: that of the man who spent four and a half months travelling one thousand six hundred and nine metres."

"And what about you?" said Pierre, "how many hours have you spent learning this edifying apologia by heart?"

CHAPTER XIX

E VER SINCE HEDWIGE'S pregnancy had prevented him from playing tennis, Pierre had replaced that sport with swimming and every morning he would go to the pool, where he met Vincent Amyot. These meetings, accidental initially, had become daily encounters and the two brothers-in-law became friends; they got changed together; that is to say that normally, while Amyot was unknotting his tie, Pierre was already putting on his swimming costume. But that morning, instead of rushing to plunge into the water, Pierre was lounging about in the sunshine with his towel round his neck, his back to the cabins.

Amyot was gazing at him.

"You've got thinner," he said.

"Unlike you," said Pierre. "That's the belly of a happy man!"

"Does that mean that you're not a happy man?"

Amyot lit a cigarette and sat on the ground; to his surprise, Pierre did likewise.

"Me, unhappy!" he said. "Don't you realize what Hedwige means to me…"

He stopped talking and stared at the murky bottom of the pool, streaked with three black lines intended for racing.

"Explain yourself," said Amyot.

"Well… to begin with, I'm only warm when I'm with her. Yes, I don't know why, but spring hasn't started for me this year. The thermometer shows over fifteen degrees and I'm living at zero…"

"It's the breeze caused by your speed," Vincent interrupted mockingly.

"…the mere presence of Hedwige gives me a warm rush. Her skin is smooth and fiery, she emits a sleek radiance like the glaze of a fine stove. Without being bubbly, she enlivens everything; she hasn't the vulgar incandescence of effusive women, she doesn't parch you; she radiates the true warmth of life, that of the woman, that of the breast, that of the heart. In her presence, it's always summer."

"You're grateful to her for giving you a child," said Amyot enviously.

"No, that's not why I find her so good and so beautiful. For she's still just as beautiful at the end of her third month; Plato says that beauty is a short-lived tyranny; with Hedwige it's a long-lasting empire; yes, Hedwige is enduring and perfect like my most treasured belongings. She is a living High Renaissance piece, a constantly rekindled, always satisfying requirement for my eyes. Oh no! Mother Boisrosé didn't cheat on quality!"

"Do you get on well with the mother-in-law?" asked Amyot.

"Oh yes," said Pierre hastily, "she's a decent woman."

"Ah, do you think so!" said Amyot, starting to laugh. "Forgive me, but the epithet is funny."

"Wasn't she kind to you?"

"My dear Pierre… she has been perfectly kind, naturally; it's just that with perfect kindness she took away my wife!"

He sighed and nodded, the still fine features of his appearance creasing into the folds of his double chin and, confronted with Pierre's questioning gaze, he continued:

"In the beginning, I tried to keep Angélique for myself— not for me alone, of course, I wouldn't have been able to do that—but at least share her fifty-fifty. For a year and a half I acted methodically, as befits a meticulous Polytechnique graduate. And then, I grew weary. Angélique leaves at nine o'clock in the morning and comes back at eight in the evening (on the evening she doesn't have dinner at Saint-Germain, that is). And she sleeps there at least twice a week."

"Hedwige very seldom goes there," said Pierre, "I forbid her to drive in her condition."

"I should be extremely surprised," said Vincent, "if Madame de Boisrosé could survive a single day without seeing one of her daughters. First of all, the Rule decrees it so. You think that you have contracted a marriage; you have contracted a disease, the Boisrosé disease: for your wife this means communal life, a siesta until six in the evening, the dormitory; for you, being led by the nose and presented submissively to Bonne, while waiting for her to grab you by your protruding snout."

Pierre, who was accustomed to being direct, suddenly turned towards Vincent:

"Is she hot-blooded, your wife?"

"She is. Only it's not focused on men. She only opens her arms to Mamicha, she only embraces her sisters, she has Saint-Germain in her blood, she stops being unfeeling there even with Uncle Rocheflamme, and I really do think that she won't ever know any real pleasure until she's in the Boisrosé family grave, because, in her will, she has refused to be buried with me. When it's a matter of climbing into the maternal bed, there's no problem! I wish you could see her hurling off her clothes. And her impassioned messages about putting an end to her solitude, the way she glances at the door of my house, at that lovely door that will allow her to rush off 'home' at last! And her weariness as soon as she returns! And her eagerness as soon as she sets off there again! Not to mention the hours that she evades me. Everything she loses in insomnia and weight when she is with me, she puts on again with siestas and kilos the moment she's gone back to her family…"

He sighed once more.

"Angélique is an accomplished lover, I'm sure of that," he continued. "She has extravagant desires that are like rages, and a prodigious lust; she can love until she draws blood, but the blood is that which she has in her veins."

Pierre stood up suddenly, knotted the cord of his swimming trunks and paced up and down.

"I suggest we found a club," he said, "an association comprising all present and future men married to Boisrosé girls. We have to stand together, for heaven's sake! We have to pit a rule against the Rule. Each of these girls is incomparable individually; they are also very beautiful all together, but I loathe having to think of them collectively. When I think of Hedwige, it makes me attribute a series of attractive qualities to the others that I had thought were particular to my wife and which, I am bound to acknowledge, don't really belong to her. It's very unpleasant! It's already bad enough marrying someone who looks like her mother; it's like living with a *memento mori*, with the ivory death's head on the table, among the festive roses."

"The Boisrosés don't look like their mother fortunately," said Amyot, "but I know what you mean. When you possess a beautiful piece of original *cire perdue*, you wouldn't want the sculptor selling his reproduction rights to a maker of chimney stacks. Nevertheless, you have to resign yourself; Boisrosé habits are stronger and the Boisrosé girls less pliable than the hardest of metals. This family is a voodoo sect in which the sons-in-law are sympathizers, not founder members. There's nothing to be done, we might as well give up."

"I won't give up anything," exclaimed Pierre, his brush in one hand, his comb in the other. "As far as I'm concerned, I'm absolutely determined to have Hedwige to myself alone. And what's more, it's already happening: she dresses in her own clothes and none of her sisters wear her shoes any longer."

"One question," asked Amyot. "Has Hedwige kept her bed at Saint-Germain?"

"Er... I think she did, just in case of a breakdown... or fog... it would be better than sleeping in a hotel."

"My poor fellow!" said Amyot, squeezing his brother-in-law's hand affectionately.

"I'm not disturbing you?" said Hedwige as she opened the door.

"You're only disturbing yourself, my beloved darling, for I was with you."

"With me?"

"Yes, I was thinking of you. I was thinking that you are relaxation."

"That's not very flattering."

"Yes, when I say it, it's high praise."

In fact Pierre, whose long strides make the house tremble during his soliloquies, is standing still, relaxing and pressing his lips to his wife's wrist in the way one drinks spa water from the place where the water is warmest.

"You're here," he said, filled with joy, "it's good."

He takes her in his arms.

"When I come close to you, not only do I feel your body, but I am in touch with all bodies. Before knowing you, I lived in isolation as though on a glass shelf in an electric machine. But now the current passes through me."

Hedwige snuggled up to him for fear of being looked at from a distance and so that he wouldn't notice her disappearing waist when standing in front of her, or her convex belly from the side. But by clasping her to him, he can imagine what his gaze might not have noticed, closes his eyes and says:

"It's beginning to show, and seriously so."

"Too bad," Hedwige replies, torn between the pleasure of appearing beautiful and pride at being a mother.

"So much the better."

Hedwige closes her eyes, happy to feel her two children pressed one against the other, because Pierre, who used to seem so strong, so Zeus-like, so striking in the early days, has, through their living together, become her child. "He's a funny boy," she says tenderly, almost with compassion, feeling indulgent and full of pity, like most women, for the incomprehensible side of their male partner, for their mysterious obsessions—for they all have one—be it gardening, civic duty, curing illnesses, war or any other mission they believe they have been given; just like those elderly retired colonels who, in order to give themselves the illusion of being busy, indulge in having imaginary mobilization orders sent to themselves. Every male thus creates a curious structure for himself in which he pays homage to a god, a demi-god, a folly. Any altar, however peculiar it may be, can be used to inspire a new zest in someone and give them a reason for living. Hedwige was not trying to delve into Pierre's motives; he was a man: that was explanation enough. Her husband's frantic pace, this invariable way he had of changing his mind, this need to take not just an overall view of things, but to see the same thing from every angle by skipping from one point of the compass to another, like our present-day landscape artists who follow the sun with their canvases in their motor cars, with that enthusiasm for seeing everything and considering nothing, for doing everything and not completing anything, for running from an occasion to an event and from a situation to an occurrence—all this was tiring, certainly, and pointless, but it was the other side of the coin to a husband who was kind on the whole, gentle, delightful at times, but devoid of any self-control.

"Poor Pierre!" Hedwige would murmur simply whenever her sisters discussed him; Pierre's name made everyone itch to speak and they even preferred to say good things rather than not talk about him. Mamicha, raising her white fringe and her august chin, added some perfidious proverb from the West Indies, a land scarcely filled with serpents, and called her daughters to come closer.

"You're too far away, I can't hear half of what you're saying."

"Here we are; we're climbing onto the bed."

And gathered together under the eiderdown, resembling on a large scale those families of dogs, cats or mice in cartoon drawings, they embarked delightedly on the agenda for the day: Uncle Rocheflamme's affair with a second-hand goods dealer of his own age ("For an old lady friend, ring out the bells," Mamicha said with a smile), the choice of carpet for the drawing room, Fromentine's new hairstyle... Hedwige was totally happy. Had she been more honest or more experienced in self-analysis, she would have realized that saying "Poor Pierre" expressed her regret at not really being able to love him. For her, amusement and variety were to be found in Neuilly, but happiness had never stopped residing at Saint-Germain.

People's separations or their lack of feeling for one another are no doubt the work of superior powers who have arbitrarily forced us into avoidable encounters, then snatched us away and cast us aside. The same oppressive and blind force which, in Bonne de Boisrosé's games of patience, prevented the kings from emerging by covering them with sevens and ruining her future prospects, also intervened to separate Hedwige from Pierre and brought her back irresistibly into her mother's little game. There are unions that the fairies, either out of laziness or through a subtle form of cruelty, allow to be fruitful yet are not blessed by them.

In any case, the fairies were not the only ones to blame; they had, exceptionally, given Pierre a brief reprieve in the course of his destiny, an hour during which, by initiating Hedwige into the pleasures of the flesh, he might have made himself master; he had allowed this moment to pass. Hedwige, disappointed by Pierre, whose clumsiness in matters of love increased day by day the more he became aware of it, was filled with all the inhibitions that Bonne, through long and patient methods of suggestion, had impressed upon her daughters as a precaution against men: man was a social necessity, a fastidious and repulsive physical burden. The beautiful, adorable Hedwige was ruined for love.

The baby brought her even closer to her mother than to her husband. Secretly, on her child's behalf, she feared this fiery and untidy father, whereas at Saint-Germain it would be pampered and cosseted: "He's a Boisrosé, he's got his grandfather's eyes." "No, she's a Rocheflamme one hundred per cent." The shoot born of Hedwige would prosper well in the warm and humid Boisrosé climate, shielded from those drying desert winds that Pierre left in his wake. In that sweet atmosphere of animal-like tenderness, in that pastoral home life, in that manger where gods could be raised, Hedwige was already imagining her mother and her sisters passing round a magnificent little baby.

In the large room with its blinds lowered so as to protect the young woman's weary eyes, a ray of sunshine filters in, caresses Hedwige's neck, a powerful and flexible column that disappears into the darkness of the feathery black hair with golden tints, and proceeds to split in two the body of Pierre who, with much waving of arms, is trying to explain what his son will be like. On this subject, he is as loquacious as his wife is laconic. The still invisible child is constantly present between them; an expression of that subconscious and frenzied imperialism of the self that constantly drives us to extend our fleshly frontiers, it stimulates Pierre and excites his avid impatience.

"Will he ever be born," he wonders, "this lazy creature, this troglodyte? For the time being, he is withdrawing like a hermit, 'feeling his life (and not his death) imminent', he confines himself to his pool, like a fish, but without the nimble flick of the tail and the rapid fins that fish have. It's inconceivable that someone born of me should be so slow! What a silly invention pregnancy is! Nature goes on its way like a doddery, elderly childminder and the doctors are unable to invent anything to speed up the event… Five months still!"

"Pierre," says Hedwige, "come and sit down beside me on the sofa. See how soft this velvet is and I'll put this batiste cushion behind your head, which will refresh you. You're flushed and your eyes are all feverish. What's the matter with you?"

"Nothing's wrong, I'm thinking of the little one. I'm happy to know he's inside you. For him as for me you're a wonderful mother; he'll have your beauty, your balanced mind. Later on, when the years have hardened him, he can if he wishes take something from me. Just think, Hedwige, he's going to be thrown among a million men, all naked, with his horoscope under his arm!"

Pierre is bent over the abyss of coming days and distant years. He sees a large-limbed little boy, moving very nimbly between four escape routes and entering the increasingly narrow corridor of the sequence of time. He sees him as a Peter Pan running beneath the tall trees. He attaches this still corpuscular fate to his own destiny.

Will he or she be dark or fair? Punctual or late? Nestlé's milk or breast-fed? Boarder or half-day? The *lycée* or a religious institution? Dim or gifted? Latin or Greek? German studies or English? Sacré-Coeur or *Sciences politiques*? Infantry or artillery? Will he make women suffer or will they dominate him? When he's twenty, who will be declaring war on whom? What will the world be like? What shape will hats and ideas have?

If you want to escape from your own self, there is no better means than a child.

"Hedwige, have you thought of ordering the baby clothes? And the nursery furniture that hasn't yet been chosen! We haven't planned a thing. I'm going to buy the baby clothes."

"Five months beforehand!" said Hedwige, who could not help laughing.

"From baby clothes to bare knees and from bare knees to trousers, it's no time at all…"

He doesn't want to anticipate the long journey from the first cry to the alphabet, from crawling games to the first tottering steps that look like a drunkard walking, from standing up and holding on to the bedcovers to running. Good heavens, what an eternity exists between the eyes of the mole and the fleeting glance of the lynx!

"Pierre le Bref," said Hedwige sweetly, "I can see you're bored, you've still got your hands clenched in your pockets. Why don't you go out? Go and do your shopping."

And Pierre went out to stretch his legs.

He talked to himself as he strode through the streets.

"Ah! If it were me in that baby's place, I'd soon be bursting through the hoop and marching head first into the future!"

CHAPTER XX

P IERRE WAS PACING up and down the drawing room.
Hedwige's face had turned a magnificent golden-
green colour.

"Listen, Hedwige, be reasonable. You need some fresh
air. Ten days by the sea will do us both good. We're
leaving tomorrow. The tickets are bought, the rooms are
booked…"

Hedwige closed her eyes; when Pierre had gone past
she opened them again, but there was a moment when he
was briefly silhouetted against the light, when he glided
between her and the window, that was so painful to her
that she shut her eyelids tightly so that she would not see
him. It was tiresome, this striding up and down, as if he
were riding on a swing after lunch. Hedwige glanced at
her husband out of the corner of her eye, ready to avoid
his trajectory. In contrast, all this commotion drove her
back towards her mother as if to a lost paradise, making
her nostalgic for the solid Boisrosé bed.

"You don't want to? But why, for goodness' sake, why?"

Her feeling of giddiness only grew. With his comings and goings, Pierre was dragging her into a waltz without music. It was a choppy passage that made her stomach feel empty and gave her a headache and an intensification of the feelings of nausea due to pregnancy.

"Oh, I know very well why. I've known for a long time that you'd prefer to die and make me pine away here than to be without your mother for ten days."

Pierre's pacing to and fro was becoming unbearable. The furniture now seemed to be rolling about, the piano was shaking and the pictures were shuttling back and forth on the walls, which were also swirling. Even though she was sitting down, Hedwige could not understand why the rug under her feet appeared to be rising upwards while the paintings were obeying some invisible gyratory impulse.

"What's the matter? You're very pale," Pierre exclaimed all of a sudden, seeing Hedwige's cheeks lose their colour and turn a shade of banana. "Have I upset you? Have I displeased you?"

Hedwige was unable to reply.

She waved her hand in a wide gesture and ran to the bathroom.

She returned a few moments later, her hair back in place, her face re-powdered, her eyes shining. She sat down next to Pierre and put her arm through his.

"My Pierre," she said gently, "don't criticize me for loving my family. Does it prevent me from loving you? Would you prefer it if I spent my time running around dressmakers' shops and going to tea parties instead of frolicking innocently in that warm tropical bath that is my family? A poor little family adrift in France, which goes largely unnoticed, which lives on its own and which does no harm to anyone. But if you wanted to drag them away, you would find you could not shift them. When I think of us Boisrosés, I'm always reminded of our mangrove trees. Have you ever seen any? No? A mangrove looks like a bundle of dead wood drifting from the shore into the sea. When we were children, paddling around at Anse à Banane, we used to try and take these bits of wood home, but our hands would immediately start bleeding and we couldn't pick anything up. Mangroves are the most resistant things in the world; they have claw-like fingers that for millions of years have clung to the earth, driven up by the tides. We were taught that we owed the fact that we were walking on firm ground to the mangrove trees. Ever since then, I've always thought that nations should be grateful to mangrove families rather like ours, to women who collectively, without any other strength apart from their fingers, endured wars, flooding, bankruptcy, revolutions, men's failures, and all the calamities."

"You don't have to behave like a mangrove tree with me," said Pierre, "I'll never let you go. Think of me as an extra root."

Hedwige pressed her warm cheek to her husband's.

"Very well, but you must do one little favour for me: buy a trinket from Uncle Rocheflamme."

"Ah, no! That would be a dangerous precedent! I don't like antiques, I only like antiquities. On the other hand, you can go and buy all his stuff if you'd like, on condition that I don't see it… The cloister is going to be sold; all that remains is to exchange signatures; the money is yours."

"Mine!" Hedwige repeated in amazement. "But Pierre, it's your only capital. You know very well that apart from the Mas Vieux and the cloister, all you have is what you earn."

"Yes," Pierre said simply, "it's my only capital and that's why it must belong to you."

Pierre threw his coat on a chair, removed his collar and flopped down on the bed, his legs spread wide; he had just returned from his morning shopping and was sweating profusely; this exceptionally warm June weather made him feel on edge and the "Year 1000 Exhibition" that he had agreed to organize was causing him problems, meetings, discussions and a great deal of work he could have done without.

"Would I not do better," he thought, "to devote my days to Hedwige? She must still be there waiting for me as she is every morning. It's at least two weeks since I last had my coffee with her."

He stood up, ready to run round to see his wife, he imagined her bustling calmly around the small breakfast table; he knew in advance that he wanted to experience that peace that only she could provide him with. To his surprise, he was overcome with a drab and lethargic sense of aversion. No, he did not wish to go and call on Hedwige: why? Ideas flitted around his head and he watched them developing without trying to marshal them; he enjoyed this shifting monologue in which absurd images—cruel, tender and bitter—jostled with one another.

Clearly, this fulfilment, this restfulness that he enjoyed when he was with Hedwige, was something he no longer required as much. Why? Was it because he knew from experience that it would be followed by a frenzy of excite-ment immediately afterwards? Just as the sea, momentar-ily calmed when drenched with oil, draws itself back all the more ferociously, scarcely had he relaxed for a few minutes in Hedwige's presence, scarcely had he fondled her soothing hands, than a sudden reaction made him stand upright. The calm that her Creole beauty gave him was nothing but a West Indian lull. "You're marvellous, my beloved," he would say, but he walked straight to the front door and, once past the door, he broke into a fit of irrational agitation.

Furthermore, he could no longer bear to see the belly from which the child would not emerge, could not emerge for four months at least. These four months weighed upon Pierre, paralysed his feelings towards Hedwige and prevented him from enjoying this woman whom he loved dearly. So he staved off his hunger by visiting museum curators and by writing lots of letters, scribbling daily with an increasingly leaky pen in halting words that were rather like sparks, in which the crosses preceded the *t* by a mile and the dots shot off well in advance of the *i*; sometimes the weary thought preceded him and he was obliged to correct the inconsistency and fill in the spaces with additions in the margin that made everything illegible. The thoughts also outstripped the words and made him reel off the end of sentences without altering the beginning. And when he shook hands he did so with a series of jolting and emotional squeezes.

The instinct that keeps the male close to his crippled female partner, however, that obliges the most fickle of animals to remain with their pregnant companions until they have given birth, drove Pierre back to Hedwige, made him stand guard beside her for entire evenings, as though summoned by an invisible force, and he would fall into a soothing slumber alongside this woman who did not sleep. But the following day, his impatience took hold of him again—his spinning like a top, his whirlwind departures, his pacing up and down the street, his sudden arrival back home making Hedwige jump, his unusual way of wandering off when he was lying beside her, interspersed with his zigzagging about and crushing insects against the window and sudden rushes to the front door.

"I'm going out," he would say. So, out of devotion, out of caution too, so as not to leave such an impetuous husband on his own, Hedwige declared that she was quite capable of accompanying him. She was uncomfortable, however, in the tiny convertible; and if they went on foot, she became breathless trying to keep up with Pierre, in spite of his touching attempts to slow down; he was always a hundred metres ahead, which made conversation difficult. Aware that he was wearing her out, like a horse, he did his best to seek forgiveness by uttering kind words and putting on the almost feminine smile that was his great attraction.

"You follow me like my shadow, my sun."

"Anyone would think you were running away from me," panted an exhausted Hedwige.

And she tried hard to keep pace with Pierre, but whereas he ran, she trotted. Their rhythm was broken immediately. She was always leading with her left foot, and he with his right. He gained ground with his huge strides and would be three, and then five, chestnut trees ahead of her. She swayed in the air that he displaced; she could hear the muffled thud of his rubber heels; the breeze clung to her legs, ruffled her skirt, blew her hat off. She had to stop at the end of the pavement to let the traffic go by; he had woven his way through! He moved easily among the delivery men and scooters unloading, the children's prams; he avoided the absent-minded man who was reading his newspaper as he walked, he steered an admirable course between the man on crutches wearing his Basque beret, the chattering nurses and the lady tugging on her constipated dog's leash.

Hedwige could see Pierre's back disappearing into the distance. How well she knew that back! How familiar those striding shoulders were, those conductor's arms! Now, he was no larger than a hare. A second later, he looked like a fleeting bacillus. Hobbling among the taxis, the buses, the cyclists, along a twisting, rolling, collapsing road, she followed the tracks of the man in a hurry who had vanished. Then, all at once, worn out and having arrived at the house where she was expected, she bumped into nimble Pierre, who was on his way back.

"Have we arrived?" she asked.

"Not only have we arrived, but we're setting off again. I've fixed everything, we're going somewhere else."

"How can one tell if one has arrived," Hedwige said one day, "if one never stops?"

The more he rushed, the more emaciated Pierre became; he grew thinner as Hedwige filled out.

Every day, she became more resistant to anything that was not to do with her gestation, more deaf to the outside world. She enjoyed her condition intimately; she relished her physical life as a pregnant woman, she descended into that silo where her harvest was stored, with a short-sighted squint she tried to decipher something in the depths of her womb and she was already listening for the first jolts. As day followed day, she was beginning to stoop under her own weight.

She was now spending entire days in bed, not saying anything, not doing anything. A colossal and welcome weariness overcame her. Faced with so much turmoil and insufficiency, she displayed joyful resignation. Although she was languishing, she knew that beneath her indolence some very intense labour was going on; simultaneously motionless and breathtakingly active, not moving a little finger, but secretly a thousand times more impetuous than the lethargic Pierre, she was collaborating with nature with all her strength, building herself up inwardly, massaging, palpating or articulating her ribs, she was applying the pointing to this tiny living machine who would subsequently only have to distend all his limbs to become a six-foot man. A surge of dazzled amazement consumed her, which her husband failed to understand. She was adoring a sort of cryptic idol, a sacred frog in her private pond, to which she paid an obscure form of worship which Pierre was excluded from; excluded, frustrated, sent back to his manly tasks. Yet he could not help returning to her and wearying her with his demands.

One morning, she saw him coming in laden with flowers, looking affectionate.

"Darling, I have a great favour to ask you."

"If it's reasonable..." said Hedwige wearily.

"I'd so much like to know what's going on inside there... to be able to pay closer attention to both of you."

"But come on, Pierre, that's not possible. Don't be absurd all the time."

"It's not in the least absurd and, on the contrary, totally normal. I'd like an X-ray, that's all."

"X-rays are not made for the enjoyment of mere amateurs," said Hedwige with a laugh. "Let me sleep now, you're tiring me. I was kept awake all night by cramp. I don't know how I can stretch out my poor swollen legs any more."

Pierre kissed her and felt sorry for her, but returned to the offensive.

"Please understand me, I want to know how things are going on inside you."

"No, no," Hedwige replied, embarrassed and jealous of her secret.

"I want to see my child."

"What a strange idea! How childish you are! What do you expect to see? A beam of light under a door?"

"I want to see this little creature and without further ado. Promise me," he said in a rage.

She gave in grudgingly because these quarrels exhausted her.

The day Pierre received the large photograph stuck to a piece of card, he leapt in the air and could not contain himself.

"I can hardly see anything. The image…"

In a mist of greyness, the bottom of the ribcage could be made out, the murky shadow of the mother's pelvis and the skeleton of the well-developed child, head low down, knees next to the chin, making a motionless somersault, with the ringed backbone filling out, and looking like a shrivelled-up Peruvian mummy, as in the most ancient human tombs, as in Neolithic earthenware jars.

"How ugly it is!" said a disappointed Pierre.

"It's beautiful," said an enthusiastic Hedwige.

A few days later, it was something else. This time, Pierre wanted to listen to the heart of the embryo beating on the stethoscope. He bent over this large inhabited cavern that was Hedwige's body, pressed his forehead to hers, plugged in the two earpieces, listening carefully for the whirr, for the delicate throbbing that was his child's heart.

"If you continue to harass me like this, he'll have convulsions," cried Hedwige in exasperation.

CHAPTER XXI

H EDWIGE WENT INTO her husband's bedroom, having made sure that he had gone out.

High-ceilinged, bright, with its fine natural lime-wood panelling, sparsely, yet nicely furnished, it was the most attractive room in the house. At the time they moved in, Hedwige had insisted that Pierre should have this room; seeing what his boisterousness had done to it, she must have regretted doing so. But Hedwige, out of loyalty, did not allow herself any regrets. She made up for this by taking advantage of Pierre's absences to slip into his bedroom and impose her order on the disorder. Left to Pierre, the clutter sprang up with the spontaneity of a virgin forest. It was enough for him to breathe and bedlam ensued. He had an astonishing gift for disorganization and truly brilliant inconsistency; he created chaos in less time than it took the Demiurge to put an end to it.

Hedwige sat down on the bed, or rather on some shoe-trees, the *Journal de la Société asiatique* and a bull—a Hittite gold idol—that had been left on the bed. Staring distractedly, she made a list of the work that awaited her. By sitting lower down, level with the chairs, she has a better view of the things left on them in successive layers. As if rubber boots and a pair of fourteen-kilo dumb-bells were not enough to crush and dirty the ancient velvet of the *bergère*, Pierre has left a suitcase precariously balanced on Hedwige's favourite chair. Furthermore, he has no idea how to pack or unpack a suitcase. This luggage has been lying there since he returned from Aix-la-Chapelle, a few days previously. The tube of shaving soap has burst and stained his ties, a flask of cognac is still leaking over a pullover whose roll-neck collar conceals some hairbrushes. Pierre was due to leave in a few days' time for Turin and he had left everything in a mess. An hour before the train, it would be enough for him to throw in a few more things to add to the jumble and shut the case without having emptied it, firstly by kneeling on it, then by treading on it. "Please, I beg you, let me do your packing," she implored him. "Certainly not! I wouldn't be able to find anything!" he replied.

Today, Hedwige merely tidies up some of the smaller things, because her belly is too heavy. She had decided that she would gradually return the room to its period style, to its original perfection, and she would stop him making faces and playing the shipwrecked victim. Hedwige adored her home as though it were a living creature and it pained her to see it ruined. A puddle of water that was now evaporating was staining the patterned oak panels of a Louis XIV parquet floor. Pierre must have been drying himself in front of the radiator. For some mysterious reason, he never washed in the bathroom. A razor blade covered in facial hairs lay in the violet cavern of the fireplace in front of which, goodness knows why, he had been shaving. And he must have thought there was insufficient light, because he had tugged away at the damask curtains, which hung, torn from their rings, and resembled a mizzen sail put up during a gale, with their broken cords looking like discarded halyards.

Hedwige, who sometimes argued with Pierre, but would never ever dream of blaming him, was for the first time consumed with indignation. This shambles was really unbearable! It was as if he did it deliberately. There was not one single pretty object that he had not broken, not one pleasant moment he had not disrupted, not one pleasure he had not rushed.

In the waste-paper basket full of cigar ash (torn-up letters, on the other hand, were placed in the ashtray) Hedwige found a box of chocolates that Placide had brought. She grew furious at the sight of these pralines, which she had put aside to give to her mother; the previous day, Pierre had eaten a few of them, without enjoying them, simply because he could not stop himself from opening the box by pulling off the silk ribbons and the gold string, and tearing the whole thing apart. He really was impossible.

Hedwige pulled herself together and felt ashamed of her petty-mindedness. Was she going to hold these trivial things against Pierre? Against Pierre, who was so generous, who always came home laden with flowers, his pockets full of funny, useful, ingenious and well-chosen little presents, Pierre who, only yesterday, had torn down some hawthorn blossom for her and the honeysuckle she loved from trees in the lane, and who had come home all scratched and with his hands bleeding. Hedwige felt moved for a second… just enough time to notice beneath the chest of drawers, from which Pierre had pulled off one of the engraved handles, a scarf that he had torn to shreds instead of undoing the knot. He had bought a dozen of them, just as he bought everything, in large quantities and, not knowing what to do with them, he lost them, gave them away indiscriminately, wrapped them around his visitors' necks, just as at table he piled all the food that was left on the plates of his guests, who had already eaten their fill and were begging for mercy: for Pierre to be happy, the plate had to be empty, the course completed, everything consumed and the meal brought swiftly to its conclusion. Generosity or wastefulness? An odd sort of generosity! Tips and never any charitable donations, bills paid twice or three times over, and never anything for grateful colleagues. "And yet he is good," thought Hedwige.

She broke off and considered this notion: was he good? Is someone good when he is not even aware that others exist, when he does not even give himself time to look at them, to pause when faced with worry, grief, anger? Did Pierre even notice when people recoiled, shuddered, frowned, or the actual fear he aroused when, carried away by one of his impulses, he sped off and people fled for fear of being knocked over by him? If Pierre were good, he would be surrounded by people; yet he was alone.

Hedwige tried to think of someone who loved Pierre, but she could not produce a single name; pals, and not many at that, but no friend. She would have liked to feel sorry for him, to invent excuses for him, but the defence turned into an indictment each time. She felt remorse; she did not feel bad about having these wicked thoughts; what bothered her was having them without Pierre realizing or being aware of them. She would have liked to confide in him and for him to justify himself. She would have liked to accuse him, sentence him and forgive him. Explanations are one of the great pleasures of living together. But to talk to Pierre heart to heart was impossible; on his better days, he listened distractedly, out of politeness, while thinking of other things. More often, no sooner had Hedwige begun speaking than Pierre would reply impatiently: "And so? Conclusion? Let's get to the point!" "To get to the point" was his favourite phrase. To get to the point of what? Can one not talk without getting to the point of things? Must one always run head down, as if pursued by the Furies? What crime could he have committed that was so horrible that his whole life should be a forward rush!

Hedwige tried hard to resist the image of Pierre that was inflicting itself on her, of Pierre pointlessly savaging objects, friendships, boxes of chocolates; she did not want to allow herself to be submerged by the great wave of bitterness that had taken hold of her when confronted by this disorder and wastefulness. She stood there gazing at the clothes from the previous day, still all muddy due to Pierre having dashed through puddles; dashed in pursuit of whom? Of what?

She tried to visualize her husband's face, his eyes and the lovely way they shifted so quickly to the corners of his eyelids, his taut nose that resembled a jib at the front of his face, his pointed and adventurous chin. But the image was fading; all she could see was a graph, a mechanical drawing, a robot with a hundred crooked arms that whirled around the room, grabbing at things, breaking them, grabbing at her, whirling her around and endangering her, her and the child.

The door sprang ajar rather than opened; Pierre was already in the middle of the room and was glaring at Hedwige, who was bent over a drawer.

"What are you doing there?" he cried, "why are you rearranging my things?"

"I'm putting them into some sort of order," Hedwige replied curtly.

"You're putting them into *your* sort of order."

"What does that mean, *my* sort of order? The whole world knows what orderliness is and that there is none where you are concerned."

"My sweet Hedwige," said Pierre, "you must realize that the notion of orderliness is very subjective. It's the outward projection of an inner state."

"So," cried Hedwige in a voice that had grown shrill, "so all this jumble, is it you? Is this your soul?"

"Why not? It's a little whimsical, but it's alive. Your own bedroom is pretty, but it looks like a Decorative Arts exhibition."

"And yours looks like a dustbin."

"Thank you... Listen," he said, more conciliatory, "I didn't come to discuss spring-cleaning, but to take you to see Madame Osiris... the clairvoyant."

He began to laugh:

"Her salon is full of women cooks, but I've been promised favourable treatment. She will tell us whether it's a boy or a girl..."

He paused. Hedwige had turned her back on him and was looking out of the window so as not to see this irritating, grimacing, fanatical man.

"What's the matter, Hedwige? Won't you come with me? Come now, pull yourself together! Whoever loves me follows me."

Hedwige turned round, her teeth gritted:

"I won't follow you."

"So you don't love me?"

"Not at this moment, certainly."

"Because of... because of my disorderliness?... Because of the clairvoyant? Don't be stubborn now, come."

He felt that he had chosen the wrong moment, that he had been wrong to insist, that by calling on Hedwige unexpectedly he had put her nerves on edge and was making himself odious, but he could not stop himself; upsetting Hedwige, hurting her and almost horrifying her were a good thing; they satisfied a spitefulness that was becoming exacerbated within him.

"Go to the clairvoyant on your own," said Hedwige, "don't look into the crystal ball, you won't see happiness there; you can read the tea leaves: your future is darkness."

All of a sudden she began to cry, her head buried in her scarf, with little choked sobs.

"I'm frightened, something's going to happen. You burn the candle at both ends. Life can't go on like this, you'll wear yourself out, you'll go mad! And I'll become a nervous wreck! There's a curse upon you. Mother can sense it too."

Pierre stopped her severely:

"Your family support me fully, I know. That's not the question. What matters to me is to know whether you're tired of me, whether you refuse to follow me towards greatness. Hurrying is my own particular greatness…"

He looked at his wrist automatically.

"There we go, now my watch has stopped! This flawless chronometer is quite impossible!"

He took it off and handed it to Hedwige.

"Have it repaired for me right away. I can't live without a watch."

Hedwige took the gold strap with its square dial and looked at it with loathing.

"My engagement present," she said.

With a violent gesture, she hurled it out of the window. Pierre stared at her in astonishment for a moment, then he leapt up onto the window casement which he closed, fearful no doubt for his black, nickel-plated perpetual-motion pendulum.

"My beautiful chronometer!" he said sorrowfully, standing in the midst of his clutter.

Hedwige looked at him with disapproval, but, having calmed down, she then said nothing.

Pierre was lost in thought; a long silence ensued. She looked at him, secretly anxious; Pierre's silences always culminated in some dreaded new initiative. She could feel the baby moving, she closed her eyes and relished the symphony that was playing inside her; flooded with happiness, she had completely forgotten Pierre's presence; all at once she felt him by her feet, leaning against her knees.

"Listen to me, Hedwige," he said in a low voice, "this child…"

"This child?"

She braced herself.

"I can't go on like this," he continued. "It's making me ill. Yes, I know what you're going to say; don't make fun of me; you're the one who's not well, but I swear to you that I am just as much and even, from a certain point of view, more so… I've thought a great deal… Just now, you were furious, but now you're calmer… and I know that you love me; don't you want to help me and release me from this torment?"

"I don't understand," said Hedwige.

"I have an idea… I've found something that can solve everything."

"But what, solve what?"

"Very well… what I mean… is that you can equally well give birth at seven months as at nine."

Hedwige drew away from him; she stared at him, speechless, her face pale.

"Yes. The child will thrive wonderfully. Keeping it two months more than necessary is absurd when one can do otherwise… Don't look at me like that… what I'm suggesting to you is, if not normal, totally reasonable at least… Hedwige, don't make that face… You haven't understood me," he concluded more slowly.

Hedwige pushed him away and stood up.

"You're the one who hasn't understood, unfortunately, how inhuman what you're suggesting is! Waiting for this baby is my supreme delight, it's what I live for! And I'm not even waiting for it; this little creature exists, just as alive as if he or she were already living with us. I could never be happier than I am bearing him snugly inside me;

everything I feel, any discomfort I experience, is sweet to me. Can't you see that I'm desperate for it to last and for the child to be perfect, and you, with your cruelty, want to take it away from me! If you were a human being instead of a locomotive, I would try to make you understand how I feel, but what's the point?"

"I beseech you, Hedwige… Please agree… It would be wonderful if you were to agree…"

She rose to her feet, firmly balanced on her large, heavy belly, and looked him straight in the eyes, no longer with anger, but with hatred.

"You're a lunatic."

"I have the address of a doctor who is willing."

"Shut up."

"Hedwige, darling…"

"Get out! Get out! I don't want to see you again."

Hedwige had become so distant, so fearsome, so Boisrosé that Pierre left, slowly for once.

CHAPTER XXII

THE "YEAR 1000 EXHIBITION", brought from Paris to Chicago, was due to open in a fortnight's time under the auspices of the Field Museum.

Pierre set off for America like a cannon shot.

He took with him some precious pieces that he hoped to sell in the United States once the exhibition was over, European booty that exacerbated the stripping bare of the Old World without embellishing the New. But antique dealers care little about such concerns: they practise their profession with the same insensitivity as the castrator who deprives the young thoroughbred of its illustrious offspring.

Pierre spent the four-day sea crossing stretched out on deck, in a state of total inertia, watching the horizon rising and falling, because for men like him there can be no half-measure: they must either be moving about at breakneck speed or else lethargic, like all those who can only find their equilibrium in movement, in aeroplanes, or in racing dinghies that depend on their own forward motion and sail on supported by something harder than a keel, by the sea that solidifies speed.

Pierre had forbidden himself to think of Hedwige: we know how little these prohibitions mean. It only required her image, kept strictly at a distance, to take advantage of a thousandth of a second's lack of concentration and creep into his visual range; and Pierre would relive Hedwige's departure for Saint-Germain, that frenzied haste when, in a flash, her suitcases were packed, filled and spirited away with a speed that Pierre himself could not have matched. He had watched all this without lifting a finger to detain his wife, almost comforted by the notion that he would not see her any more. The separation would not be long, six weeks at the most, which, by affording him a change of surroundings and keeping him busy with work, would bring him, without his noticing, to the delivery date so eagerly awaited. Thanks to this journey, Hedwige would live, Pierre would live. He admitted to himself honestly that he exhausted her more than any great sorrow could, more than any long illness. When she cried out "You're killing me!" she was not speaking figuratively; she felt that she was in danger of dying, and the child with her. Each day he crucified them a little more.

Could he have restrained himself?

"No, I can't. I can't get my breath back, I can't slow down, I can't stop; the entire drama of my being is contained in those two words: *I cannot.*"

The crossing of the Atlantic by steamship, New York and its feverishness, the energy Pierre had to expend as soon as he arrived in Chicago and the rapid success of the business dealings he had been involved in, made him feel much better. The very day before the opening, the Western museums had acquired everything he had brought from Europe, including the Mas Vieux cloister, which the city of Chicago had bought and paid for cash on the nail, having long been jealous of the little French cloister of the same period that overlooked New York, from the top of Washington Heights.

Since people were surprised that he had not waited for the opening of an exhibition at which he would doubtless have found collectors whose private offers might have been higher than those of the museums, Pierre replied: "I have never made money except by selling too early."

"I was wise to come," he told himself. "America agrees with me. This dry, golden autumn stimulates me.

"I like the rhythm of these great urban ganglions, the excitement of the traffic and the bouncing of the elevators at the top of buildings as straight as avenues; the conductivity of all this American material puts me in a state of healthy intensity.

"Life is easy here; there is so much good humour at every level of this cosmopolitan overexcitement! After all! Here is a country where everything lives at the pace of the Stock Exchange. I can escape from the continuous crucifixion of the old continent which used to get me down. In this way I can prove what I have always maintained, that frenzy can espouse order, and that firmness cannot stand in the way of passion."

Two weeks went by, then a month. Pierre was no longer having fun.

"It seems to me that my admiration for quick-start police motorcycles with their sirens that give them the right of way, and my enthusiasm for the easy attraction of avenues that are straight and uncluttered with cars, is exhausted.

"I'm beginning to become blasé about the pleasure of signing bills everywhere instead of wasting precious time handing over and receiving money. Is it rather sad to see the appeal of new things fade like this? I am scarcely aware any more of how satisfying it is to find telephones in every room instead of 'having a phone' as one does in Paris... and

I no longer go into raptures about the convenience, very relative furthermore, of being pursued by long-distance calls as I move around each day.

"Nor do I take any pleasure in seeing a boy from the Western Union appearing as if out of a box the moment I ring, to take my telegram that I can no longer reconsider, which I regret immediately afterwards.

"Yes, all this is convenient… but not essential. A simplification of the daily task, that's all. It's the work of Slav and German immigrants; they have organized their new nation according to ultra-fast methods, the former out of laziness and the latter by being practical. But they have not succeeded in endowing Americans with the tragic meaning of life, by which I mean its brevity. They are actually idlers; in this, they have remained Anglo-Saxons."

The man in a hurry soon realized that not only did he not care for all this comfortable transatlantic galloping around, but he even took pity on it.

In reality, there was no galloping at all.

And the day even came when American apathy infuriated him even more than French disorganization.

"Before the Americans, who ever thought about relaxing? Everything here is an excuse for parties and dawdling…

"The United States is the largest unemployment work-shop in the world.

"It's Sunday twenty hours a day.

"To say nothing of standardization, which has reached such perfection that everything stops all the time.

"A New Yorker is always free for meals.

"All American women are dying of boredom."

Pierre visited Wall Street on a day following a wave of panic: the slump in business appalled him.

"How could I have thought at the beginning of my stay that America lived at a Stock Exchange pace!" he wondered.

He walked through the Chinese district: they were letting off firecrackers in honour of Lao Tzu. In Harlem, the centre of the darkest idleness, the Negros slept all day long. In Chicago, crowds lounged around for hours on end, beneath the first of the spring rainfalls, just to watch gangsters being buried or film stars getting married. Only the Italians from Cicero, once the importers of *farniente*, toiled.

"From the moment of my arrival at the wharf, from the moment the immigration officer with preposterous slow-ness checked the questionnaire containing the seventy-two queries asked of immigrants, up until my departure when crowds of friends will come and laze around on deck, not because they like me, but because they have nothing better to do—it was, it is and always will be like this. With every voyage, the steamship brings back from Europe Yankee idlers who are half asleep, drunk or who out of careless-ness have remained on the wrong side of a gangway that has actually been drawn up and lowered again ten times over. America, a land discovered by people who had zest in them, consists of nothing more than hold-ups, vacations, strikes and gaping onlookers.

"If I had to stay here," he sighed when he saw New York again on his return from Chicago, "I'd die of ankylosis and paralysis. I must leave without waiting for the end of the Exhibition.

"Leave for where…

"For the lethargic Orient?

"For languorous Rio?

"For indolent Oceania?

"For the stillness of Tibet?

"A little organization, for heaven's sake! A little concen-tration. I must know where I want to go; let's close our eyes, let's imagine these journeys. Where do I feel drawn to out of a deep-seated need…? Obviously, to a railway station first of all; a train, no matter which one! The circle line? Going round and round New York endlessly? Come on now, I am in full possession of my mind, after all… What

I need is something to do immediately, this very day. I can't remain in this room, it would drive one to suicide!"

All of a sudden, he remembered having accepted an invitation from an important daily newspaper to fly over New York at sunset this same evening. He was saved.

"Let's go," he exclaimed joyfully, "let's go to this very American occasion."

Pierre arrived at the elevated railway. Four parallel lines ran south-east to north-west, the two outer ones for the stopping trains, and in the middle, four tracks reserved for the express trains. He took the stopping train.

The time? Shortly after the ebb tide that had already emptied the business district.

The place? Downtown, where the first streets start, in the direction of the Bronx, that is to say New York's back of beyond; along one of those parrot ladders, vertical avenues, crossed by side roads, that lead to the north.

The setting? A suspended iron bridge with a plunging view over dirty windows, low roofs and, further on, over offices and clean windows, brilliantly lit hotels, apartments that were initially simple, then more and more luxurious, and then, once more, humble ones.

Pierre is almost the only person in his carriage: a few office cleaning ladies, some delivery drivers hanging by one arm from the straps—all these people immersed in their evening newspaper as though in a printer's bath. A toothpaste advertisement provides travellers with a mirror in which Pierre inspects himself.

"I look very well."

Even though he is only in his early thirties, it is hardly credible, so drawn are his features, so greying is his hair at the top of his skull, beneath his black hat. His nose has become a bird's beak. Not only has his face lost the youthful and charming glow it once had, but his physiognomy, that is to say the unchanging part of our face on which doctors or gypsy women base their diagnoses or prognoses, had much altered during the trip. His forehead has become wrinkled like a beach at low tide, the wrinkles have merged with his flesh, leaving blue gaps at the temples, and the bags beneath his eyes are those of a man who is worn out.

"This train stops at all the stations, yet it appears to be moving really quickly. One is so close to the houses that the sight of all the windows right in front of you is like so many punches in the face."

Pierre is sitting down and not doing anything, but he has the feeling that he is being active. These windows that flash by strike him as moments from a life that will never return. The electric rails draw him onwards with the same imperious invitation as the logic that hurls him into the future. Restrain himself? Never! Let others get bogged down in their individual labyrinth, become entangled and lulled into this and that course; he knows he is gripped by a power vindicated by supreme necessity.

Having arrived at a main station, he changed trains and caught the express.

"I'm inexhaustible; no sooner do I move onto this line than I'm already thinking about being in the car that is waiting for me. How I love this noise of the wind whistling in my ears! What I'm doing excites me and urges me on; I forget about anything that delays me; I'm quite content to live in the following moment in this way. I don't exist, I pre-exist; I'm a predated man; no, I'm not a man, I'm a moment!"

And so his troubles do not leave him! He is building his mental constructions in that vast wasteland, the future. The closer he gets to them, the land shrinks back. Pierre will end up by building on a wild ass's skin, on a diminishing asset, as narrow as the rock upon which New York stands. In any case, the city and he have no foundation, they are rootless: weak and unsteady like the present moment.

The express went at a faster speed than the stopping train, but because it no longer skimmed the houses, one didn't notice them. Pierre was amused by this illusion of appearing to go more slowly by going faster.

"The train still sings its own song, a sort of popular

refrain from the axle, an opera chorus tune from the rails: 'On we go! On we go…!' Perhaps the aeroplane in which I shall be sitting in a few moments' time will make me feel nostalgic for this train? It may even explode in the air, lose a wing, catch fire? 'Monsieur rushes about too much,' Chantepie said to me when, in my haste, I banged my head against the breakfast tray. I'd already like this plane to crash.

"I can't keep still any more… I'm missing all the stations, these stations my train passes through without warning, without crying 'watch out' or '*gare*' (what a strange expression!)"

Pierre burst out laughing at this ridiculous thought. A rather dreadful laugh.

His face was pale. His fingers were shaking. He was becoming an exaggerated version of the person he was. This caricature of himself at this moment, in this hit-and-run train suspended above buildings that were gigantic and had no authenticity, was nevertheless the most accurate expression of the truth. He who believed so firmly in the straight line was spinning around dead ends, his exuberant soul, his scatterbrained imagination and his bogus mentality lost in mazes. Like everybody else, this emancipated man carried his master on his shoulders.

*

The cars were waiting on 155th Street.

Pierre, together with the guests, climbed into a superb promotional vehicle which sped off. The speedometer touched 150 kilometres an hour without one noticing, with the nonchalance of a child's scooter.

Cemeteries. Tombstones. Golf courses. Mausoleums. The last trolleybuses. Summer restaurants. Not one tree. A stiff breeze. A copper-coloured sunset.

Woodlawn Cemetery... Pelham Park... Casanova...

A nasal voice in his ears announced the names of places, of beauty spots along the way, but Pierre was not listening or looking round. An inner chill froze his limbs.

"I don't feel well," he said to himself. "No matter... Let's be in a good mood... This excursion is delightful, only somewhat long... Let's be alive... After all, my tragedy is a comic drama, not a cosmic one."

Having made this effort to pull himself together, he began to feel anxious again.

"I feel more out of breath than if I'd done a five-hundred-metre sprint... When I get back to Paris I must see a doctor."

They arrived at the aerodrome. The wind had dropped. The windsock was pointing towards the lawn. A fine aeroplane, as platinum-coloured as a film star, the Lockheed Superbus 999, was waiting for them, surrounded by photographers.

They took off.

Powered by four engines, the plane rose into the sky as straight as Jacob's ladder while the stewardess placed in front of them, on plywood tables, some drinks that were tilted by the perpendicular ascent, tilted as when one drinks.

"It's really strange," thought Pierre, "I've travelled in succession on a stopping train, an express, a fast car and a state-of-the-art aeroplane, that is to say I've increased speed each time, and the faster I go the more things appear to slow down. We're doing five hundred kilometres per hour, and it seems to me that we're not moving. Here I am suspended in total space, detached from the world; everything becomes never-ending; the bigger it is the less it moves; the port barely drifts out of sight because it is enormous; the sea becomes stiller the more it becomes ocean.

"I probably didn't see the universe looking turbulent because I was looking down on it. We only go fast at ground level. As soon as I step back to take a look at my old planet, it seems dead to me. Speed is a word invented by the earthworm."

All at once Pierre felt a terrible pain in his left side. He searched for a cause, because he liked to understand in order to guess what might happen next.

"We climbed too quickly," he thought.

Abruptly, his pulse fluttered and his body grew limp. It seemed to him that a suddenly exposed gun was firing at him from point-blank range. A two-hundred-kilo weight fell on his thoracic cage beneath which he crumpled, as if his ribs, which had become concave, were going to touch his backbone. He wanted to resist this dreadful feeling; the more he tried to expand his chest, the more he felt himself pierced by a burning thrust. It was as though a spear had remained stuck inside his body.

The plane banked to the right and showed its passengers the marvellous sight of the new docks in the Hudson with all the jetties, which resembled the rays of an aureole, whereas the tip of Manhattan, which was made to look as though it was on fire by the setting sun, was dipping its bows like a red-hot iron into a sea streaked with barges, lighters and tugs bewigged with black smoke. Pierre saw nothing; he could no longer breathe or move his neck.

The pain reached his shoulder, passed under his armpit like a sling, and made his arm numb as far as the elbow, as far as his little finger. He sweated, his teeth chattered, his temples were trapped in an iron door that was closing. He had no time to think: "But wait a minute, I'm not going to explode in mid-air," not even time to call out: "Go down, because I'm dying!"; he would simply pass away in his seat without anyone being aware.

What a comfort it would be if the four engines had suddenly exploded and he had been hurled down from a height of ten thousand feet!

He clenched his teeth, his eyelids, the palms of his hands, the small of his back, his nostrils, his toes; he squeezed one part against the other, just as the oyster clamps its shells tightly against attack from the knife, everything in his body that was paired or twinned. One moment he was bent double and the next he was huddled up and rolled into a ball so as to allow the torture as little surface as possible.

The stewardess, wearing white and heavily made-up, passed down the aisle and brushed against him without him being able to call or cry out, so immobilized was he by a needle of iron, so much did it seem to him that the slightest movement would cause him to break apart, the slightest pause in his resistance smash him against the partition.

Explosions took place one after another inside his head, alarm bells that reduced him to pieces. He pouted so as to keep his lips away from his teeth, which would have sliced them off instantly. Stabbed, battered and ripped apart, his only thought was to curl up small, to huddle up while waiting for the attack to end. Be it life or death, at the point he had reached either could only mean a reduction in his suffering. A paroxysm of this kind does not endure. The organism either yields or it recovers.

All around him, people were exclaiming. The passengers were rushing over to the west side, their faces lit up by the sunset like Sioux wearing warpaint; their gazes were converging below; noses were flattened against the windows the length of the aisle; shrieks of admiration echoed against the metal partitions. Sparks crackled: interviews were being given over the cordless phone.

All of a sudden, Pierre had the impression that rescuers with large shovels were digging him out of the avalanche that had fallen on him. The oxygen was filtering into his lungs once more, his pulse was steadying itself. A moment later, he could even expel the air from his ribs, which could now move again. The spear that had perforated him still hacked into him as it withdrew, but at last it came out. The nails were being removed from his Cross.

He subsided into feelings of well-being and he set foot again among sensations that were unpleasant but ordinary: nausea, headache, intermittent electric shocks in his hands and feet. The shadowy cone which he had entered ebbed away and the light reappeared as soon as he was able to open his eyes.

"Death is a slow and weighty animal," was his first thought, once he found he was free of pain. "When I almost killed myself in a car at Saint-Vallier, I had already understood this."

His attack had lasted for quite a while, since the sun had set and the aeroplane was now returning to its base. Wrapped in his overcoat, with his hat over his eyes, no one had noticed him.

The plane was already lowering its undercarriage, rather as pigeons that are about to land on a roof extend their legs, hidden beneath their bellies.

Just as Pierre was setting foot on the cement landing area that was surrounded by reporters, the organizers insisted he say a few words in the microphone about his aerial impressions. Still shaking, still alarmed at having been in such pain, he did not know how to refuse.

"Every time the genius of one man has conquered the inertia of matter, his parents and friends have dismissed him as restless, God has punished him and fate has struck at him. In short, everybody is always in agreement that Prometheus should be chained to his Caucasus, everybody including the vultures and the journalists."

Nobody understood a thing about these words spoken in a panting voice, in an inarticulate language, by a "French guy" who shuffled from one foot to another like a turkey on a hot plate. But they were taken for enthusiasm.

CHAPTER XXIII

Pierre hopped on the first ship leaving for Europe, even though he had booked his cabin on the second.

Curtailing your schedule is unwise: you are greeted by solitude. Not being expected, Pierre found a Paris unconcerned with him, an empty apartment, an absent wife. Not even a note from her. All that the concierge handed to the new arrival was a bundle of administrative bills, each more threatening than the other, and meter readings. Hedwige's cupboards were empty, she had taken away her dresses, her underwear, her furs. She had never been back. She had had her post forwarded to Saint-Germain.

According to Pierre's calculations, the birth was due to take place in a fortnight's time. Separated from the present, evicted from the future, he sat down in the centre of a drawing room that had become as vast as the steppes, feeling astonished at the havoc that absence can bring; his trunks, one tall, the other long, set down their geometrical shapes with complete lack of consideration among the fretted, grumpy-looking armchairs. Picture frames, which can never remain straight, had been cast more askew by the stillness than by any earthquake. Movement can justify disarray, but disorder that is dead is far more distressing than the most inextricable living mess. The gramophone, with its broken records, looked as though it had received a punch from the piano, the telephone cord had become entangled like ivy around the feet of the standard lamp, the inlaid floor panels had become slightly unstuck due to moisture in the ceiling, the ceiling that was "full of 'oles", as Chantepie would say.

The clutter of objects, the dusty emptiness of this room and the ruined furniture were for Pierre an image of the discord between himself and Hedwige, of the disorder of their love life.

"What would Hedwige say if she were here?" wondered Pierre.

Pierre did not dare call her. He went and prowled around Saint-Germain, waited for her to emerge, and exhausted himself waiting for something that did not happen. He wrote a great deal and sent none of it off.

The less he dared, the more overexcited he became.

Finally, he telephoned his brother-in-law at the office.

"Hello? Pierre here."

"So you're back!"

"How is Hedwige?"

"As well as she can be in her condition."

"When is it due?" asked Pierre.

"In two weeks' time."

"Another two weeks! Are you sure I can't see her before then?"

"I don't advise you to," replied Amyot. "The doctors disapprove."

"Then is it because she's very ill?"

"No, even though she was in a wretched state when she reached us, after she had left you."

"Does she really not want to see me? Does she still hate me?"

Pierre spoke with such passion that the sound of his voice made the microphone crackle, splutter and explode.

"They're afraid," Amyot continued, "that you might do her more harm than good."

"How do you know?"

"I know that Hedwige prefers not to see you…"

"Is she happy, at least?"

"Yes, indeed, very happy, very well looked after. The whole family is there, as you may imagine. They've put a mattress on the floor for the duty nurse and they cook dreadful Negro stuff on the stove."

Pierre exploded:

"So, she doesn't miss me?"

"Not much," Vincent Amyot replied phlegmatically, without appearing to notice his brother-in-law's agitated state. "Not much, not much… She'll be just as wonderful a mother as her own mother was. Basically, that's all that matters to them… How I wish Angélique could have given me a child! You've never understood the Boisrosés: they're vegetables. With Hedwige, at least, you have a plant that is happy to reproduce."

It was agreed that as soon as Hedwige went into labour, Amyot would call his brother-in-law.

Pierre reverted to his solitary stamping around. Nothing stirred in his home apart from Chantepie, whom he had asked to come back. The lift was out of use, the clocks had stopped, the electricity had been cut off. It was the middle of the All Saints holiday period: three million Parisians, bearing chrysanthemums, had set off to suburban and regional cemeteries.

Pierre was bored; he wanted to go out, drawn by the summer weather of St Martin's Day and driven by the violent shock of having nothing better to do, but his legs were numb and he felt breathless and very weary. Along with this sense of languidness came a tiresome feeling of sickness throughout his body, a feeling of deep disgust.

"Midday on All Souls' Day… who on earth can I ring?"

Placide was away. The Mas Vieux was too far. The only recourse in a situation like this are foreigners.

"I find Regencrantz fairly entertaining. I shall invite him."

Pierre had, as it happened, found a letter from the doctor in the post. Regencrantz described his most recent disappointments and the story of his last visa: it was from Labrador that he was now expecting one that had been too long delayed. He was no longer living in Bordeaux, but in Marnes-la-Coquette, with a doctor friend; working for a pharmaceutical products company, his job was to put calves' liver in pills.

"Is it you Regencrantz?"

"Dear Pierre Niox!"

"Come and have lunch."

"Impossible, I'm on duty over the holidays. But why don't you come over here and share my lamb chop."

Pierre dashed off to Marnes and was reacquainted with the wandering Jew's floppy handshake and his passport adventures, filled with dreary incidents. Strengthened by a time-honoured experience of misfortune, Regencrantz knew how to use it, philosophically, to adapt to every situation. Pierre, in turn, described his trip to America in a gay and lively manner.

He ate lunch with his elbows on the table, bent over the tablecloth like a skier on a snow run. With his spoon held out, he lunged at the soup which, in German fashion, the doctor had offered him, and he kept his head over his plate. Regencrantz listened to him, arching his back and slumping farther and farther back as the meal progressed.

"By the way," said Pierre, "a strange thing happened to me while I was in New York. As a doctor, it would be of interest to you. Although I have an iron constitution, it appears that I am not suited to flying. And yet this isn't the first time: I've flown a good many times. Would you believe that in the course of a very short flight, I was overcome with a peculiar ailment, a sort of attack…"

"What do you mean? An attack? Explain yourself better. A headache? Buzzing in the ears?"

Pierre described his blackout while flying. He would normally have related it in a couple of words—as he did with anecdotes that he reduced to the minimum or the stories that he dashed off and summarized so quickly that no one ever understood them—had not Regencrantz, in his anxiety, plied him with questions.

"Will you allow me to listen to your chest? Not here, there's too much noise… I should also take your blood pressure."

After lunch, they went into a nearby building and walked up to the laboratory.

Pierre undressed and bared his chest. Regencrantz listened carefully, in the way people do when they eavesdrop.

"And now, the X-ray."

Regencrantz pressed his face to the frosted-glass screen. The shadow of Pierre's heart rose above the diaphragm with each intake of breath and then dropped down again. In the darkness, Pierre could feel the cold of the glass on his naked chest and he could see Regencrantz's bald head following the motions of his thorax, like a collector searching for the signature on the work of a master.

"Now, lie down here. Don't tense up. Let yourself relax."

An electromagnet crackled behind the screen. In a tube, on the phosphorescent quartz filament, of the type of orchid colour we associate with lightning, Pierre could see a sort of magnetic signature developing and being repeated in interrupted quavers, a bright and irregular cast of his breathing.

"They are my heart's cries expressed luminously," he thought. "What on earth can my heart have to say to that old rabbi Regencrantz?"

In the pitch-darkness, Pierre watched with amazement as the secrets of his body were made legible, his pulse transformed into a coloured ray, his heartbeat covered in sparks, his entire life diverted into this tube.

The doctor switched on the light in silence.

"Well?"

"Are you sure, Pierre Niox, that you had only one attack of the kind you have described to me?"

"I'm certain of it."

Regencrantz nodded absent-mindedly, looked at a note, opened and shut some drawers.

"Come now, Regencrantz, why are you asking me this? Talk to me, for heaven's sake!"

"Given the condition of your heart, I would have thought that you had already had five or six attacks," said Regencrantz hesitantly.

"The condition of my heart? So is something wrong with my heart?"

Regencrantz replied with a wave of his hand that signified nothing, that was merely the outer reflection of an unspoken thought.

Pierre considered the matter. Snatches of medical conversations at the end of dinner parties, items read in magazines or dictionaries all fused together.

"Bend your knees two or three times, if you would…"

"I get out of breath quickly," said Pierre, "but that must be lack of fitness."

"Yes, indeed… Why not?"

"Come on," said Pierre abruptly. "What is it? Tell me what it is straight away! Vasomotor problems? No? False angina? Heavens… the real thing?"

Regencrantz nodded as he pushed away the X-ray machine, which was on a track, with his shoulder.

"And even… well developed, apparently?" Pierre continued insistently.

"By taking care, avoiding muscular strain… keeping an eye on your blood pressure… What's your previous medical history? Nephritis? Scarlet fever?"

"Regencrantz, I don't like being made a fool of… You have either said too much or not enough. You care for me as a friend. Don't make that odd face. What I want to know is whether I'm done for or not. Are you sure it's not intercostal?"

Regencrantz's lips opened, ready to give a harsh verdict.

"Classic stenocardia, unfortunately."

In a deep silence, Regencrantz could hear a blackbird whistling, a car pass by. But none of Pierre's senses were focused on the outside world any longer.

"I know it's relentless, but sometimes one can live for years," he said very quietly at last.

"Sometimes," replied Regencrantz, without much enthusiasm.

Pierre had plunged into a murky, suffocating world where no light or sound reached him.

"How should I consider my attack? As a warning?"

"Yes."

"I'll have many others… I'll know when I'm nearing the end… I'll know, won't I?"

Regencrantz lectured him.

"No chlorides… No tobacco… No staircases."

"None of that is of any interest to me, my dear Regencrantz. One thing alone concerns me, you must understand: I absolutely insist on knowing at what time death will knock at my door."

Regencrantz said nothing, watching Pierre constructing his assumptions like castles of cards.

"What!" Pierre continued, pressing the point, "I really will see death approaching? Don't tell me otherwise, I have arrangements to make."

"Your heart is really thumping. Your left ventricle is not a friend you can depend on when times are bad: that is all I can tell you with any certainty."

"I'm not asking you to cure me, Regencrantz, I know that one doesn't recover. I'm simply asking you to mark out the path… to tell me as precisely as possible how many attacks will there be along the road that leads me to… the cemetery."

"In your heart's present condition," Regencrantz replied slowly, "if I'm to tell you what I think deep down, I don't believe that you would survive another attack."

"The next one would finish me off?"

"Oh, no…" said Regencrantz hesitantly.

The conscientious doctor prevailed over his friend.

"It's very likely," he said drily.

Pierre raised his arms as though he were sinking.

Pierre goes home.

He is a prisoner here between his four walls.

Up until now, the reassuring, breathing parts of a room for him are not the walls, but the doors and windows, because doors open onto what is new, doors allow you to leave; windows are friends; you can cast your eyes through windows, you can throw money out of them, you can communicate with the living. Pierre no longer expects anything at his door; he no longer pays any attention to that window that overlooks a labyrinth with no exit.

He repeats the conversation with Regencrantz to himself: "Do you mean to say, Regencrantz, that the next time… ?"—"It's likely."

Not a trace of mobility or agility in Pierre any longer. He appears to be stuck in cement. He enjoys thinking, but he has lost his sensitivity, he no longer moves around. His footsteps seem as useless to him now as cries from the bottom of a dungeon.

Everything is blocked. There are guards at all the exits. No means of escape.

CHAPTER XXIV

A DAGGER THRUST to the heart: the victim takes a few more steps before falling down dead. A great misfortune can strike and numb simultaneously in this way, paralysing our emotions and anaesthetizing the imagination, while our intelligence goes on ticking over.

The physical assimilation of the disaster begins much later.

We carry the impact within us like a deferred ending whose practical applications we lie in wait for as we glimpse the infernal machine.

Pierre did not fall asleep until the morning. He had spent the night trying to comprehend, forcing himself to translate, no longer into words but into mental images, the great adventure he had embarked upon. He was not in pain, he was not shaking. It seemed to him that all this was happening to someone else. When sleep came, Pierre welcomed it like someone taking opium before enduring torture.

At nine o'clock he woke with a start, thrown from his bed by that sinister music that had not left him when he was asleep and that kept repeating Regencrantz's words: "It's likely… it's likely… it's likely."

"What's to become of me?" he said to himself out loud.

Hearing his own voice piercing the silence, he was seized with a nameless terror. The threat of losing his mind suddenly loomed over him. For the first time, he considered how destructible he was, how easy to upset, how fated he was to be destroyed.

"I am doomed."

He repeated these words, imagining his defeat, his decline and the advance of the invisible enemy towards him.

He remembered stories about people sentenced to death: some show off and curse their executioners, some set themselves up as heroes, while others create fear around them. Pierre envied them: their death had a human aspect at least, a human cause, a date set by human will-power. They are part of what is known and is even commonplace. It is men who have convicted them, men who will come to their aid or who will execute them. Up until their final moment, they will be dealing with men, men for them to plead with or stand up to.

He was entirely on his own and was waiting for something that was absolutely impossible for him to imagine.

"A masked death," he wondered.

He leant against the wall, his eyes staring. Before him,

on the tablecloth, set out lovingly the previous day, lay his most recent acquisitions: a gilt chalice, a sacramental ambry, a length of Sicilian silk.

"What am I going to do with all these?" he said to himself with a perplexed air.

Mechanically, he unfolded the silk, the colour of dried blood.

"It's like the colour of Hedwige's dress."

The thought of Hedwige struck him with such force that he staggered. He felt pain for the first time. It was so unbearable that he feared he might die then and there. The frightened reaction of someone who was very ill spurred him towards his bed where he lay down, breathing carefully.

The mid-morning sun warmed his feet, but he no more felt it than he heard the sparrows singing or the pair of doves cooing. With open eyes, he carefully preserved the calm expected from darkness and closed eyelids. A sense of peace came over him suddenly, the doldrums of the tropics, when the sails of yachts are limp and their reflection in the still water looks like a vampire with its head hanging down from the ceiling.

Fear had left him; fear projects itself into the future and for the time being it was impossible for him to think of the future. A fleeting joy came over him at the thought that his death was a purely individual adventure and one that would only happen to him. (Morally and materially, Hedwige was taken care of.) Was it because death was to cut the thread of his days so prematurely that fate had caused him to live alone so much?

"I'm going to have to organize my life," he said.

The absurdity of this remark made him smile.

"Organize what is already no longer… And yet if I were a believer, what wonderful days would lie ahead!"

A phrase of Turenne's came back to him: "I should like to place some time between my life and my death." Pierre had moved into this no man's land. It was up to him to make God's kingdom out of it.

But he had always lived without God. Uniquely focused on day-to-day realities, the materials for his future constructions, lacking any metaphysical anxieties and indifferent to death, which he never graced with a single thought, he neither denied nor accepted the afterlife; he was simply not bothered with it, having other things to do, frenziedly having to pursue a destiny that had now left him alone beside the grave.

"I can't go on automatically, like a doddering old fool, doing things that I won't see completed. How shall I fill my time?" he asked himself in a loud voice.

Ever since the previous day he had constantly been talking out loud, as if to disturb the silence before it became eternal, and also so as to remain on good terms with this outmoded self who would soon have no voice at all. When words are very solemn, one is inclined to say them aloud; and for Pierre, nothing could be light-hearted any more.

"I was a man of action," he said. "What shall I do now?"

He forced himself to review the occupations that were still possible. For obvious reasons, almost everything was precluded: how could he do sport, go on journeys, take trips, do any gardening, do business, make plans? Even reading, for other people a relaxation, an education, a time for reflection and daydreaming, was an acute form of action for him, because he read so that he could take part wholeheartedly in the most spirited exploits of great sea captains, explorers, adventurers, his heroes.

"Action presupposes the future before all else. Regencrantz has wiped out my future. The future was my life. How shall I live without life?"

He felt himself lost in a foreign land, a land without clocks, a land whose language he knew nothing of because no one speaks there in hours, minutes and seconds, a land in which present-day money no longer has any currency, where the words "precede", "follow", "early", "late" no longer have any meaning. He seemed to have lost all depth. Something vital, something essential had deserted him.

"It's funny," he said dreamily, "I have the feeling that I've been operated on by myself."

Not for a moment did he think of looking after himself in the way the doctor had prescribed. Whether he died immediately, in a month, in three months, what did it matter? Even yesterday, the future was for him an infinite space in which his fearless momentum was driving him beyond all weariness. Placing a limit on infinity was to deny it and to instantly destroy the patient.

"I am in a void in which I recognize nothing. I've been marooned in mid-ocean, without any possible rescue, on a rubber mattress…"

Pierre was amazed that he did not feel the distress of someone who is shipwrecked. An entirely new feeling of apathy came over him and caused his eyelids to droop. He dozed off.

He had a dream: he was dead and he was keeping watch over himself, astonished to see a Pierre Niox who no longer moved. It was appalling, this body solidified by the disappearance of life, this man in a hurry suddenly pinned, weighed down for all eternity. With a knife, he opened the veins of this corpse and saw that no blood flowed. In one of those symbolic puns that are the wordplay of dreams, Pierre murmured:

"The man who was squeezed for time really has been squeezed to the last drop!"

Rooted to the spot, he contemplated his funeral mask,

his wordless mouth, his soft, pasty flesh and that inner smile, half mocking, half blissful, that the dead have. That expectation, so full of hope, which had been his life's true companion, had deserted him. His speed of motion had forsaken him… And nobody would ever know how quick he had been!

"How are you feeling?" Pierre asked his double, and the latter responded without opening his plump white, swollen eyelids, which looked like poached eggs.

"Well. Still much calmer."

Pierre awoke with a start and remembered his dream. It was true that nobody would ever know how quickly he had been able to move. No one would ever be grateful to him for the efforts he had made always to be more dextrous and more nimble. He would watch enviously as flowers were laid on the tombs of the great men who were his neighbours. "I, too, was a hero in a way, a sunny and invigorating man," he would cry out, "and one who has cracked the whip a good deal to bring nature out of her rut! I, too, had some merit!" But they would pass by without hearing him.

He had lived too quickly to be noticed.

The telephone rang for a very long while, so long that Chantepie himself heard it and rushed in:

"Monsieur is not replying to the phone?"

"No. Switch it off. Tell the concierge that I'm away to any callers. I don't want to see anyone. You yourself, Chantepie, make yourself as invisible as possible."

Pierre remained alone in the empty apartment, alone with a lucid intelligence sustained by a sick heart in which the blood that normally gushed from left to right only came in dribs and drabs. All the time, he could see on the wall, as he had on Regencrantz's screen, a large, dense aorta, petrified and almost rock-like. All he could feel in his body was his ever-watchful heart, balanced precariously on its tip, like a spinning top. For how long would the little oscillating movement continue to function?

Every evening, after going to bed, lying in the silent house as he did when he used to wait in vain for Hedwige, Pierre vaguely wondered why he felt shattered. What treasure had he been robbed of? Yes, it was true that due to swift action, due to the hasty procedure, carried out with more devastating speed than any of his own efforts, something had ended the moment Regencrantz's head had nodded, something that was no doubt his raison d'être. Pierre was just beginning to sense that that indefinable thing was Time, his beloved Time, which was deserting him.

He owed everything to time: his originality, his verticality, his expansiveness. In losing that quantifiable ether that he strode through in buoyant, joyful leaps, he had lost everything.

"Now," he told himself, "begins the harsh ordeal of surviving, of persevering, of waiting. Me, waiting!"

Over the following evenings, Pierre did not go to bed, preferring to spend the night in an armchair. He did not dare lie down for fear of hearing his heart thumping; as soon as he laid his ear on the pillow, he could nevertheless detect, in the silence of the night, that rumble of thunder, scarcely audible though it was, that terrified him. He remembered the last moments of old Boisrosé, with his mouth open like a fish at the bottom of a boat and that halting breathing of a dying man; the Mas Vieux clearly did not bring happiness.

The thirsty runner, who swallowed up the hours like an ogre and drank up the miles as the earth drinks water, had already come to a stop. He had been blamed enough for being mechanical! With the machinery now broken, the car in the ditch, the motor reduced to silence, Pierre could have walked through a countryside full of gentle creatures and left behind these petty squabbles with human beings that his weaknesses had landed him in. But his fading strength no longer provided him with the means.

Rather than regret a happiness he had never experienced, Pierre might have felt remorse for having sought his sensual pleasures in speed and for having mowed down everything in his way had not merciful fate made him the gift of a child. In the hands of this creature still to be born, he would leave his debit balance and the task of paying his debts to a world that from now on would continue without him.

Once upon a time Pierre used to go to bed without going to sleep; now he went to sleep without going to bed. Sitting up all night, his eyes open, he watched the calm intensifying.

Each morning he repeated the same activities; he washed very slowly, contemplating with disinterest his dumb-bells, which were the same shape as the globe is on the opening pages of atlases, in just the same way as he considered the world itself, without any desire to lift them up any more. Then he would go out and walk along the banks of the Seine at a strolling pace, at times when there are no pensioners around, times when you meet no one apart from fishermen with rods and old men wearing capes, their white silk scarves knotted beneath their white beards, and who look after small children in garden squares. At the age of thirty-five, he was experiencing the *De Senectute* and he was walking about like an old man raising his gaze to look at the houses.

Having become extremely frail himself, it was the outside world that now seemed to him antiquated and destructible.

"It's unbelievable how everything has changed!"

And day by day, he grew increasingly weary of it.

He could feel the soothing sensation invade his being, which no longer struggled, even though his entire life, on the contrary, had been nothing but struggle and his powerful, essential warmth had come from the friction of his personality with the wind, with men, with everything that stood in his way. Today, even the memory of this heroic revolt against enemy forces had been obliterated. Vanquished, he let drop his weapons. It was a kind of joyous defeat that he fully supported. He possessed true despair, which is to say that total absence of hope that resignation and peace bring, not that violent regret, wrongly termed despair, in which a shadow of hope is concealed, just enough to prolong our resistance and our dreadful convulsions.

Ever since the day when, having passed a local ambulance with its flag, its bell and its frosted-glass windows, he had imagined himself falling down in the road, being picked up and dying on the spot, Pierre no longer went out.

"I must live a further fortnight," he thought to himself.

The time required to see, to observe his child, to hand him the "baton" in that relay race in which father and son run against time.

Frightened of stairs, wary of steps, terrified even of pavements, he stayed at home without stirring so that he, too, could be sure of surviving. From his bed, he watched the purple showers, the iris-coloured clouds, the shafts of harsh light over Paris, and, in a direct line with the dome of the Invalides, the Eiffel Tower adorning the Montsouris park with a grid of iron mesh.

All his expectations were dead and buried and his frenzy had abated. His nights were spent reading. He rediscovered Bossuet: at the *lycée*, he had come to adore the great panoramas replete with the smell of incense and gunpowder, those broad glimpses of the lives of children of the nobility that "show all the extremes of human affairs". Today, he preferred to pause over the less dazzling passages, on the muted pages in which Bossuet's voice subsides after his outbursts: "The shepherd finds and captures his lost sheep…"

Leading an empty and limited life, only one view remained to him—the sky, the sky in which he discovered, reflected in vapours, all the earthly attractions of the world he was about to leave, flags, cathedrals, swollen snowscapes, islands in the ocean, continents that formed before one's eyes and unravelled a moment later; all those shapes that one recognizes in passing here on earth and that quickly fade away, flooded him with their unreality.

What detachment! He remained lying on his back, like the sleeper in summer, never wearying of searching for excellence behind the fleeting clouds. One day he found it.

Then, prepared to be patient, he stood ready to wait for She who is always on time for her appointments.

A phone call from Amyot: Hedwige, transported to rue Mozart, had had a daughter.

Looking very pale, Pierre walked slowly, very slowly, down his staircase.

"It would be too bad," he thought, "if I were to collapse down there, if the guard going off duty were not able to give the password to the guard coming on… I am going to see my daughter and it's important that between here and Auteuil nothing should happen to me."

He took his car, raised his foot from the clutch very gently, without letting his tyres, worn down from so much prior acceleration, skid. It was a time for saving money and looking after things. He was holding his steering wheel with an unsteady forefinger; anyone would have thought he was frightened of crashing on the way.

He arrived at last at the clinic. It struck him as remarkable that a man who was about to die should come and haunt the district of Paris in which most children are born.

He stopped at the porter's office and had him make a phone call. He was asked to come up.

He crossed a garden area where nurses were taking the air and where convalescents were manoeuvring themselves about in their own wheelchairs (this method of crawling along made him shudder).

He walked along corridors where trays of stewed apple and biscuits, and bunches of roses removed from rooms overnight, were laid out on tables, among different-sized vases and burettes.

A lift, as vast as an operating theatre, let him out at the second floor. He noticed the baby-scales: it was the maternity floor.

In a moment, he was going to see a small bundle with clenched fists that would look like an elderly, red-faced grandfather, and which would be his daughter…

He reflected that this child would come out of the clinic in two weeks' time, that she would take her proper place in the world, that he would not see her eyes gleam at the sights of all the jewels, just as Aladdin's lamp gleamed at every wish, that he would not take her to the ball and that she would not be in love with him.

He sat down on a painted metal chair, waiting for the nurse who had gone for dinner to return. He could have entered without being announced, but between him and that door—which many men would have charged through with emotion and haste and with legitimate pride at seeing the gift of creation realized that makes an artist out of every father—between him and Hedwige there was a chasm that he could not bring himself to cross. He gazed at the door level-headedly, with the cool detachment of a yogi. With that cruel lack of curiosity that those who are about to leave this life show towards those who are staying there or entering it, he thought of Hedwige just behind that door, less than ten metres away from him, and he remained seated, not feeling the slightest surge of affection for her, without any emotion, without a trace of that abounding passion that had urged him to go and call on his wife. At Saint-Germain, at the Mas Vieux, she had been for him—the most frenzied, the most anxious of men—a symbol of peace of mind. Now he had found a more perfect peace of mind away from her and without her. Death is more soothing than the most sedative of partners.

Hedwige was no longer necessary to him.

*

Behind the door, a child's cry. From the other side of life someone was calling.

Pierre could barely hear the call; he was like a dead man who, through his tombstone, deep in a forgotten cemetery, could hear the cock crow.

"My seed has germinated," he said to himself, "and I am prolonging myself…"

For one last time he almost felt himself living as he did before, that is to say urging himself on, but it was more a vague memory than the reflex itself. He stood up and took a step on the polished linoleum. The newborn baby was still wailing. It was a very tiny human bleat.

"She already has her own song," he thought.

He pressed his ear against the padded wax-cloth material. He could hardly hear the child any more. He was already on the dark bank of a river, and on the far side he imagined a tiny creature with a large head, with the body of a tadpole and bones that were still soft, who was waving at him, giving him a very vague wave that was neither a farewell nor a hello or a "come back"; just the sort of wave you might give if you were allowed only one, one simple wave of recognition, as if to say: "I'm here, I've arrived, you can go away and not worry."

Pierre took no further step forward. He did not open the door. His hand lay motionless on the door handle.

He listened again, but he could hear nothing apart from breathing as regular as the human tick-tock of the heart of this same child that he had once listened to through her mother's body.

"I feel very calm," he said. "Now there's a little watch that Hedwige will not throw out of the window."

The nurse must have forgotten him. Pierre had forgotten his own existence: it was a very long way behind him. He had done his time. His heroic frailty no longer urged him onwards, but now drew him backwards. It seemed to him that he had already left this earth, which he could still see, but without it belonging to him any more.

The man in a hurry had reached the foothills of eternity.

He hesitated a further moment in front of the white door. Should he go in?

"What's the point…"

He shrugged his shoulders, turned around and went back downstairs.

THE END

Paris, November 1940—March 1941

Notes

1   The École Nationale des Chartes is one of France's prestigious *grandes écoles*. It provides training for librarians and archivists.

2   A mocking reference to Madame de Sévigné and the tone of her letters to her daughter, who married the Comte de Grignan.

3   A pioneer of French aviation (1901–36) whose plane crashed mysteriously off the coast of Dakar.

4   The best-known auction house in Paris.

5   A graduate of the prestigious École Polytechnique.

6   'Silent cloisters, monastery vaults/ It is you, dark caverns, you, who know how to love.' (Alfred de Musset.)

7   An allusion to the typically southern hero of Alphonse Daudet's burlesque novel, *Tartarin de Tarascon* and its sequels.

8   Precursors of the *Guides Michelin*, the *Guides Joanne* were a series of guidebooks named after their creator, Adolphe Joanne. After 1919 they became known as the *Guides bleus*.

9   Untranslatable pun. In French *à l'arrêt* means "stationary", whereas *être aux arrêts* means "to be under arrest".

10   In French the word *coureur* can mean "runner", but also "womanizer".

AN ART OF LIVING

A LETTER TO PAUL MORAND
FROM A CLOSE FRIEND

From *Lettres de château* by Michel Déon (Gallimard, 2009)

After a freezing winter, the heatwave of summer 1976 came like a second omen. Who was to blame? The gods? We had fired them. The politicians? They were on holiday and, in any case, they turned out to be the most surprised of all. The press was not yet riding its climate hobbyhorse, which it desperately depends upon for survival. It was not a matter of climate change or of planetary disaster, but of those people dying from indifference, some frozen, others wilting or starving. By printing two-column head-lines on their front pages, newspapers were certainly able to exaggerate the prospect of a world reduced to a ball of ice or a burning desert. An elderly man is not averse to contemplating the notion of this kind of devastation.

In 1976 Paul Morand was eighty-eight years old, my

own age, which today, in 2008, may perhaps draw me closer to him, not that we were ever very far apart, in fact. In one sense, we share the same curiosity: how much time is there left?

Five years previously he had published *Venices*, bringing his work to a close, leaving behind odds and ends in his bottom drawer, but resolved solely to maintain his *Journal inutile* [his "pointless diary", as he himself called it], which stopped on the 10th of April 1976 with his replies to questions posed by a women's magazine:

> ELLE: "What do you think of love today?"
>
> I: "It's the age of the caveman."
>
> ELLE: "What will follow it?"
>
> I: "The age of the barrack room (Mao, Brezhnev)."*

In May 1976, we were expecting him in Ireland. He would be travelling with Claude Gallimard, whose firm published both of us. On transferring flights at Heathrow, where the plane for Shannon was delayed, the departure board announced a shuttle flight leaving for Jersey, a place he did not know. He gave Claude the slip and jumped aboard. It was to be the final flourish of a traveller who behaved as though he were being pursued by the Devil.

---

* Morand is making a pun on the French words *cavernes* and *casernes*.

We know what happened next: Brittany, his wandering around in the Mini Cooper sports car (Paris to Vevey in six-and-a-half hours), from Les Hayes to Bourdonné, from Brittany to Switzerland, from the Château de l'Aile to avenue Charles-Floquet and the emptiness of the vast apartment where everything reminded him of his wife Hélène. Heat discourages one's determination, including the will to go on living. Ever since her death, surrounded by friends though he was, his life had been beset by grief. On the evening of the 22nd of July, the hostile or merciful hand of death gripped him by the throat. He still had enough strength to be driven to the Hôpital Necker, where he died on the 23rd.

We had, of course, been sorry about his volte-face at Heathrow, while at the same time we understood his reasons. As far as Ireland was concerned, an article about hunting in *La Revue des voyages* and a short story, 'Bug O'Shea', had said a great deal.

For him, there remained the Unknown: Jersey.

Up until his last breath, this nomad would reject a French cemetery. His family was buried in a grave in Yerres.* The prospect of finding himself—should we say "waking up?"—in some confused mass, in serried ranks, among the tombs of a large city and having "enemies or strangers" roaming around appalled him. It is understandable. In Trieste, he had

---

* A small town some twenty kilometres south-east of Paris.

chosen "a sort of forgotten pendulum above the Adriatic ogive", the funerary monument to Hélène's family. She was already buried there.

He was delighted to be accepted in this refuge even though he risked being regarded as an intruder:

"It is," he wrote, "a noble stone pyramid, six metres high, a piece of Italian eloquence, above which an angel twice as tall as a human opens a black marble door to the afterlife, as thick as that of an empty safe."

At the same time as he changed burial places, he changed dogmas:

"I shall be watched over by the Orthodox faith towards which Venice has led me, a religion of joyful stillness that continues to speak the language of the Gospels."

He was not frightened of death. He dreamt of it as though it were another life:

"Perhaps there are kindred souls who wait for the deceased and greet them with cries of joy, like newborn babies, on the other side of life…" (1930)

It is true that he did not envisage this final resting place without a few luxuries or liberties. He was born into a well-to-do middle-class background—his family was "radical"—that society so well depicted by Gide or Martin du Gard. At the age of eighteen, after a flirtation with Marxism at a time when it could still be considered chic, he was induced away by the influence of Hélène and that disillusionment which awaits all the world's great "seers".

"Would anyone," he noted sadly, "wish to take responsibility for my suicide or for doing my work?"

One of his last letters illustrates the tone of a correspondence that never became bogged down in generalizations:

FROM P.M. TO M.D:

11th November 1975

Thank you, cher Michel, for your letter of the 25th which arrived the day after a small stir caused by Castries' speech. He spoke of "a Gaullist gathering… a disparate hotchpotch". Debré almost left the Coupole when Maurice Schumann was admitted…

FROM M.D. TO P.M.,

THIRTY-THREE YEARS LATER:

March 2008

Cher Paul, there is nothing to stop one from replying to the same letter twice. The first reply is probably lost. The second rounds it off many years later. If I dare respond to your "cher Michel" with "cher Paul" after addressing you goodness knows how many times with the traditional "cher ami" it's because we are the same age at last: eighty-eight. The years in between have slipped away in the sands of time. Wisely, Paul, you would not have stopped growing older and I would never have caught you up and so at about this time we would be celebrating your 120th birthday. This is also the day that I dare to use your first name. A step not taken lightly. From Venice, in 1974, you complained: "In Paris there's no longer any difference between the pavement and the road: at parties I lose myself among so many first names…"

They would lose themselves in the company of Cocteau who, to hear him talking about his circle of friends, lived in a kindergarten filled with Loulous, Jeannots, Francettes, Zizis, Dédés… I forget, having failed to ask him, which infantile names he used for Stravinsky, Diaghilev, Picasso or perhaps… Einstein.

I notice you have begun to use the familiar *tu* form of address. As a respectful friend I should not display too much humility, even though I find it hard to use *tu* myself, but anyway… let's try. Your time clock stopped at eighty-eight years. Mine also stands at eighty-eight. We are therefore on a relatively equal footing. It's worth pointing out that this number eight has clung to you since your birth. In 1988, you would have reached a century. Reduced to ashes, you have remained tremendously fruitful. I should have made a note of everything that has been published: new editions, unpublished work, updated material, correspondence, preparations for a *Pléiade* edition, and the *Journal inutile*. You have probably never been so much in the public eye since you left us. The volumes of my Morand collection bristle with yellow bookmarks. If I pick up any of your books at random, one of these bookmarks unveils a sentence that catches the eye:

"I should like to die at the age of eighty-seven, thus a further two years of reasonable life, although without much interest."

The trouble is that one doesn't make up one's mind about anything apart from considering suicide as a cowardly but comfortable solution. In this context, who, from the age of five, has not wanted to hang himself time and again, to bleed himself dry or to drown? Our most enduring sorrows stem from childhood. The rest of existence is spent either defying them or rectifying ruins. Oh, I know, remorse, regret and alarm signals blight our later years, but I can see, in your case—apart from brief confessions in which everything is played down—some wonderfully ribald stories: "… sperm still abundant".

Life spoilt you. Even the little games at the Académie amused you. Having taken your seat much later than me, you didn't have time to become blasé or even get irritated. Elected in 1968, you died in 1976, barely eight years later (still that dreaded eight) whereas I accrued thirty years of attendance beneath the Coupole, from 1978 to 2008, in the eighth *fauteuil.** Yet another eight, a sign of fate that should not be overlooked. Of those who took their seats with you, there are only four survivors: Druon, Ormesson, Lévi-Strauss, Marceau.† The secret plotting and the political-literary manoeuvring that went on did not have time to tarnish your satisfaction, following two rebuffs, at being one of the forty. Hélène cared about the Académie as much as you did, if not more. Beneath the aura of the *Immortel*, there is a ferocious struggle for seats at the table. There are certainly the beginnings of many violations of protocol, and hostesses no longer know by heart the dates of election which the hierarchy determined. You did not serve as a young Protocol Attaché in London (1917) without soon understanding the sensitivity of a milieu that frequently has no other proof of its existence on earth. A photograph

---

*   Members of the Académie française—the *Immortels*—are only forty in total and are elected to numbered seats or *fauteuils* on the death of a predecessor.

†   This was written in 2008. In 2014 only Jean d'Ormesson survives. Maurice Druon and Claude Lévi-Strauss died in 2009 and Félicien Marceau in 2012.

of you, probably taken in London, shows you in uniform: white silk trousers, shoes with buckles, tailored frock coat. A visiting card is clipped to it: "Paul Morand, Attaché au Protocole" and, below, in your own handwriting: "What a pretentious young man!"

I never enquired about your behaviour during the sessions at the Académie, at the entrance to the hall and on the way out. Did you maintain the traditional silence of the "newcomer" for a year and only speak when you were asked? Did you, at a doorway, allow Jules Romains or Guéhenno to pass first? They loathed you and led a fairly spiteful campaign against your election. The letter which I partially quoted—the rest will come at the end—refers to a brief episode in the guerrilla warfare that our colleagues waged. In his response to the speech made by Maurice Schumann (I should say his "thanks", according to our rules) the duc de Castries could not stop himself making a cutting remark about the spokesman for Radio-Londres during the war. It was true to tradition and the malicious Castries did not miss his opportunity.

One imagines you being rather discreet, adopting a mounting hardness of hearing out of reticence unless, as Ramón Fernandez suspected in an article in *La NRF* (1941): "One senses a kind of timidity about Morand, which explains a good deal."

Wherever you happen to be, your first "timid" reflex is to discover how to get out of the trap. At the Académie this can be somewhat complicated unless one is struck off, a rare event over almost four centuries. Ancient traditions protect us from Supreme Power just as Supreme Power protects us from the rules of the Kings' Courts. A pity that the Académie should suffer from the vices of democracy over its elections. Your friend and protector, Philippe Berthelot, under whose direction you started out at the Quai d'Orsay during the First World War, said that "democracy is the right of fleas to devour lions".

I've been dipping into *Journal d'un attaché d'ambassade (1916-1917),* that contemptuous indictment of one of the myths of our time, a myth that has unleashed so many terrible wars and buried entire civilizations. Your pessimism is reassuring. In this diary, maintained so methodically when a hectic life left you with little time to sleep, your mind was quick to seize the core of the matter: the confusion of a nation involved in the first of the great massacres of the twentieth century which was governed by men who behaved as though they were running an electoral campaign. We remain in the wings, the main stage is obscured. Pot-bellied, superfluous generals pass through, at times covered in laurels, at others treated as codgers and fools.

Where are you during this tragedy? While a charnel house is being constructed at Verdun, you are at the Medrano Circus watching an act in which performing geese do a Spanish dance. The Ministry hasn't sent you there, that Ministry in which you are the perfect civil servant, skilfully organizing your free time. At lunchtime or dinner the chances are that you can be spotted at the Ritz, the Crillon, at La Pérouse or Maxim's. Wealthy and often titled ladies, already in possession of highly secret decisions made by the Cabinet who sat that very morning, hold open table. Marcel Proust joins you for the pudding course. Rationing isn't much of a problem. On the two days a week without meat, you console yourself with lobster and fish. If there's no white wine, you drink champagne. A young and extremely rich Romanian girl, a princess moreover through her first marriage, entertains a great deal and is invited on other days to join the inner circle. Her shrill, peremptory voice is not frightened of coming out with outrageous remarks. Some of her utterances seem to you Heaven-sent: "A man who is not unfaithful to his wife is not a man."

So might marriage not be a prison after all? A door still remains open. They go out to admire the moonlight and they return at breakfast time. Who would not jump at such a guarantee?

At times, you embarrass your staunchest friends. The deftness with which you escaped the butchery of 1914–18 leaves an unpleasant taste. Your friend Valery Larbaud, ruled out of active service on account of his bad health, offered his services for several months emptying chamber pots and serving meals on trays in a Vichy hospital before taking refuge in Spain, in Alicante, to work on his book. The family he lodged with included some very lively young girls. They made him run a few risks, rather less serious ones than those experienced in the trenches by the men of his generation, but nevertheless… How we might have wished that Péguy, Alain-Fournier, Codet and so many others could also have escaped the slaughter! The sacrifice of your life—or even just a left arm, which your friend Giraudoux considered a lesser evil—would not have shortened the endless killing by a single day. Your death, on the other hand, would have deprived the age of a portraitist so brilliant that he might have been taken for its creator.

To those who had the cheek to ask you what you thought of yourself, you replied apologetically:

"People think me subtle, adaptable and intelligent; quite the reverse, I am blunt and foolish."

To what extent would you have liked the quite compelling portrait of Lewis in your first novel to be your own?

"Lewis entered the room heavily and sat on the ground, laying two large, steaming boots by the fire and settling his dog, which gave off a foul smell, between his knees; excessive fastidiousness led him to appear as though he was shunned in elegant places because he quite enjoyed giving the impression that he was rough and ill-mannered."

However you may have behaved, dear Paul, no one would believe you. Or were you, rather, thinking of the way you treated women when in your *Journal inutile* you noted sharply:

"I'm a shit."

Said none too soon! Did Hélène not give her blank cheque? It would have been very grudging of her to blame you for affairs that were foreseen in your agreement. The fact that she may have suffered as a result made her love you all the more. She was not made of marble. In your fictional works, which are sometimes transparent—the new generations, or whoever they were, not having inherited their parents' skills—the preliminaries are brief. It's depriving oneself of the best part.

I open… *Ouvert la nuit*. No single favourite story, they're all gems. 'La nuit nordique' has delighted me ever since I was a teenager. Aïno, a cool Scandinavian girl, yields to the traveller's fine words on the shortest night of the year in Sweden:

Aïno gripped her hands around my neck.

"You're an international swine," she said.

I took her in my arms. She remained there the rest of the night, for the sun, after a quick shower, was already bustling about.

Since I complained to you that such a night was far too brief, you came back at me:

"Ten minutes is a long time. Two would have been enough."

Women were never angry with you. They treasured your notes, which were often written in lead pencil, which was easier to rub out. In the inscription to a press officer, I recall: "To X… in memory of the Savoy, affectionately, P. Morand." Not exactly a cheap hotel. The drawing rooms in which these beautiful ladies entertained you bear witness to your lightning passage through a life that had come to a halt following your departure (or your flight, if you prefer). Your photograph could be seen everywhere, on mantelpieces, on bedside tables, in a desk with drawers that contained expeditious love letters from you, and in particular the photo that I like very much: three-piece suit, an elbow resting casually on a dresser beneath a delicate portrait of a young girl by Marie Laurencin; sometimes you are in a bathing suit or dressed as a deep-sea diver on the Passable beach at Cap-Ferrat, or now and then wearing dungarees at the wheel of a racing Bugatti, the famous 57. One of your former priestesses owned a bronze bust of you and used to say: "According to the mood I'm in, I tap him on the cheek as I pass by or stroke his forehead." Would you ever have written such a poignant story as 'La Mort du cygne' without your intimate relationship with Josette Day, the one-time ballet student at the Opéra before she became famous as a film star thanks to the close attention of Marcel Pagnol and her friendship with Cocteau? One of these ladies whom I shall not name said to me: "I am Hécate!" To be as precise as possible, she was not the only woman to make such a claim, and, perhaps, at the time that *Lewis et Irène* was published, there may have been a woman who claimed to have inspired the character of Elsie Magnac, the earlier version of Hécate. Elsewhere, in the same novel, people thought they recognized a famous fashion designer who protected herself admirably from the ogres of finance. This lady friend was not very pleased when, at a fancy dress ball given at her private mansion in the Faubourg Saint-Honoré, among the Pierrots, the cardinals and the Punches, you appeared in evening dress and a white tie, immaculate apart from one minor detail:

a strip of shirt-tail was sticking out from your fly-buttons. Lewis himself could not have provided more of a shock. I take the liberty of reminding you of these scraps from the past and from your books, since novelists easily forget their waxen or flesh-and-blood characters after having imprisoned them for life in two hundred pages. The reader is a better keeper of memory than the author.

Your short note of the 11th of November 1975 has occasioned a very long reply. I can sense you longing to go outside for some fresh air, but I should like to add a comment about the body of your work that reflects you like a revolving mirror.

Hiver caraïbe, *Bouddha vivant*, *Air indien*, those portraits of cities, *Londres*, *New York*, *Bucarest*, reread today are perfect faded snapshots akin to Lartigue's beautiful photographs.

You make little of your travel writing. Wrongly so. The world deserved the very rare example you provide of a simultaneously loving and lucid eye. These tales are your roving memory, your silhouette standing out amid the chaos.

Whenever a writer sees "other people" he ceases to inspect his own navel.

I was saying that your note had occasioned a long response to which, for all your chronic impatience, I should like to add a word about your books. A tornado suddenly shattered this work that was so self-confident and we probably then assessed its vulnerability, which made it more precious still. An accident along the way humanized and sensitized it. Did it need this? Perhaps it was necessary for it to move forward openly and less hurriedly. Let us refer to Ernst Jünger's diary, kept during the years 1991–6:

> Politics is the pox of literature, writes Paul Morand. An excellent maxim that he himself did not adhere to sufficiently, still less so his wife. I had put them on their guard. He was one of those writers on whom his youngest disciples relied, however much they may have compromised themselves politically or morally.

In fact, you did not affect politics, politics affected you. You made fun of it thanks to a scepticism inherited from Philippe Berthelot, your sponsor as well as Jean Giraudoux's at the Quai d'Orsay. A senior civil servant serves the state and the state decrees, well or badly, its political policies. At a particular moment in the history of France, our state was split in two as if with an axe. It had two half-heads. We hesitated between serving the one or the other. Millions of lives and their futures were caught in two nets. This time, luck was not on your side. From being First Minister in Berne, you found yourself virtually on the street. In Switzerland:

… the knot on which saws are broken; invasions have shaped
it like a joiner's plane, obliged to deflect in the midst of the
grain.

In exile? Not really. Let us say rather: in purgatory. One
gets out eventually. In the meantime, borders are closed
or closely watched, you are struck off the ministerial list,
your salary is suspended, in Romania the Soviets confiscate
Hélène's income, in France publishers show caution and
your books have little success except in bibliophile circles,
which is a far better sign of posterity than you might think.

Not destitute, but you could be seen pedalling on an
old bicycle to do your shopping in the market. Hélène
and you nibble away together. The winter is particularly
harsh and you shiver in gloomy rooms. By great good
fortune, the Lausanne municipal library in the canton of
Vaud is a warm shelter. Deprived of geographical space,
you spend the afternoons there consulting the histories of
Europe and Asia, the greatest possible escape. A copy of
Montociel, rajah aux Grandes Indes is inscribed to Josette Day:
"… this account of a journey during a time when I no
longer travelled, Paulm. 1944–6." *Montociel*, unfortunately,
was a failure as a novel. One does not look for the "new
Morand" there. In another book, you write to the same
person: "… this journey in time, her devoted Pmorand."

The two condensed signatures, which already look like text messages, recall *L'Homme pressé* [*The Man in a Hurry*]. The pill is not merely bitter, it is sad, as you had foreseen in 1931:

> There is something lovelier than Paris; it is nostalgia for Paris.

In the full ripeness of his years (fifty-seven), a man whose books flew from one success to another was unwisely approaching the Tarpeian Rock. You responded courageously with the writer's supreme weapon: some masterpieces, *Le Bazar de la Charité*, *Milady*, *Parfaite de Saligny*, *Fouquet* and one of the greatest and most dramatic novels of the twentieth century: *Le Flagellant de Séville*. *Venices* would be the testament and farewell to the friends of your youth, to the ghosts, to a miracle of serene beauty, the city that overcomes everything that is ponderous:

> In Venice, my insignificant being had its first lesson on the planet, as I emerged from classrooms in which nothing had been learnt.

There were a few of us who, in our early years, were able to recognize a memorable elder colleague who was threatened by the baseness of current events. Of those young friends, practically none remain apart from Jean d'Ormesson and myself.

For all that, the *Journal inutile* does not always spare us. There is something healthy about that and it reminds your friends of relativity. Fortunately we are no longer at an age when we wound each other with chilly words. Our warm caresses did not blind you and I can imagine, being restored to favour, the irritation with which you swept aside these caresses. Including my reply to your own 1975 letter whose ending you have probably forgotten:

> … Jean d'Ormesson is on his way to 200,000 and nothing is going to stop him. Kléber is at France v. England. Solzhenitsyn did not care for Nabokov. He has turned his back on Russian exiles living abroad. For him you can only resist in your own country (what a justification for Vichy, by the way!). When are you coming? I'm going to make some brief visits to Vevey but it's hard to leave a distressed woman who is on a protest strike against life. Cabanis' book on Saint-Simon is a success, mainly because people haven't read any of it.
>
> P.S. I realize that from the start of this letter I've been using the informal tu. Would you mind if this slip of the pen became the rule? I admire your life together; a good team.
>
> Tibi, semper, Morand.